THE NOT SO QUIET LIFE OF CALAMITY JANE

THE NOT SO QUIET
LIFE OF CALAMITY JANE

K. LYN WURTH

FIVE STAR
A part of Gale, a Cengage Company

**LIBRARY OF CONGRESS
CATALOGING-IN-PUBLICATION DATA**

Names: Wurth, K. Lyn, author.
Title: The not so quiet life of Calamity Jane / K. Lyn Wurth.
Description: First edition. | Waterville, Farmington Hills, Mich. :
    Five Star, a part of Gale, a Cengage Company 2020.
Identifiers: LCCN 2019041833 | ISBN 9781432871352 (hardcover)
Subjects: LCSH: Calamity Jane, 1856-1903—Fiction. | Women
    pioneers—Fiction. | Frontier and pioneer life—Fiction. |
    Dakota Territory—Fiction. | GSAFD: Western stories. |
    Historical fiction.
Classification: LCC PS3623.U785 N68 2020 | DDC 813/.6—dc23
LC record available at https://lccn.loc.gov/20190418

First Printing: January 2021
Find us on Facebook—https://www.facebook.com/FiveStarCengage
Visit our website—http://www.gale.cengage.com/fivestar
Contact Five Star Publishing at FiveStar@cengage.com

Printed in Mexico
Print Number: 01   Print Year: 2021

For my dear sister and true friend, Laura

ACKNOWLEDGMENTS

Thank you to Martha Jane Cannary for being rowdy enough to catch my writer's eye, and then for leading me to wonder how, as a solitary child on the American frontier, she survived.

Linda Wommack, Tammie Jorgensen, and Megan Joy supported me through the moments when Martha Jane drank too much, became unresponsive, and flummoxed me. Thank you for your discussions, questions, and responsive readings.

James D. McLaird and Richard W. Etulain decided Calamity Jane deserved meticulous research and clarification. Their resulting definitive biographies, *Calamity Jane: The Woman and the Legend* (McLaird) and *The Life and Legends of Calamity Jane* (Etulain), provide rich historical documentation of this indomitable woman of the West. I hope this story honors their scholarship. Thanks also to *True West* magazine for regularly stoking my devotion to this slippery heroine.

I send special gratitude to Tiffany Schofield, acquisitions editor at Five Star Publishing, for welcoming my work. Thanks also to Diane Piron-Gelman and Cathy Kulka for their encouragement and surefire editing skills on behalf of Five Star.

Now for my writing co-conspirator and husband—Dave loves to play with story and ask questions that improve my fiction. My devoted reader and champion, he supports my health and well-being. Without him, there would be no novels under my name and no truly happy ending.

Martha Jane's story is in part about sisters—how they

struggle, but also how they love, support, and endure. Sisters understand as no one else can. That's why this one is for Laura.

PROLOGUE: FIRST THINGS
COLD AND BLUE

1862, Mercer County, Missouri
Baby sister screams red and cries herself dry, then goes quiet, cold, and blue.

Ma please come home, come home, I cry, but she don't come so I cover the baby with an apron and curl up in this corner. Come home. But Ma said she can't take it anymore, the bawling babies and no husband who cares. Papa's been gone, how many sleeps? Where is he? Ma won't say, just curses his name and spits on the floor. Then she goes.

If only Grandpa James could wake up, break open his black coffin, and climb up out of that hole. He always had a kind word. A song about a bluebird. A shine in his eye. He even smiled when Ma got loud and flounced her red petticoats, as long as she baked his buttermilk biscuits light and poured honey over.

"A man can forgive a lot," he'd say, "for a butter-melting, feather-light biscuit. And besides, a good woman's got spunk."

But he got too old to live, with big warts growing on his hands and face. The wasting disease took him to Jesus, leaving me with a gambling pa and a ma who loves to drink and dance. With baby brothers and sisters who stink up diapers, cough, and run green snot out their noses, leaving nobody but me to change and wipe.

And Lord, how they cry. Poor babies, thirsty for the milk done dried up out of Ma's titties, but all they get is brown liniment bottles of sugar water and whiskey. Before she goes dancing, Ma mixes it up and snaps on the rubber nipples. Tells me to feed them when Grandpa

James's pocket watch looks like ten, big hand up, little left-side hand cocked high. Not before, or they won't sleep all night. But oh, how those babies cry while I bounce them and sing, "Oh Susanna." I'm waiting with the warm metal up by my ear—tick, tick, tick.

I'm only six, but I got my mind made up. I'll never take a husband or get babies of my own. Won't listen to them screech or watch them get sick and die. Won't call a stranger to say last words over the dirt. No, thank you.

I'm fit to be tied, tired, and mad. Ma should stay home, wash some diapers, feed them. But she yells Papa let her down again. It ain't her fault. Crying, "That man always lets me down."

Charlotte Cannary is pretty as those ladies on cameos, with high, pink cheeks and golden hair. Looks like a doll but comes on like a working man, cussing, drinking, smoking cigars. Men stare at her, figuring how scared they ought to be, but can't leave her alone.

Pa's timid as a cupboard mouse, skittering when she cusses him. He winces when she says those words, "You let me down." Shrinks into his pale chest, the white part under his shirt not sunburned from farming, like the egg top of his head. You can see his little blue veins pump there, down to his sun-browned, leather neck. He maybe was handsome when they got married, but now he's just sad, and sad ain't handsome at all. He lets her run wild. Still, I love him. At least, I did 'til he went on this last toot with our money. Now I'd like to punch him in the nose.

I got to agree with Ma about Pa sometimes, but she's a bad mother to let this baby die. I don't want to cry, so I bite my lip and blink. Scuff my heel on the dirt floor, scratching for an answer there to what am I going to do.

This was a pretty baby, too, with sandy curls. She could've grown up to be a good sister, but Ma acts like babies are nothing. She has more than she wants, then lets them slip through her fingers like flour. I swear she dropped that last one in the outhouse hole. It chokes me to think about it, so I look at Grandpa James's watch. The hands still ain't right.

I get up and kick the blankets rumpled on the floor and knock over the broken-legged chair. Breathing on the smoked-up glass, I rub my sleeve to clear a spot to see out, but I only see myself in the dark, reflected, and the candle behind me. These things I'm thinking shine with hard, clear edges, like I'm seeing them for the first time, and I study on them to keep from looking at that dead baby under the apron. One tear slips down. Just one, I tell the baby Ma never named. That's all I got for you. I'm surely going to need all the others.

Ten comes around, so I feed the living ones. They shove crumbs in their mouths and suck loud and hard, clutching on to the bottles like they're life, and I guess they are. One child is nearly five, the other only a year. I try not to think their names, so as not to love them, but I do.

"Damn, diggity damn. You are too sweet not to love, especially you, Cilus. Don't you die. Nobody gets to die, you hear?"

When their bellies get tight and full and their eyes droop from the whiskey, I tuck a dirty blanket over them. It ain't enough to keep them warm, but it's all I got.

Damn, diggity damn.

It's dark and damp and stinky diapers sting my nose. My stomach pinches, empty. Yesterday's bread is like a year ago. I should've kept back a little of that whiskey milk for myself, but that's mean. You can't starve the babies.

I spread my toes apart, stretching my feet, then my legs and arms. I crick my neck and close my eyes. Men shout and sing outside, drunk-happy and dangerous, stumbling past our tent. I'm scared to sleep with only a knot for a lock, where anybody can rip open those flaps. Anybody already did.

I got this piece of broken glass wrapped in a rag, for a knife. I'll use it if that man comes back, the one who came last night, who

11

pushed me down and made me sore down there. He won't sneak up on me again. He won't leave me feeling shameful, scared to tell Ma. Her voice yells in my head anyway, that it was my fault, for not being ready.

"Ma," I whisper, but I know she won't come. I tell myself it don't matter. I got this piece of glass.

I press my finger to the glass tip, then suck off the drop of blood. No, siree, I won't get caught again. But my eyes are scratchy, closing. I hum, "Oh Susanna" but can't finish the tune.

I can't stop myself from sliding there, to colors so clear and bright, they stay like blurred tintypes or a magic lantern show after I wake. Pictures turn to feelings, taking me far from this here damnation.

Another here spills in when I close my eyes. Dry, rocky hills wear old green coats of grass, not bright and leafy, but dusty, dry, and wide, dotted with blue and red and yellow flowers. Purple, rumpled-blanket mountains shrug up behind the hills, rough with evergreen whiskers, wearing sharp white hats. Blue sky bubbles high and clear as water to quench a body's thirst, and this forever opens so far, I can see what's coming. To run if I need to or to stay if I like.

That horizon I walk to is teasing, wandering away. It knows my name. It's soft, too forgiving to cuss or beat or tie me down with a rule. More than a place, it's an invitation. A story somebody wrote for me. A new land to cross and follow, like a dream.

★ ★ ★ ★ ★

PART ONE
1860s, LITTLE GIRL WEST

★ ★ ★ ★ ★

CHAPTER ONE
THE IDEA OF MOVING ON

1864

Their conveyance is smaller than most, more of a cart than a wagon, but Martha Jane's heart beats faster. She lifts her chin when a better-dressed boy passes and scowls at her tattered dress. Pa's going to get it right this time. Their shameful days are over.

For once, Pa got lucky at cards and brought his winnings home, so at a St. Joseph mercantile he lays down money for bags of flour, potatoes, corn, and jerky. Baking soda, lard, dried apples, and raisins fill boxes and tins, stacked as high as Martha's shoulder. Complaining there's not enough space in the wagon, Ma's packing and repacking. After washing and folding every tattered sheet and dress like it's new, she stuffs their goods into hinged boxes on the wagon sides. The breakable goods, she wraps in gunnysacks and pads with straw: a framed picture of Grandpa James, clear bottles of whiskey and vinegar, and two kerosene lamps. Waving the kids away without any curses, Charlotte smiles to herself and even hums as she works. Martha stares, wondering if there's always been a good, happy mother stowed inside that woman, waiting for hope.

At night, they wedge planks across the wagon bed and lay a straw-stuffed ticking on top. Concerning that bed, which looks softer than anything Martha Jane's ever slept on, she sees Pa wiggle his eyebrows at Ma. He announces that, more often than not, the kids'll sleep outside, under the wagon. Ma pooches out her lips at him and slaps his tickling fingers, cussing the air blue. Looking grouchy, when Martha Jane ought to feel put out, sleeping on the ground. The girl tells herself, for kids, life just ain't fair.

With a strange feeling that, in all the hullabaloo, she could be too easily left behind, the girl doesn't leave her father's side. Drawing squiggles in the dust with the toe of her new brown boot, she listens to him dicker with a Norwegian farmer over the livestock: two horses, two oxen, a milk cow, and a goat. She's impressed to see Robert Cannary spend more on guns than on anything else. There must be danger ahead. Thieves, maybe. Indians, for sure. She doesn't ask.

When they return to Ma with the goods, the woman tugs her pin curls and hollers curses at her husband. Says, "Aw, hell, so we'll starve, while the big man plays the brave soldier." Martha Jane hides behind the wagon, picking splinters off the new wood, peering around the canvas, and listening to the argument. As if too much has suddenly changed, it satisfies the girl to see her mother tumble back into herself, disgruntled and almost violent, yet familiar.

"The Henry repeaters," Pa explains in a low voice, "will keep us alive if the Pawnee, the Sioux, the Cheyenne, or Arapahoe come screaming down. Thirteen shots without reloading will be the difference between life and death." His eyebrows rise with righteousness, and his hands weigh like hammers on his hips. *So it is Indians,* she thinks. Martha smiles to see him hold his ground, while her mother turns away with pressed lips and an angry shrug.

While Charlotte sulks, Pa leads them to a pasture outside of St. Joe, to teach Cilus to shoot. Popping glass bottles off fence-posts, Pa says it's not fitting for a girl to fire a gun, and her mother'd have a fit, but he scratches his gray-red sideburn and winks at his girl as he walks away, leaving Cilus to teach her.

Seeing that wink, Martha Jane, who's already forgiven him so much, forgives all. With Ma always cutting Pa down, she reasons, he has to say one thing and mean another.

Pa loves her, his red-headed girl, the best. Or he ought to, Martha Jane believes, because she's seen the harm of his ways, yet, like a good wife, she always stands up for him. When she looks at Pa, her heart could bust open, its hot flesh-knot too small to hold the pure love of a girl. Especially today, with his new boots shining and his face set to the future, making things better for his family, Pa seems not a bad man, merely a weak one.

With Cilus curled around her for support, Martha Jane sighs, raises the gun, and shoots. On her third try, she hits and shatters a bottle, believing it a sign of her new power. Her faith and love can be her father's cure, and so, in turn, her family's salvation.

When everything's piled in the wagon, it amounts to something considerable, more than they've ever possessed. Martha Jane feels rich, even a little proud. She leans close to the wagon to smell the fresh-cut pine and runs her fingers over its splintery, gapped corners. The Cannarys may look like poor folk next to the bigger, outfitted wagons, but the family's hope makes their rig add up to something better, what it might become, instead of what it only is. Martha considers how it is, to believe in what you can't see, and likes how faith makes her feel. Older, and strong enough for a new adventure.

So it doesn't bother Martha Jane to ride near the end of the train, with only a small canvas stretched over short hoops, or to notice how their six heads bump the short canvas when they sit. It's more of a home than their shacks in Iowa or Missouri ever felt to be, and clean, to boot. No mold, no rats, no fleas. It smells as new as their dreams, a rolling possibility.

Leaving the cart and oxen for his tiny, cigar-smoking wife to master, Pa proudly mounts the long-legged bay and rides ahead. Cilus and Martha Jane ride double on the dappled, skittish colt they name Henry, after the rifles, because of how he startles into a run without a kick to his ribs. Martha's older, but Cilus is bigger, so he rides behind, with his arms wrapped around, to hold her. The horse throws them twice before accepting them. They circle back to where Ma drives the wagon, cussing ahead at the wagon and back at the babies. There's no end of squawking and whining coming out of there. Martha and Cilus wink at each other and sigh for gratitude to be grown, eight and six years old, and riding free.

With the rifle they share, they take turns sighting and firing at rabbits for that night's stew pot. The Henry is heavy, over nine pounds, and they soon feel their small arms toughen, their muscles building to heft its barrel to eye level, to train it on their targets. They love the gun. Pa lets them ride free in case they run into Indians; at the first sign of trouble, they're to ride forward to bring the extra repeating rifle and ammunition. He warns them, too, not to waste what could feed or save them on greasy prairie dogs and shivering leaves.

At first, Martha Jane shoots wide of nearly every target, but when she does hit something, she forgets the misses. She cherishes the dizzying, chest-busting-open sense of being not a helpless child, but a girl on the verge of the woman she'll be. She feels her ignorance, having never been to school, but scans the prairie for what she needs to know, and life obliges her, spilling out quiet lessons for her benefit.

While skinning rabbit and pheasant carcasses, Martha studies the hot, tacky blood that spills crimson from white vessels, and nearly violet from blue ones. With the tip of her knife, she penetrates the silky membranes, separating them from fur and bone. She sees what holds life together, and what happens when it ends. Hearing the holy sigh, she senses the mist of soul that hovers over a newly dead creature, then drifts away, and she wonders, *to where?* She feels her own life beating in her neck, her ears, her wrists as never before. Pictures the blood, a river running hot and fast when she walks, and then slower when she sleeps, and Martha Jane feels the wonder of her body growing, crossing the world. Before learning to hunt, she'd always been afraid, but now she cradles the Henry in the crook of her arm. There are the tickling possibilities of a new land under her feet and the bubble of sky expanding above, to give her courage. She kicks up her bootheels, takes long strides, and holds her chin high.

Martha Jane begins to think she's been fed bullshit; life isn't only one thing or another, and it's sure not how her folks make it sound. Fencing a child in with rules and beating her with fists and sticks. Leaving her alone, so strangers use her in the night, like she's nothing. Martha sees it now; life can be anything bright and new if you get up and go, dropping your old self behind. As Iowa and Missouri's poor farms, towns, dirt, and shame fall away behind the young girl, she won't look back. It thrills her to discover you can forget whole parts of your life, just by deciding. The revelation turns her inside herself to seek a voice, a new authority. She finds the idea of going as nourishing and juicy as fat, to chew on.

A few days west, Pa rides ahead, claiming to hunt, but Martha's belly lurches, knowing; he's falling backward, and, by nightfall, he'll huddle in a poker tent to gamble away what coins he didn't spend in St. Joe. The trail may seem a different place, offering different hopes, but for Robert and Charlotte, it could be one more chapter in the same story. Martha grits her teeth against her parents and their desperation, vowing it won't be hers.

Sure enough. Pa's still away as the party calls a halt and makes camp, so Ma corrals the kids, the cow, the oxen, and the left-behind colt. Alone, she shoulders the cooking and chores. She doesn't look so gay now, as she did in the city. Charlotte's red petticoat drags its muddy hem. Sweat shines on her face, her eyes are red, and dark circles smudge her eyes. Shameless, she slips her flask from her garter for sipping, careless of who leers at her naked thigh.

To escape Ma's temper, Martha and Cilus ride out for buffalo chips. The homesteader advice leaflets recommended them as the best prairie fuel, but there are none, and no buffalo to drop them, either. Both absences disappoint Martha Jane and give her further cause to doubt grown-ups' advice. She and Cilus break low limbs off creek-side cottonwood saplings and pull up rushes, thinking they're better fuel than nothing.

Ma cusses a blue streak at their offering, batting greenstick smoke out of her watering eyes and singeing potatoes in lard with salt pork and dandelion greens for the children. When Cilus begs for johnnycake, she won't touch the corn meal or flour, but cries, "Not with a thousand miles ahead and a no-account husband, so pipe down and swaller those taters." Ma hardly ever cooked back home, so the food is poor. She burns the potatoes black on the edges, but leaves them crunchy, half-raw in the middle. She always uses too much salt. Yet the charred mess tastes different to Martha Jane, somehow better from their tin plates in the clean air, and she bolts it down.

Martha Jane's never been so light, so free, or so happy, but her mother's temper is gathering like fat, black clouds, so the girl pitches in with Lige and Lena, the two remaining babies. She wipes their dirty bottoms with wet leaves, bundles them in clean gowns, and tucks them under quilts for the night. She pats and sings until their thumbs fall out of their sagging, wet-petal mouths. Because she's the oldest girl, it's her duty, and like it or not, she is her mother's hope.

After they sand-scour their plates and hear Charlotte sigh an end to work, Martha and Cilus slip into the lavender edges of the darkness to play beyond the ring of campfire light. With one eye on the camp, they see Ma light a cigar, pull out her bottle, sprawl into a camp chair by the fire, and drink herself down. Now and then a man wanders by, talks to her, takes an offered sip from her flask, and laughs. The other women of the wagon train chat around their fires, clustering while separating from Charlotte. Different place, same story, Martha Jane sees, swallowing hard under the everlasting shame.

When the moon is straight overhead, Martha and Cilus return. Carrying their mother's snoring, flopping, sweating body into the wagon, they settle her onto the mattress beside her snuggled-in babies.

Brother and sister sit by the fire, poking it into a flickering fever with willow sticks and letting it warm their faces red. They pass their mother's whiskey back and forth, egging each other on. Choking down the last inch, feeling the heat run in lines down their thin little chests, they laugh about the whipping they'll get if Ma remembers she didn't finish her whiskey. They wonder at the tree line along the creek, how it ripples like water, up and down, near and far. The flames lick out funny, too, with better blues and greens flashing up in the yellow. Cilus's dark eyebrows wiggle like caterpillars, and Martha can't stop giggling. When he pulls a face, she says, "Watch out, or it'll stay that a-way." He snorts, loses his balance, and almost tips into the smoldering coals. That seems funny, too.

When Pa returns in the morning, he finds them humped together near the ashes, cherishing each other's heat like pups. They wake to shouts and loud thumps from inside the wagon, and babies screaming.

Martha and Cilus stretch. Rubbing their throbbing foreheads, they spit bitterness into the dust and head for the creek, to gather more tinder and sticks.

Riding with her brother, Martha Jane's annoyed with her skirt, the way it rides up her legs. She won't sit side-saddle like some city lady, only to land in the dirt should Cilus decide to jump Henry over a ravine. She's also noticed the way men look at her and understands there is trouble in their seeking. Unlike Charlotte, Martha Jane would refuse their eyes on her stockings and bare skin. Praying Ma won't notice, she scissors a petticoat down the middle, front and back, so it'll split and cover her legs on both sides. The split petticoat works, covering her even when her skirt rides up. Still, Martha Jane envies the boys and wishes for trousers.

To learn to control Henry without Cilus, she gets up while it's still dark. One difference between boys and girls, she's noticed, is boys are taught to do things, while girls are kept helpless, with no lessons for important things. It's ridiculous, because helplessness is surely the road to ruin for any child. And if the damned world won't teach her, she'll figure it out.

Saddling the horse alone while standing on a stump is almost too much for her. For days, her shoulder muscles feel torn and swollen, but she doesn't complain, and soon she gets stronger. When Henry's ornery with her, she takes his face in her hands, rubs his star, and looks him in the eye until he settles down. She brings him stolen apples, so even when she rides with Cilus during the day, Henry favors her, confounding Cilus and delighting Martha Jane.

She starts to think of Henry as her own horse and feels jealous when Cilus takes the lead. She doesn't like resenting her brother, the one person she can count on, so she ignores the dark feeling, the frozen stone in her chest.

When she rides Henry alone under the stars, she finds something new. Alone is a way she's never been, and, once she experiences it, the more she craves her own edges, the silence, the mood, and the luxury of deciding for herself. Every minute of her life, she's had to obey or argue with somebody, usually Ma. She's always responsible for the others, after Ma goes down.

Rage burbles up in her chest. *It's not right,* she tells herself. *I'm just a girl, and it's her job, not mine.* But Martha Jane wants to be good almost as much as she wants to be herself, so she pushes anger down, too. Still, during her dark morning rides, she imagines pointing Henry west, letting his thumping hooves carry her away, never to return. But she's just a little girl with nothing. Even if she took the rifle and some supplies, the world wouldn't abide a girl child on her own. Some do-gooder would snap her up, make her a servant, or send her home. Worse, Indians might capture her for a slave, like in those horrible fireside stories.

Not yet, she tells herself, *but the day will come for me to ride away.*

Nickering Henry away from camp, she shivers at the bright moonlight casting shadows in front of the Platte cottonwoods, and the possible predators there. She rides through them, to the bank, and from a high rock studies the satin water, twisted like a girl's hair, with its sand-bar plaits. Hills rise and fall on either side of the glistening water, as if the land is a soft throat throbbing, rushing with heartbeat and breath.

She's never been here, and has never seen where she's headed, but Martha Jane feels her own breath and heartbeat quicken, as if she's going home.

Next afternoon, she and Cilus kick the horse harder to join Pa farther up the trail. Eager to escape their mother's demands that they carry and play with the babies, they pass wagon after wagon, sneaking peeks into their canvased interiors. Wondering about other people's lives.

It's not as dusty up front where the men congregate, upwind from the churning wagon wheels, but Martha Jane and Cilus fear being sent back if Pa sees them. So, once they spot him on horseback, they drift to the company's edges, like geese on the flare ends of migratory *V*s, less noticeable to the train leaders. Out of the swirling dust, they wander, loosely tethered, yet free.

Beyond their mother's voice and their father's guilt, the riders slow down to study wildflowers: the papery yellow ones low to the ground, the leathery pink ones like ladies' hats, and the clustered white ones like lace. They follow unusual tracks in the dust to hidden, meandering waterways. It's not hard to find their way back; they need only follow the shouts, whistles, curses, bellowing oxen, and cracking whips. Their company plods below that yellow cloud, its dust a new filth on the hem of the blue curtain sky.

The skinners driving the mules and oxen are a slumped, bleary lot, leaking tobacco juice, blasting farts and oaths. They capture Martha Jane's imagination, and she wonders out loud to her brother, "Where do they come from? How long did it take them to get so dirty? Did they ever have mothers?"

He laughs and shakes his head. "From hell, their whole lives, and I bet not."

"See how they move them?" Martha Jane hollers back over her shoulder, poking Cilus in the ribs.

"I never guessed oxen got tender parts on top," he admits, shaking his head. "Just down underneath." Cilus shifts on the saddle, wincing.

"That whip moves 'em along, all right," she says, noting where the whips sting to make the oxen giddyup. She might need to know someday. She pictures her own small hand curled around the leather bullwhip handle and her shoulder drawing it back. Good thing she's getting stronger from her midnight rides. She likes the way the whiplashes curl back like *S*'s, like dancers in the air, whizzing and firing forward to pop knots on the oxen's hides. She imagines the lurch of the wagon, the thrill and the power of making a solid thing move against its stubborn nature.

"Someday I'll do that," she mutters, knowing it's a strange wish for a girl. But it's her own peculiar idea, and precious for that. She hasn't much else to hope for.

The idea of moving on is strange, fine, and new in the girl's heart. Tough and sturdy and as sure to grasp as a saddle horn.

Cities or little farm towns with their broken-down houses have always owned Martha Jane. Her first sights were angled farmhouse rafters, shack corners, and crooked doorways. Her first smells—smoke, urine, offal, and mildew. Too many days, food was stale or moldy bread and, before that, milk tempered with whiskey, sucked through a rubber-teated glass bottle, left to curdle in the baby girl's crib. Martha knows Ma did that for her, because she did it for all the babies after, to keep them quiet.

Even when Martha Jane could walk out of those houses alone, she could only see hammered angles and rivers of waste, reeking of humans packed too close together. Between buildings, flies swarmed and crawled, and, from her doorway, she could see no clean, uncrowded spaces.

But here with Cilus wedged behind her on the saddle, feeling warm and secure in his brotherly arms, Martha Jane tingles with a new sensation. The horse gives her a plodding, sweet rolling rhythm of moving forward. The wind hurries past her face, blowing her long hair behind her and drying her sweat, sometimes lifting her blouse up from her ribs. These sensations rock and carry her, as if nothing is meant to stay in place for long.

The whole wagon train rolls west, rarely staying in one camp more than a night, unless an axle breaks, and, even then, it's an inconvenience and sensed as against an unspoken rule, to stay. It's movement that matters. It's the West that means something, the idea and place each body's longing for.

The sun rises behind them every day, showing that where they've come from isn't good enough, and wherever they stand is only a starting point, so pack up and get going. Next to her secret night rides, and even after only a few hours' sleep, morning is Martha Jane's favorite time. She rolls out from under the wagon, shakes the grass and sand off her bedroll, and races Cilus to begin the day.

Martha Jane stirs up coals and throws on twigs, heating up the cold coffee for Ma, who's always hungover and slow to start in the mornings. Martha wipes the babies' bottoms and ties on dry diapers. She wrinkles her nose, shaking out and rinsing the filthy rags in the creek, then hangs them from the back of the wagon to dry. She feeds the little ones cold porridge so they'll stop crying, while Cilus harnesses the team. By then, Ma's had her first doctored coffee and grudgingly faces the world, so Martha Jane and Cilus saddle their horse. While Ma nurses the baby, and before she can think of another chore for them, they ride away. If Charlotte calls after them, Martha Jane pretends the wind in her ears deafens her.

There's a line, Martha Jane tells herself, *between being good and being too stupid to be happy.*

The girl breathes in the rising dust and the lingering scents of clover and smoke, greeting another day on the trail. The dew darkens their boots, and the horse is a little fresh, snorting and prancing, ready to run.

There's nowhere Martha Jane would rather be than moving west.

★   ★   ★   ★   ★

She watches, listens, and pictures it in her head, and it makes her giggle. The grownups grunt and moan while their children lie under the wagon, pretending not to hear. It's the same thing horses and cattle do, Martha Jane knows, but how it all works with people gets tangled in her imagination. Cilus raises his eyebrows, says he knows all about it, but the girl doubts his purported wisdom.

Then one of Pa's gambling friends, Mr. Dandridge, corners her in a grove and backs her up against a tree outside camp. Sliding his hand up her skirt, he touches himself and tells her she's a pretty little thing, land sakes.

She kicks him away, trying not to look, and, with her heart pounding so loudly she can't hear the details of his curses, she trips and crashes through the underbrush like a hunted deer. Too late, she unsheathes the little knife she keeps tucked in her waistband, the one for whittling sticks. She didn't think to grab it when his hands were on her, and she cusses herself for being scared thoughtless and blind. She calls that man every dirty name she can think of and promises herself, next time he'll be sorry.

Tears streaming down, Martha Jane kicks stones out of her way. She can't hear Mr. Dandridge following her, but she stays in the open, where people can see her. There's some protection in that, but she liked the streamside thicket. Now he's gone and spoiled it and made it a dangerous place.

Martha Jane calls down hellfire, piles, and a pox on Mr. Dandridge. May he suffer boils where the sun won't shine. She mumbles and swings her little blade at the space in front of her until she's wrung out.

Back at their wagon, Ma notices the clean tear tracks on her dirty face, pinches the girl's chin in her fingers, and asks what's wrong. Martha Jane won't tell her, not until Ma slaps her so hard she blurts it out.

"A man tried to touch me."

Ma leers, then hits her again. "Don't be egging on the boys, you little tramp."

"I didn't. I was gathering sticks," she cries, ducking as Ma cuffs her again. This blow breaks open the girl's lip. Martha, reeling back, dabs the blood on her sleeve. "It ain't my fault!"

"You get in trouble, nobody's gonna blame the man. It's always the girl's fault," Ma whispers, digging her fingertips into Martha's arm. "You've got the devil in you."

Ma shoves her out the canvas opening to stumble down the step, then turns back to the chicken she's plucking. "You get a baby in you," she grumbles, "don't bother coming home. That's all I got to say."

Martha runs, boiling over, now as mad at Ma as she is at Mr. Dandridge. Forgetting her fear of the cottonwood grove, she plunges back into its shade. There she practices drawing her knife, slashing at the man's and woman's faces that hover in the air ahead of her.

After that morning, she's alert and on the lookout for it, so she notices more. Men drink so they can do things, then plead innocent after, saying they were drunk. That very night, Pa does the same with his gambling. He loses half their cash at dice, to Mr. Dandridge, of all people, then blames the whiskey for the wrong he's done.

Ma yells at Pa so loud, people stop carrying their water and tending their fires to huddle, gossip, and stare at the Cannary wagon. Martha and Cilus ride their horse away, faces burning in shame. There's no privacy in the camp.

Martha Jane nurses her rage. She tells herself she didn't ask for what Mr. Dandridge did, and her mother's false accusation puts the girl more squarely on her father's side. She feels sorry for him, yoked to that woman. She's sorry for all of them, with

Charlotte as wife and mother.

Worst of all, the girl thinks, blushing, *Ma's a hypocrite.* Martha Jane's seen her going off into the woods with at least three different men, then walking back out alone while tucking coins in her belt. Probably all these staring people have seen her, too. Maybe she's making back what Pa lost, but still. Now, the girl figures, men like Mr. Dandridge must imagine Martha's for sale. The daughter of a loose woman must be loose, too. She curses her mother with tears in her eyes, then asks God to forgive her, because a good girl doesn't do that. And how she wants to be good, or at least better than folks say.

For a week or so, Martha Jane stays near Cilus for protection but soon feels too needful for solitude and wanders off alone. Riding at night or walking alone in the woods, she keeps the loaded rifle with her. Neither Mr. Dandridge nor any other man will catch her again, because she's wise. For extra luck, she rubs dirt on her face and doesn't wash as often. A little stink can only help, here in a world where little girls must beware.

The more she pays attention, the more Martha Jane wishes she were a boy.

CHAPTER TWO
CHARITY

1864, Virginia City, Montana

The church lady is young. Like the others, she's dressed in black, but her silk shines like a beetle's back, with sparkly beads and ruffles, so she's got money to share. Charity itself, this new one's here to help the poor. The woman may be new to looking down on folks, but the girl sees from her pooched-out lower lip, the older birds in the starched, black, cotton dresses already taught this new one how to whip kindness like a lash. With one kid glove, she holds out the butcher-paper parcel, but her nose wrinkles and she holds her breath. Perched the way crows do on a board outside Martha Jane's tent, she balances, her shining, button-up shoes above the mud.

"Take it," she urges, bobbing the package up and down like a worm before a trout. "There's a proper dress, stockings, and shoes about your size. But first, the soap and hot water," she reasons. "You must wash before you put on clean clothes, or what's the point?" She laughs, her voice cracking. As if, *of course you understand.*

Hot water. That sounds like hard work, hauling wood and buckets, then building a fire, and the little girl's arms are tired from bouncing babies. She eyes the loaf of bread wrapped in a dish towel as if it's a baby, enfolded in the lady's other arm. She'd swear she smells some smoked cheese wrapped up, too.

Their last food was four, maybe five, days ago, but she's scheming for Cilus, Lena, and Lige. They cried themselves dry last night after three days of sipping water, their bellies cramping and mouths moving like chewing in their fitful dreams, huddled with Martha on the pallet hopping with fleas. Ma and Papa are six and seven days gone. Ma's gone walking, begging men in the camp for her whiskey and cough medicine, while Papa rolls dice and plays faro. He says that's how he provides, but he doesn't bring any home.

The littlest ones started calling Martha Jane "Mama" three days ago.

She studies the crow-lady's face. She needs that bread for them. She's eight, after all, and can stand the pinch and dizzy spells, but at five and two, for the babies it's too hard. And Cilus, turning seven, is a big boy who needs more food. He's gone pale, his arms like sticks, and his lips cracked to bleeding.

Martha Jane wonders why church people value soap more than food. As if God Himself would go hungry, so long as He could smell like roses. But God, however He smells, is a stranger to her, distant as a planet unseen and unnamed, while the shivering of her brothers and sister under her blanket is close, worse than the fleabites she's scratched raw.

She reminds herself to be polite, forces a smile, and pipes up, "Well, I thank you kindly for the dress and soap, Ma'am, but I got me no water to wash, and no fire to heat it. If it's all the same to you, I'll take the bread."

The lady's nose rises, and the corners of her mouth go down. "Don't be impertinent."

Martha Jane sighs and brushes hair out of her eyes. "I'm sorry, Ma'am, but my brothers and sister are starving." Feeling rage like a cold stone in her chest, the girl wipes her running nose on her sleeve, lifts her chin, and looks the church lady in the eye. "I don't ask for myself," she says, thinking hard, knitting her eyebrows together and striving to be well-spoken, "but they are but tiny children and should not . . . suffer so." *Or die like the others did,* she thinks, but holds back the words. This bird could still fly.

The crow tips her head, swallows, and blinks. Shifting her weight, she wobbles on the plank. One shoe slips near the mud, but she's forgetful of it and holds Martha Jane's gaze.

Behind the lady's bright-blue shine and long lashes, the girl sees the flicker of a heart. Hard, pink lips soften to let out a long-held breath. Eyes glisten and fill. Her tall, black figure sways as if the dusty breeze fingering her curls could knock her over. She whispers, "Oh, my."

The girl feels the moment contract, nearly disappearing as all possibility rushes inside it. Now, now. She drops a weak curtsy, holding her torn dress hem like wings at her sides. Like a lady, but not. She thinks, *I will bend or kneel or crawl as low as it takes. Even into the ground.*

Behind her, inside the tent, a baby coughs.

She whispers, "My name is Martha Jane Cannary, Ma'am, and I thank you for your kindness." She lets the skirt conceal her dirty hands and the sins they signify, then drops her eyes. The humble and the hungry can only wait. This is a thing she feels she's always known.

The lady fumbles both packages, releasing them from her shawl to fall at Martha Jane's feet. Untucking a handkerchief from her sleeve, she whirls on her heel and raises a gloved hand to her mouth. Mud splatters up.

She's crying, thinks the girl, who bends and caresses the paper. *Good. Go cry, black bird.*

Dabbing her eyes, the lady goes where Martha Jane, glancing up, imagines they all must gather for comfort when charity finishes, when it fails.

CHAPTER THREE
POTTER'S FIELD

1865

The fever burns through Cilus fast, burning red spots onto his neck and belly. He doesn't cry or complain, and, by the time Martha figures how sick he is, he can't stand. She holds a can for him to piss in and dabs his hot brow with a wet rag, but he pales and turns his face to the wall.

She paces the streets, knocking on doors, begging for soup and medicine, but as soon as she mentions the fever and the spots, doors slam in her face.

She scrubs her face and hands and braids her hair. She offers to work in their houses, to empty their chamber pots and scrub their dirt. They size her up and answer, "No." Maybe they read her desperation, her plans to swipe food from their pantries and tonics from their cabinets.

For three days, Cilus burns like an exploded mine. On the fifth day, he won't answer her whispers or sigh at her song. As she changes and sponges him, the babies cry, but she ignores them. At least they can still cry.

"Ma will come home soon," she lies to Cilus. "She's out getting medicine for you now." If he hears, he knows it's whiskey she's out getting, for herself. But maybe she'll share a little with her sick boy, should she stagger home. Pa, well, he's been gone for two weeks. Gambled himself broke, probably. Martha doesn't talk about him. Because they believed him better than

Ma, he's a darker discouragement. No better than a hole in the ground.

She recounts stories as if Cilus can still hear her behind his cooling white mask. She brings back for him their good days riding Henry, coming west. How they gathered firewood, shot at prairie dogs, sneaked off at night, and drank by the fire. How he's her best friend and, damn it all, he can't step out of the memories they share. And although she knows better, she tells him he's too young to die.

"Don't leave a hole in me," she whispers in his ear. Closing her eyes, she slows down her breaths to match his. His chill awakens her with the morning.

Martha Jane begs a miner in the neighboring tent to lend his back and shovel, to help her bury her brother in a potter's field. With no wooden cross to mark Cilus's head, the girl chooses a stone sparkling with quartz and mica, the size of a loaf of bread but so much heavier.

After Cilus, with the baby now just four weeks old and the other one born on the trail west, eighteen months, that leaves four mouths to feed. Martha Jane cusses and prays for her mother to stagger home, to bear some of the weight, if not any guilt. The next minute, Martha pictures knocking down that good-for-nothing with a chunk of firewood, on sight. She lets herself hate her parents because hate may not be food, but it makes her stronger.

The neighbor who helped her bury Cilus told her bad water probably killed him, and Martha Jane should boil any water for the babies. That might help, if they didn't already catch it from their brother.

Martha rips long, soft strips from their mother's old petticoat to tie the babies' right ankles, anchoring them to a stake inside the tent. Lena's old enough to hold the infant and mind the other two, if she doesn't have to chase them different directions.

Lena, devoted to Martha Jane, promises to keep the little ones untangled in their straps until Martha gets home from begging.

One day's scavenging amounts to a garbage meat bone to boil for soup and a stale loaf from the hotel kitchen to soak in the broth. Martha Jane strips off a handful of dry beans somebody left on stalks over the winter, in their garden.

Over a fire outside the tent, Martha blisters her fingertips on a hot kettle. She boils the nasty-sweet, turning ham bone, chunks of bread, and the beans into mush the older ones can lick off their fingers. She dabs some on the littlest baby's lips, but the tiny tongue thrusts it out. For Lena and Lige, Martha Jane kept back the bread heel, breaking and giving it like communion.

She takes nothing for herself and tells herself the gnawing in her gut ain't so bad. Thinking she hears her mother's voice, she glances up at the door, but nobody's there. It's like that now; she hears bells, whistles, all manner of things that aren't there, along with the crying and sniffling that never cease. Martha Jane turns her face from the fussing infant with a thought that's hard and true, that should make her cry, but doesn't: the little ones will probably die anyway, so from now on, she'll give it all to Lena and Lige, who still have a chance.

Cilus is dead and buried a week when Ma staggers home. Martha Jane ignores her, and Charlotte slaps her face for disrespect. "What? You gone deaf?"

"Count us," Martha Jane wails.

"What?" Charlotte demands. "What do you want from me?"

"Count us," she insists, and Charlotte shakes her head, looking with bleary eyes over the staked children huddled on the bedding. Blind drunk, she shakes her head.

"You don't even see he's gone," Martha chokes, sweeping aside the canvas flap to flee the tent.

Why do only good people die?

But two days later it's Charlotte sweating in the blankets, and Martha's dabbing her mother's brow, her rash. She won't speak to the woman but tends her in silence.

Charlotte tosses and moans. Martha wonders what her mother sees as tears run down her dirty face and into her ears. Her eyes rolling left to right, Charlotte mutters, "Damn him," and, "Why?"

As Charlotte fades, Martha tamps down her rage with fear, now not so sure she wants the woman dead. She's not much help, but she is the mother. Somebody to hope for, at least.

When Charlotte convulses, Martha dribbles whiskey out of the bottle into her mouth, to ease the jerking and shaking. Charlotte mutters, "My good girl."

The knot in Martha's throat sends pain into her ears, and she stumbles out of the tent. She won't let that damned woman see her cry. By the smoking fire, Martha blinks, locks her heart, and whispers, "If you're going to die, get on with it. I got work to do."

Going to her neighbor, Martha asks him to spread word through the gambling tents, for her Pa to come home, that his beloved wife is dying. Pa won't come, she knows, but as she hoped, the neighbor pities Martha with a chunk of side pork and a fistful of flour from his stores. Hearing a baby's cry from Martha's tent, he adds a tin cup of goat's milk to his offering.

Martha's so numb, so grateful for his little kindness, that when the man spreads his fingers over her chest, feeling too early for the start of her womanhood, she doesn't slap him. What else has she got, to thank him?

36

CHAPTER FOUR
JUGGLE AND DANCE

1866

Still, it was hard to see her die; even a bad mother is a buffer, a threadbare blanket you tug close to protect you from the world. A scrawny tree, offering a little shade. A brightly colored, staggering bird, Charlotte had stood between Martha Jane and some men, at least, by flapping and drawing attention to herself.

Yet hadn't she, by her absences, prostitution, and binges, published her family's weakness and her child's vulnerability?

When she thinks of her mother, Martha Jane senses how both are true and chokes on mixed rage and gratitude.

But now Virginia City can see, want, and even pluck at will the unprotected child. Men's eyes travel up and down her body, with her delinquent father nowhere near to threaten hunters away. Carrying water or wood, Martha Jane pretends she wears a tortoise shell. She steadies her trembling hands and quivering chin outside their rat-infested shack, that supposedly better place Pa moved them after Charlotte's death in the tent. Pretending to be unaware, Martha Jane's not sure which pains her more, the men's lust or their wives' whispered condemnation.

Night and day, her father gambles for gold he's too proud or lazy to dig, sluice, or pan. Drunk on cheap whiskey and a convert to luck, he won't save enough to buy a miner's tools, nor could he drive himself to break a sweat. The treasure he does hold, he can't see; Martha Jane's love hovers over him like abandoned mist in a canyon. It's his, whether he claims it or not, because Robert Cannary is all the world has allotted for Martha Jane.

She tells herself nothing's changed. She's still the family's hope, and still unable to bear it, but she squares her shoulders under the load. All she knows is, she loves them, even as she resents their raw-throated cries for food. For them, she haunts the storefronts and streets, begging coins.

A one-legged man named Joe, his one shoe deep in mud, leans his weight off his peg and beckons Martha Jane off her begging corner. Terror chilling her neck, she shakes her head, but he crooks a finger and swears not to touch her.

"Damn it," she mutters, glancing left and right for competitors. She just yesterday fought off two pint-sized pickpockets to claim this corner, but, too curious to resist the smiling man, she slogs over, cussing the heavy mud coating her cracked shoes. Stopping six feet away in case the stump's a trick and he means to grab her, she huffs her exasperation at the greasy man. "What? I ain't got all day, mister."

He laughs, tells her to simmer down, and suggests she can do better. Coaxing her near with sleight of hand, stories, and songs, he shows her how to juggle and make a stone or penny disappear. How to dance a jig, to turn her begging into a show.

"Call out funny things," he teaches her. "If you're smart, they'll give you more."

He teaches her how to compose verses that rhyme, and then, how to whistle a tune.

He frowns down at his peg, then hitches back and forth in a comical approximation of dance. "Don't laugh, little girl. I was good at this. Can you picture it? The shuffle-tap-step and spin?"

Martha giggles, tries, and feels clumsy, but his earnest praise warms her cheeks.

Joe nods and advises, "Toss out jokes and riddles. Tell them how handsome and beautiful they are, how smart they must be, to be so successful. When they give you something, cover your heart, curtsy, and say, 'Thank you,' but wink and smile like you're glad to be you, not them, with all their troubles. Bless them and promise to pray for their souls. You don't have to do it, mind you, but they'll watch next day for your happy face and, even before they find you, they'll have your coin in hand."

Martha Jane practices the rhythmic tossing and catching, the stone thrown from behind her back to come down into her front cupped hand. She lifts her chin, forces a spark into her eyes, like the one Beggar Joe gives her.

Joe disappears from Virginia City a week or so later, before she can report back to or thank him, but she's learned well. With a ready joke, she draws the attention of passersby to her quick, 1-2-3 performance. She polishes her banter, learns how hard to push, and how far. Nickels and dimes rain down on Martha Jane, enough for bread and milk for Lena, Lige, and the babies.

It curdles something in her to consider how Joe was more of a father to her in a week, than Robert Cannary had been over nearly twelve years. She misses both men, now, still holding out hope that her Pa will love her back someday.

Whenever she thinks she hears Joe's song or cough on the street, her heart clutches, then falls in disappointment. The street wasn't so lonely when he was here, and he looked out for her, chasing swindlers and drunks away. But with Joe gone, she tells herself, there's more business left for her.

Martha keeps a little money back to buy a violet-scented bar of soap and keeps it in a tin box in her pocket. Remembering the crow-lady, the girl washes her hands and face before she works the boardwalk. People may pity a poor girl but will cross the street to avoid a filthy one. Ma never cared much about cleanliness, and Joe never made a lesson of it, but Martha figures this out for herself.

One kind man in a red brocade vest asks her why she's so poor she has to beg, why her mother and father don't feed her. Martha starts to tell him Ma died of fever, but then she feels inspired.

"Well, sir, she died on our way west, in an Indian raid. I threw myself between her and that bad Injun, but he tossed me aside like I was a rag. Then he buried his hatchet in my dear mother's golden-haired head. And my Pa, he . . . it breaks my heart to say."

Martha Jane touches the corner of her eye and nearly smiles, pleased with her word concoction, but the rich man's mouth presses into an uncertain frown. Fastening down her delight, she presses her lips together and coughs up a dry sob.

He sucks in a deep breath, fighting emotion, but his eyes shine as he draws three quarters from his vest. "Poor, brave child," he mutters, dropping the coins in her palm. Not on the ground in front of her, she notices, but in her hand, the way one decent person pays another.

She shakes her head, stacking, sliding, and clicking the shining coins as he walks away. Funny is good. But then there's pitiful and brave, a new combination to unlock hearts and purses. There's so much to learn about folks in this world, and how to move them one way or another, to get what you need.

In any case, it's clear—the truth has little authority or effect. It seems that virtue, if indeed it is one, is better left to ministers, schoolmarms, and rich folk who can afford its perils.

Little girls on their own best learn to lie.

CHAPTER FIVE
GIVEAWAYS

1867

Pa's run up some awful gambling debts in Alder Gulch, so he orders Martha Jane to pack only what they need. He mutters about vigilantes coming with a rope.

"But we've got a judge in the territory, Pa," Martha argues. "Folks don't go around lynching anymore."

"The hell," he says. "You're a child, and you'll tell me how things work?"

Martha sighs and changes the diapers. Instead of rinsing and packing them wet, she tosses the soiled rags in the trash-filled alley. Pa's breathing down her neck. "Hurry up, gal, hurry."

He's surely upset somebody important this time.

"Where we going?" Martha Jane asks, knotting the last bundle and handing it to him. "And how? We got no horse or wagon, and I can't carry everybody."

"Don't get smart with me," he mutters.

Seems Pa has a little gold nugget and some dust he didn't mention to the people he owed. With hungry little ones pecking around his legs like chicks, and skeptical Martha standing off to the side, he bargains with a stage driver to transport them to Salt Lake City. Right then and there, before the scheduled run.

Salt Lake City, Martha thinks, *to the Mormons?* She's heard strange stories, how they pray with secret signs and ceremonies, and every man takes several wives. The stage route to that city is notorious too, for robberies and kidnappings.

41

Martha Jane has half a mind to dig in her heels. Let Pa deal with these children on his own; he and Ma made them, so let him feed them. Seems she has all the responsibility of a mother now, but none of the rights, not even to know what's happening.

No wonder Ma drank.

"Pa, I don't think—" she begins to say, but he swings around and slaps her mouth. Tasting blood, she lowers her eyes and blinks back tears.

"He don't mean nothing by it," Lige says, tugging her sleeve. "You shouldn't aggravate him."

"Well, you're aggravating me," she whispers, punching her brother's shoulder.

Pa finishes haggling and opens the stage door, climbing in first and leaving Lige and Martha Jane to sort out and lift up the little ones. When she does climb in, she takes the seat farthest from her father.

The stage no sooner gets up a head of speed through the low, grassy hills, than it stops to water or change the horses.

"These watering stops, at the ranches," Lige whispers, "is where folks got murdered and robbed by road agents, not three years ago."

"They don't do that anymore," Martha Jane protests, only half believing.

Pa glances at them, smooths his mustache, and nods agreement, but he doesn't look sure. Every few miles, he sticks his head out the stage window into the flying dust, to look back. His long side hair flies up like wings and every time he settles back in his seat, he licks his fingers and pats it flat over the top.

"Anybody following us?" Martha asks.

Pa sniffs. "I'm taking in the scenery."

"Sure," Martha Jane says, rolling her eyes.

"You show some respect, little lady. I'm keeping you, your

sisters, and your brother safe."

Martha Jane doesn't say, *from trouble you brought on us.* This isn't the first time Pa's ducked collectors. Her father leaves bad debt behind him the way taking-off birds squirt crap on the ground. He hardly ever came home to their little tent or shack for that very reason, and Martha Jane finally made a game out of giving false names and turning away angry men with far-fetched excuses: he's gone to Rapid City, he's run off with a dancer, or, he up and died of the French pox. Half wishing he'd done one of those things, she'd also be half hoping he'd remember and come home to his girl.

Pa's useless, she thinks today, looking out through the veil of dust at the pale green-and-tan aprons fringing the rocks and ridges. It pains her to think it, but since Ma died, he's failed her completely. Her love for him is no more use to her than the newspapers she can't read, good only for crumpling to wipe babies' bottoms.

The farther south and west they go, the more the soil reddens as if it's soaked in blood. Martha Jane shudders, then falls into fitful dozing, dreaming of wearing a ruffled wedding dress, suddenly some Mormon's thirteenth wife.

Martha Jane remembers Missouri's buildings and farms as a jumble, like a child's stacked and scattered blocks on the green grass and brown fields. In St. Joseph, where they'd stocked their wagon, there'd been some nice houses with lush lawns, shrubs bearing flowers, and even a few picket fences, but even that city stank. Mining towns, with their flowing sewage and filthy tents, were worse yet.

But Great Salt Lake City looks like God himself mapped out and built a town with perfect square after square of homes and businesses, all of it clean as a whistle. On the main thoroughfare, a spired building raises its decorated arms to heaven. Pa tells her that's the temple, where the Mormons pray.

The stage barely bumps on the wide street that's been leveled and bricked smooth. Every house shines white or yellow, with gardens and fruit trees shading the well-dressed, walking people. Most of the ladies wear drab colors like doves or modest calicos, while the men top their outfits with vests and nice hats. They're clean, every last one. Nobody looks pinched or hungry. Children run and play tag around the houses, some pausing to tuck balls under their arms and eye Martha as she peers out. One tall, blond boy waves, and Martha waves back.

Downtown, the plateglass windows are so clean they flash blades of sunlight into Martha Jane's eyes. The stores she can see into stock dresses, suits, cans of food, dolls, balls, and tiny, lifelike wagons for children's play.

Low-slung, blue-gray mountains hunker over a sapphire lake that gathers water from several streams, like arms that hug the city.

"Glory," Pa murmurs. "It's just as they say."

Glory, is it? Martha thinks, disgruntled and eager to argue with Pa, who sports a four-day stubble, reeks of sweat, and ushers nothing but trouble through this heaven's gate.

"Do Mormons gamble, Pa?" Lige asks.

"I think not," Pa answers, bouncing a squalling baby on his knee.

"Then what in tarnation are we doing here?" Martha Jane blurts, and the answer is another slap. She dabs her lip, swollen twice its size from Pa's nerves on this trip, and wishes she could slap back.

When Pa herds them into a bath house, Martha Jane wonders how much money he's kept back. Two women making *oogey-oogey* baby talk carry off the grimy infants to spiff them up, as Pa and Lige enter the men's bathing room. In the other, Martha Jane and Lena have a big copper tub to share. With a bar of soap, a wash rag, and all the suds she can rub up, big sister sends the little one into fits of giggles, donning scoops of bubbles as ear baubles, beards, and mustaches.

Soon Pa stands outside the room, rapping and calling, but Martha Jane sinks down so only her nose pokes above water, staying until goose pimples blotch purple on her arms. Only then does she climb out to rub down Lena and herself with the scratchy gray towels beside the tub.

It seems a shame to put on dirty dresses, so Martha dips them into the bath water and wrings them out. Then they're too wet to wear, so she rolls them in the damp towels, then flaps both frocks up and down until they're only damp. The dresses cling to their rosy, damp skin, but should dry soon in the summer sun.

"For God's sake, Martha Jane, come out or I'll come in, whether you're dressed or not," Pa threatens, pounding again. One of the Mormon ladies shushes him, then raps on the door and sing-songs, "Hurry, young ladies. Time's up!"

"Coming," Martha Jane calls, finger-combing tangles from Lena's blonde curls, then braiding her own red-brown hair. Squinting at herself in a chunk of brushed steel on the wall, she can't get a clear view. She wonders why there's no real, glass mirror in here. Maybe Mormons don't look at themselves. Like some Christians, maybe they're proud of not being vain.

Lena and Lige complain of hunger, but Pa explains that, because of the baths, there's no money for food. *Just like him*, Martha Jane thinks, *not to plan ahead*. What's more important? Martha fumes and bounces the littlest baby to quiet her.

He marches the kids to a big house in the temple's afternoon shadow, a white, porched home crowded with tall shrubs and flowers. Fat, black-and-yellow bees buzz on the orange, blue, and white blossoms.

Pa straightens his tie, smooths his mustache, and pokes Lige and Martha Jane, telling them to stand up straight and be polite. "Meaning," he adds, "shut your yaps." After he raps on the door, a lady in an apron and hair kerchief answers.

He's well into his speech about orphans and destitution when Martha Jane gets the gist. He's hoping to give them away.

The lady sighs, tilts her head, and listens.

"No," Martha Jane blurts. "I don't want to . . ."

Pa glares at her and she glares back.

"You can't," she says, but Pa ignores her.

"She's bright. She'll take to your religion real quick," he says to the lady, forcing a smile.

Martha Jane glowers at the woman, who tilts her head like a dog, then narrows her eyes. They slide off Martha Jane to widen over her baby sisters. One's toddling across the porch toward the flowers, while the other's sucking her fist, fixing to bawl. Pa plucks baby Liza out of Martha Jane's arms and holds her up for the lady to see. Liza's little bare feet kick the air.

"Like hell!" Martha snorts, turns on her heel, and storms down the porch steps. She knows Pa won't dare beat them in front of such good people, so she beckons Lige to follow her. What will happen later is another matter, but she won't be handed over like a slave.

When Pa stomps down the steps holding Lena's hand and without the two babies, Martha Jane unleashes on him, punching his ribs, his chest, arms, and legs. Any part she can reach, she pummels, grunting and crying, "I hate you! I hate you!"

By the time she thinks to run up the steps to claim her sisters, Pa's clamped her against his chest, pinning her arms to her sides. He whispers in her hair, "Hush, Martha Jane. Hush."

She goes limp and sees Lige and Lena staring at the ground. Finally, Pa lets go of her, and, when he walks down the sidewalk, she swears she won't follow. But Lena and Lige do, running to catch up and each child taking one of his hands.

"Goddamned traitors," she mumbles, wiping tears with her sleeve. She trails behind, leaving nearly a block between herself and the others.

He rents a cheap hotel room, leaving them hungry. Pa tumbles onto the bedspread and falls into deep snores, with no apology or explanation. Martha Jane pulls back the covers and settles Lige in bed beside Pa, then makes a little pallet on the floor for herself and Lena, between her father and the door. While the other two children sleep, Martha Jane pinches herself to stay awake. Against the dim moonlight that filters through the lace curtains, she watches her father's gray profile.

She curses him. She hates him. She can't believe what he's done.

Too tired to keep vigil, she startles awake in the yellow-lit morning, knowing, before she looks up, what she'll find.

Pa's side of the bed is empty. Like a cat, he stepped over her and Lena in the night.

When Lena and Lige wake up, they don't talk about it, but beg breakfast from Martha Jane. She picks sleep crust out of her eyes and mutters, "Robert Cannary, damn you to hell."

The room was paid for only one night, so Martha leads Lena and Lige back to a farm she'd spotted, coming into town. At night, they sleep in the hayloft, gulping milk straight from the cow's rubbery teat and gathering fruit from the orchard. Martha Jane knows it's only a matter of time before the farmer finds them, but she hopes he will be kind.

On the third day the farmer, whose name is Eben, catches Martha Jane stealing eggs. After raising a hand to drive her out, he thinks again and whispers a prayer. Looking up to the hayloft, he calls out for the others he senses hiding there. Until Martha calls, they stay behind the bales.

K. Lyn Wurth

Invited into the house, Lena and Lige keep stone faces as Martha says their parents are dead. After consulting with neighbors who are also childless but admit they can't afford the charity, the kind Mormons ask all three children to stay.

A week later, while riding in the new family's wagon in town, Martha sees her father reeling in the street. In a town where Martha Jane assumes there's no liquor and no saloon, her Robert Cannary's found a way to fall down drunk in public. It's the Cannary curse. Wanting to pity him and hoping he will see her, she looks into his eyes. He spins and falls, giving no sign that he recognizes her in her new dress and bonnet. Martha Jane breaks her gaze, faces front, and doesn't look back.

Later that week, she eavesdrops as the farmer and his wife discuss that poor man in town, how he took a fit and died. So, they say, are the wages of sin.

Martha feels a knot in her throat but swallows it down, refusing to cry over Robert or Charlotte again.

They make her work hard, which she doesn't mind so much because there's always food, but the farmer and his wife clearly prefer Lena and Lige, petting their heads and giving them new, Mormon middle names. When they look at Martha, they bite their lips and shake their heads, calling her down for running through the house and blurting out her every thought. They tell her children should be seen and not heard. She tells them that's horseshit. They insist a lady doesn't use those words, so, just for spite, she lists every bad one she knows, adding a few original combinations of her own, until their faces pale.

The first time she runs off, she returns to the house where Pa left her two baby sisters. From the shady porch, she peers in the bay window past the parted lace curtains, pressing her nose against the cool glass to watch them toddle and play on the rug

48

together. There's nobody else in the room, so she raps on the glass, but they don't look over. They're wearing clean dresses and little leather shoes. Their cheeks are rosy and already look rounder. Martha Jane wants to bust in and take them back, but it sickens, weakens, and yet pleases her, how they're better off without her.

She sniffles and rubs her sleeve across her nose as she walks back to the street. She aches for her kin, but she can't imagine the farmer and his wife welcoming two babies, simply to please naughty Martha Jane.

She sometimes tries to be good, the way a person would try on new clothes to see how they feel. But even when she thinks she's doing well, keeping most of their rules, she gets whipped with a willow switch for some little infraction. Outraged, she turns the air blue, and this invites more whippings. Martha Jane can't rest her whole sore bottom on the seat of a chair. Struggling to keep faith, the Mormons force smiles that don't lift their eyes.

Late evenings alone in their parlor, when they think she can't hear—which is the only time she's listening—they call her a tribulation, while she calls them worse. They discuss how she's too old to save, at eleven, and well past her innocence, having theologically lost it when she turned eight years old. Martha ponders this. Mormons seem to believe there's something magical or blessed about being seven or younger. They confess some hope yet for Lige, if he's baptized soon, because he doesn't argue and works hard, while Lena's still within her age of grace.

Lena and Lige seem to fit here in Great Salt Lake City, secure with bread, a roof, and hope of a Mormon heaven. But Martha Jane's lost nearly everything and everybody already and trembles in dread of losing more. She slips away from her kitchen chores, though, to pass hours in town, being herself: juggling, honing jokes, and performing magic tricks for passersby.

After scraping together a dollar in one day, she figures she could manage snatching away Lena and Lige, caring for them better than Robert or Charlotte did. She could teach them tricks, and together they'd have a little circus. Martha dreams she could hold her family together with the same big personality that gets her in hot water with the Saints.

She tells herself, once she saves up twenty dollars, she'll hightail it out of this hard-polished, squared-off, flower-decked heaven. She'll take her family back to some lesser paradise, maybe Montana or Dakota, where rivers run in muddy canyons, dust sparkles with gold, and a girl like Martha Jane can cuss a blue streak, appreciated and unrestrained.

CHAPTER SIX
PRIVVY MATTERS

This here butt-smoothed wood seat is a far sight better than hanging bare-assed over a downed log, scraping my tender girl-parts on bark and then picking thistle stickers from where they ought not to be. Heaps better, even considering a few cobwebs and hornet's nests up in the corners. See, lately I'm sneaking into outhouses, careful not to let the doors slam and announce me when I'm done.

These here Sears and Roebuck pages are smoother than leaves and don't give a girl a rash. Great Salt Lake Mormons do keep their outhouses in fine condition, some even mud-caulked against the wind, with lime to scoop in after, to block the stink. I suppose some folks might read these nicer books instead of tearing out their pages, but I got no such inclination, letters and words being near impossible for me. I ain't ashamed. I just ain't bright in a bookish way, or so that Iowa schoolmarm told me.

Staring out a knothole in the wall, it comes to me how some of my best ideas rise with the stink of my own shit. It fills me with a sense of being and belonging in the world to smell myself, and in these little boxes, I finally get some time alone to think. Just to be myself. Away from people I'm begging from on the street. Away from Lena and Lige. I love them but gosh darn, they drive me crazy with whining and worry and awful chatter about how I ought to do this or that to please the Mormons, instead of things I like, which without fail displease them. As if I give a tinker's damn to please those pious and peculiar folks, men who got no more sense than to take a passel of wives, or lots of women sharing—and surely fighting over—one man.

51

Seems they show poor judgment in the most basic matters where common sense should apply, but to my brother and sister, the Mormons who took them in and give them three squares a day can do no wrong.

Those young ones boss me like I'm not the oldest, like I didn't ride west, a true pioneer, while they still crapped their diapers. Diapers that I, by no coincidence, scrubbed on river rocks. Why, I'm near enough to twelve years old to spit on it.

But in their new comfortable abode, my brother and sister fear I will cause them to be cast out. So I try to oblige, to not talk back or cause trouble, which runs counter to my nature. Worse, the father in that house is even quicker to slap me than Pa was. Never thought I'd see that or think of my father again with any gratitude.

So here in this shithouse, I breathe in the good stink of what's parted from me, what I need not carry anymore, and consider what comes next. I got a good street business going, making a good dollar a day and that's not bad, but it ain't enough. I spend a dime on a stale roll every noon so I need not daily suffer that farmer's wife's burnt kidney pie. Where on earth does she get so damned many kidneys? Must be cheaper by the dozen at the butcher shop. I don't like the taste or the rubber squeaking on my teeth, even if I'm rumored to be an Irish girl, going way back in Pa's line. There's just some animal parts a person ought not put in her mouth, however traditional they may be. Lena and Lige wipe bread on their plates, though, to sop all the gravy, like Mary cooks the best food ever served. More poor judgment there, so maybe they're becoming Mormon, too. Perhaps these sorts of changes in taste and in religion happen without warning—another reason to keep up my guard.

I figured to teach Lena and Lige my street tricks to get them out of that house, but Lena can't toss a ball or catch it to learn to juggle, while Lige is too all-fired shy. His face gets red when anybody looks at him and he grumbles about begging being shameful. Lena says she'd rather work her fingers to the bone as an honest girl, and I tell her, sure enough with a greedy Mormon husband, don't worry, she will. Too proud, both of them, they won't put on a funny show for anybody, won't even stand beside me while I perform. Being took care of all their lives, they still got pride, which virtue I find the shamefullest thing of all.

Shifting on the wood seat creaking under me, I flick away a daddy long legs and consider the prospect of thievery. It pains me to keep things legal, when I see there's profit to be made outside the law. Why, just today in a grocery I saw a little scamp half my size shove past me, lift a ham, and hide it under his shirt, bold as brass, scot-free. His belly ain't the one growling now. Still, there are the fires of hell to consider, and I hate to turn to crime until necessary. While it re-assures me to have a plan of last resort, I am not desperate yet.

As for practical matters, the sheriff in this town is fat and slow, and in a pinch I could surely outrun him. But these Mormons are so righteous, so ready to point out and punish sin, some do-gooder'd surely nab and hold me 'til the lawman caught up. There's surely a better town for crime than this one. Anywhere, probably. And if I get caught, the hardest consequences could come sooner than hellfire for me and will hurt more sorely than jail. Thrown out of the farmer's house, I would anger Lena and Lige and lose what family I've got left.

So I dance and juggle and dodge their rules and pious ways, stay-ing out until dark and they're too tired to punish me.

I pick up the catalog and page through. Everything a body could need or want, a treasure house on paper, here in this book. It only makes me more upset, to think how little we got, us orphans, and how hard it is for a child, innocent of no crime, to find her way in the world. There's no justice in it.

I hear a house door slam and slide the catalog to the floor, set to yank up my drawers. If some rightful owner is walking back here to use this privvy, I'm caught and won't have time to wipe. Best thing now, to wait and knock the intruder flat with the flung-open door.

But I hear a throat clear, a barn door slide open, and horses snorting and trotting out, so I settle back into my thoughts.

What if I'd been born somebody else? Would life be this hard? I let my piss run hot out of me, splattering. This hole's filling. I may need to scout out a new one, because the smell's getting rank despite the lime. Not, as Ma liked to say, that beggars can't be choosers, but that's exactly what riles me up. Why wasn't I born into a house with my own hole to crap in, or even, dare to think it, with indoor plumbing? Water through the walls and shit floating out. Why the hell not? Lots of children get good things without lifting a finger.

What is it about me that's so undeserving? Did God look down on me and say, "I'll make things hard for Martha Jane Cannary. She'll be hungry and have to shit in the woods or other people's outhouses, all the days of her life." It don't seem like God would decide that, if He has any justice or mercy at all. So, it means my being in this state is not God's doing, but man's. Almost for sure, some man's. And so it's righteous to fight my lot with all my wits and anger. Maybe even to break the law, if I've got to, to balance things out.

I feel much better now. Ripping out and crumpling a page, I come to think there's more than one helpful thing a girl can experience in an outhouse.

CHAPTER SEVEN
CALFSKIN BOOTS

The tweedy, buttoned-up man notices the woman's pretty ankles, then reaches out to help her off the stagecoach. On his arm, the lady steps over the mud. Martha Jane notices the smile under his waxed mustache as he escorts that woman into a restaurant.

From the window Martha watches, her stomach growling.

White bread shines with yellow butter. Steaks drip red-brown juices, snuggled in with little round potatoes and carrots cut like coins. When the lady pushes away her half-full plate and dabs her lips, Martha wants to dash over to snatch what's left. She doesn't. The folks in there are so clean, they must smell good. Martha Jane sniffs one armpit, then the other. Damn, she's out of soap.

After the man walks the lady to the hotel staircase, he saunters down the street. Martha stays ten feet back, wiggling and limbering her fingers to lift that pocket watch that throws circles of reflected light on storefronts as he passes. Deciding that's too risky, she follows him into a store, guessing which pocket holds his folding money. When he stops to stare at a pair of ladies' boots on display, he jingles change in his right trousers pocket and bites his lip.

After the rich man wanders one aisle over to look at hats, Martha steps up to the boots on display. Molded from white calfskin, the shin-high, laced beauties make her catch her breath. Stitched blue forget-me-nots and pink roses grow up the sides, heel, and over the top, with shiny gold threads lining the leaves. Wearing them would be like walking in a garden. That leather looks soft as butter, but when Martha Jane reaches up to verify it, the watchful storekeeper raises his broom at her, so she skitters out.

She ponders the hard question: if she had the money, would she buy necessary bread or lovely boots? She's still seventeen dollars shy of her twenty-dollar goal, to free Lena and Lige from the Mormons, and it might as well be a thousand. Maybe she needs another plan. Should she steal the boots for herself, to catch that rich man's eye and a hot meal? For what those boots are worth, she could sell them and buy her own meals for a while. Still, getting caught stealing something that pricey could land her in jail.

The next day, Martha Jane spies the flowered boots on that same pretty woman. Surely the rich man bought them for her, as a gift; it couldn't be what Ma used to call a "co-in-sid-ence." Martha envies the lady, and her lost chance curdles bitter in her mouth. When the woman, who Martha sees now is not much older than herself, lifts the hem of her skirt, flowers bloom.

So the world is a big market, all buying and selling. Martha Jane may be only a girl, but she knows already, every last thing has a price. What did those boots cost the lady? What did she give the man, to pay or thank him?

She follows the woman-child to the hotel but doesn't follow her inside. Instead, she walks around to the back door where hens cluck in coops, laying eggs or waiting to be plucked into dinner. Broken bedsteads lean against the wall. Piles of rotting vegetables stink, too far gone for Martha Jane to bother picking through. When the back door opens and a cross-eyed boy empties gray water from a dishpan, Martha calls out, "Hey."

"Hey yourself," he says back. "Whatcha want?"

"You work here?" As soon as she asks it, her face burns. *Of course, dummy,* she chides herself. *Why else would he be pitching dishwater?*

"Yup," he says. He doesn't tell her she's stupid or shake his head. He lets the screen door close behind him, drops the dishpan upside down on the step, and settles on it. He's bigger than Martha, probably older. His shock of black hair has a skunk stripe offset on the right, and his eyebrows nearly meet in the middle, above his disconcerting eyes. Martha Jane can't tell exactly which part of her he's looking at, but he's looking.

"Whatcha want?" he asks again, pulling a cigarette out of his shirt pocket and striking a match on his overalls seam. As he lights and puffs, Martha wonders if the cigarette is good, if she'd like it. She decides not to ask him for one, because she wants something else instead.

She explains how she had this beautiful pair of boots before her Ma died, but the banker took everything from her house to sell for Pa's debts, even her flowered boots, and that lady staying at the hotel somehow got them.

"They're mine," she lies. "Can you get them back for me?"

He laughs below his shoulders, his skinny chest pumping under his checkered shirt. Blue curls of smoke twirl out his nostrils, fogging the stripe in his hair. "That's a whopper if I ever heard one."

She insists so hard and so loud that it's true, she starts to believe it. They are hers, by right of seeing and wanting, if not by earning. Desire burns so hot, so deeply in Martha Jane, it is a kind of owning.

His brown, misaligned eyes blink at her. She stops talking and waits, recognizing that he sees her as clearly as anybody ever has and knows her for a liar. He doesn't turn away but lets her squirm.

"Well, hell," she finally says, kicking a food-crusted can at a red hen. "You helping me or not?"

He pinches the end of the cigarette to snuff it and tucks it back in his pocket. "What'll you gimme?"

Martha shrugs and lies some more. "I got nothing to give."

He squints and grins. "Maybe later we'll think of something."

Martha considers this. She studies her own busted boots, the brown leather caked with dry mud and split open so the soles flap like old ladies' tongues on Sunday. Last time she asked Eben, he told her because of her cussing and sassing, she didn't deserve new ones. So much for any hope of honest gain. This boy could get what Martha Jane needs, but she shies from an open deal. Papa always said to nail down the terms of a wager, surprisingly good advice coming from a lousy gambler.

"I'll make you johnnycakes so good they'll break your heart."

"Johnnycakes?" He picks his tooth, spits, and laughs again. "Well, ain't you a wonder. What's your moniker?"

"Martha Jane."

"I'm Ralph." He shakes his head. "Martha Jane, it'll take a hell of a stack of johnnycakes to buy a pair of boots. Not to mention the hell to pay, if I get caught."

Bastard, she thinks. *He's no friend.* "Never mind," she says, turning to go.

"I didn't say no. Come on back."

She studies him, wary. He's going to tease her now, maybe chase her and twist a pinch on the soft part of her arm or her nipple, the way boys do. But he doesn't. Instead, he studies her broken-down, busted boots like they make him sad. His shoes are old but polished, and the soles look solid yet.

"Little girl," he says, standing and picking up the dishpan. "You done broke my heart with your story. When that lady takes off her boots tonight, if she sets 'em outside her door to be polished, I'll pinch 'em for you."

Now that Ralph's agreed, the boots, lovely as they are, seem too small a thing to ask for. People never agree, but you keep asking anyway, seeking favors great and small. Nothing prepares a girl for kindness, for "yes." What if it's Martha Jane's only wish for a lifetime? Would she ask only for boots? Maye she could get more.

But these—they are more than they appear. The boots are a garden, comfort, and a new way to walk through whatever comes.

"Thank you," she says, grinning. "You get those boots for me, I'll call you King Ralph and fry up johnnycakes all the rest of your days."

Ralph, unlike most people she's known, is good as his word. The next day, he meets her at the kitchen's door with a brown paper parcel. "Not even broke in to her feet, they're so new," he says.

Watching her tear the paper, he rolls and lights a smoke.

"This is the nicest thing anybody's done for me." Martha Jane blinks back tears. She drops the old shoes off her feet and ties on the boots, turning her ankles one way, then another, to admire the embroidery.

"Look a little big. I could sell 'em for you, split the take." Ralph chuckles, little curls of smoke drifting from his nostrils.

Martha Jane glares. "You just try and get these off me. Anyway, I'll surely grow."

"Fine, then. They're your feet. I squirreled away a little honey, and the cook's napping, so you best get in there to fry up some 'cakes."

Stepping lightly to the kitchen door, Martha Jane laughs. "They'll be fluffy as clouds."

Coming back the next day to sit with Ralph on his morning break, she finds he's gone, fired for some reason. The boy who took his place eyes Martha as if she's gutter trash, despite her lovely boots. Martha Jane cusses the little lord, then sets out to see what she can pinch from the Main Street stores. People have been passing by her little comedy show, tossing no coins today. She's feeling nearer her last resort.

Outside the store where she first saw the boots, a man grabs her arm. Her heart races, fearing she's caught, but it's Eben, the farmer who took her in.

"Where have you been, Martha Jane?" His voice is kind, but insistent. "You can't run wild this way. Come home."

"You don't want me," she retorts. His sigh and his weary eyes confirm it, so she adds, "I'm no good."

He takes a deep breath and lets it out. "You can be good if you try," he says, releasing her and thrusting both hands in his pockets. "We'll ask the bishops about getting you baptized. Lena and Lige have received this grace already."

Martha Jane studies his broad face and neatly trimmed beard. His blue eyes are kind, but his good intentions make the little hairs stand up on her neck. "You baptized them?"

He nods. "They're Saints now, gaining a heavenly reward."

Damn. Strength runs out of her arms and legs, and she reels, about to faint. Her beautiful boots feel too heavy to lift, to run. She's worn out. Freedom is a hard responsibility and a burden, and the girl reconsiders the sweet hope of being a child, with someone else taking care. But these Mormons worked her hard in their house, more like a servant than a daughter. They claimed they only beat her to save her soul, but that kind of religion makes no sense to Martha Jane.

She steadies herself and throws up a challenge. "I can't believe in Brigham Young. None of the rest of it, neither, far as what you told me."

"In time," he says. "It will come to you." But he shakes his head, and his eyes drift off her face. He never looks that way with Lena or Lige, never so hard or impatient. That expression is a loose lid over a beating or a slap. Martha admits it to herself; when she's not pretending to be somebody else, she rubs people raw. Born wrong, never to fit in.

"You're kind to ask," she says. "I'll think about it."

"You're a child. You don't decide, you obey. Come along." His voice hardens, and he grabs for her, but she dodges his calloused hand.

"Tell your wife I won't scrub her piss pots anymore," Martha answers. Turning on her shiny heel, she darts through a gaggle of well-dressed children and escapes him.

CHAPTER EIGHT
BETTER THAN HUNGER

Outside Great Salt Lake City, high on the far side of the lake, she finds folks more her kind—a cluster of rag-tag men and women and dirty children camped in tents. They've tried to claim property near the Mormon city but can't dig in. Whenever they marked their plots, men on horseback who call themselves Danites pulled up the stakes and ordered the would-be settlers to move along, if they have no formal part in their church. This is Brigham Young's country.

It's a restless group, like gypsies who move from the lake, track the streams, and ascend the mountains above the city. They long for their own promised land but have no leader. These wanderers from Missouri absorb Martha Jane the way ground drinks water. She finds with them a sort of family, but not one person tells her when to come or go. They're generous, ladling their watery soups, and she shares her scraps with them. The liberty and safety suit the girl's needs.

At night, they bring out banjos, fiddles, and mouth harps to play and dance around a fire. As long as they're out of sight of the Saints' true city, the avenging Danites won't bust up the party. After enough whiskey, the drinkers whisper about Brigham Young and the power of his church. Some of them had been Mormon but drifted away for reasons Martha can't discern, though she hears mention of a massacre in Mountain Meadows, years ago.

It's clear these vagabonds both crave Brigham Young's touch

and fear his reach, as they would the arm of God. Some of them, still pious, won't drink the whiskey, and they still wear their temple garments, a peculiar underwear they believe will keep them free from sin. Martha Jane wonders if Lena and Lige wear temple garments now.

In the firelight, the drinking men gather courage to sing a ballad that tingles Martha Jane's spine, a lament of John D. Lee. One line remembers men, women, and children who died like melting wax on the word of Brigham Young. For their courage to sing against that fierce Lion, Martha Jane trusts the exiles.

Leaving their bottles beside tree stumps so they can dance, the men unwittingly offer Martha something she can't refuse. The strong drink gives her a light, free, and familiar feeling, taking her back to Cilus and the trail. After several swallows, the whiskey makes her cry for him and her other lost brothers and sisters. Eventually, though, her cares drift up, away, with the campfire smoke.

Joining the other dancers in a reel, she forgets for an hour that her siblings lodge in strangers' houses, learning a new religion. She unloads her obligation to save and feed them, to fix everything, the duty she's carried all her years. As if she were those children's mother. The whiskey returns her childhood and steals her worries, so she sips what she can. She dances, and the older boys twirl her as if she's pretty. One tries to steal a kiss. She imagines being free, a woman grown.

In the light of dawn, her head throbs from the whiskey, but she keeps the lightness and joy of the dance. She picks up chores in the camp, glad to work when she's not forced or beaten. One woman gives her an old, cut-down skirt and shirtwaist to replace her grimy, tattered ones. But in the ash and dirt of the camp, her fine boots darken to gray, the flowers fade, and she forgets how they looked, when new.

The boys who tried to kiss her at night are polite during the day, but they wander off to practice shooting and wrestling. She follows, hiding behind trees to watch, and soon figures she can shoot as well as some of them, and better than most. She studies how they spin pistols on their trigger fingers, slipping them into rough leather holsters. She likes how they push their hats back on their heads and let hair fall down in their eyes. Tossing back the dregs of last night's whiskey, they pretend it doesn't burn their throats. Shoving each other's shoulders, they cuss and laugh, while their sisters back in camp churn butter and scrub. Martha Jane feels sick with envy. She doesn't only want to be among them, she wants to *be* them, possessing their swaggers and skills.

The camp women are kind, but conservative in their ways, murmuring about Joseph Smith and living at Great Salt Lake again. A few of them are sister wives, loving their shared husbands even beyond Brigham Young's command. They warn Martha to stay away from the boys, to act like a lady. They hand her needles, thread, and scraps of calico, and dough to knead. As the girl fumbles, the boys' pistol shots and laughter pierce her with injustice, that she should be locked down in camp. After she drops the cloth or dough and wanders off several times, the women begin to talk about her, instead of to her.

To hell with them, she mutters and recovers some cast-off boy's trousers to wear. She tucks her hair into a hat and challenges the fellows to a shooting match. They laugh and tell her to go cook their supper, so she takes on the biggest boy with a roundhouse punch. He rubs his jaw, squints, balls up his fist as if he'd punch her back, then busts out a laugh. The leader, he overrules the others; she can stay.

She's too wise to outshoot them every time but fires wild three times out of ten, to spare their feelings and yet earn sufficient respect. When the women corral the boys for the heavy chores, gathering and cutting firewood, Martha matches their work and earns her place in the camp, if not in the mothers' good graces.

She's happy to have crossed over into a way of being that's real for her. She keeps her dress, though. She'll wear it when she pleases, and only then, and won't again let anybody narrow her down.

But her sense of self only makes things worse, and her stay with the former Mormons ends abruptly. When an older boy gives Martha Jane too much attention and a kiss on the cheek, rumors circulate that Martha Jane's a bad girl. Even among folks who've fallen off the religion tree, Martha stands judged.

"But I never," she objects, to find nobody's listening.

The mothers form a calicoed wall around their innocent boys, ordering Martha Jane Cannary to move on.

She drifts to a rough camp where men put on no religious airs. They're miners on the move, mule skinners out of work, a trapper who can no longer breathe at high altitudes, and one scarred, educated runaway slave from Carolina. Martha Jane sidles up to their campfire as if she belongs, hefts a cast-iron skillet, and sizzles up johnnycakes and bacon for everyone.

Great Salt Lake City's only a few miles downhill from this rascal camp, but Martha Jane feels farther. Her ties to Lena and Lige are loosening. These men drink, cuss, chew, and spit like the miners she knew in Virginia City, so she feels, for the most part, at home. But her body's changing inside her boy's clothing, and she feels the men's dark, sexual heat, even when they avert their eyes.

Then one man crosses the line. After everyone else is asleep, he pulls aside her blanket and settles in. Half-asleep, she feels his hands inside her trousers, and it's all she can do to shove him off. Leaving behind all she owns, she flees the camp into moonlit trees.

Next morning, she stumbles back into the city, arms scratched from brambles and knees bruised from falling on stones. Trembling from her close call, she knows what the man wanted, what he seemed ready to take by force, and also knows she's not ready. The hands in the dark surprised and panicked her, having believed herself brave enough for anything.

When she arrives penitent on farmer Eben's front porch, he blocks the door. But his wife, sweet, round-faced Mary, claims to see a change in Martha Jane.

"You're humbled," the woman says, touching Martha's greasy hair.

"I need help," the girl admits and casts her eyes down. "I need me some kind of mother, after all."

Mary nods, steps aside, and against her husband's objection raises a finger to his lips. "I'll deal with her, Eben," she insists.

Lena and Lige rush up to her with hugs, while Eben shakes his head, unconvinced. "She's just hungry, not sorry at all," he mutters. "And look out. She's got lice crawling in her hair." His wife, coursing with motherhood, doesn't break her smile.

She tries. She really does. Martha Jane polishes the grates, washes windows with vinegar and balled-up newspaper, and scrubs the dusty porch with a boar's-hair brush and suds. She even rinses the piss pots, those "never agains." She labors until her knees throb and her hands bleed, vowing to keep Mary satisfied, for taking her in.

But Eben catches her smoking behind the barn, scolds her for riding the old mare astride, and slaps her for talking back. Despite his repeated warnings, she slips out of her dresses and into trousers whenever he leaves the house. He raises welts across her back with a leather strap and insists Mary wash out the girl's mouth with lye soap when she swears, so often Martha Jane's mouth feels raw.

Finally, Eben refuses to keep a hoyden under his roof. He orders her out, leaving Mary, Lena, and Lige in tears, but Martha relieved.

"Being good is too damned much work," she mutters, turning her back on her brother and sister, who hang on the porch rail, sniffling and frowning.

Martha Jane stays inside the city limits now, afraid of grabby men who hunker in the hills and on the trails. She knocks on doors, offering to do housework or cook. At the right moment, an overwhelmed mother hires her for cleaning and laundry. That situation ends in less than a week, when the oldest son steals his father's watch and blames Martha Jane.

Wandering off the main streets, Martha's surprised to find a few saloons. It seems not everybody's Mormon here in the holy city, and there's even a liquor store, not far from Brigham Young's temple. Of course, as he reminds the Saints in the *Deseret News,* true believers refuse coffee, tea, and intoxicating liquor. Despite his admonitions, the saloons and City Liquor store thrive, and Martha finds strange comfort in that; maybe there's room for the likes of her in Great Salt Lake City, after all.

Martha Jane charms Saul, the jovial, chubby owner of a Jewish mercantile who spots her for the orphan she is and welcomes her to his family's table. She finds the Jews of Great Salt Lake to be generous, feeding her and offering shelter as the nights get colder. The girl sees the security and contentment of their children and daydreams of bringing Lena and Lige here, to this loving home.

For a month, Saul overpays her to sweep and stock shelves in his tidy store. For Martha Jane, this is a revelation; Jews aren't greedy or selfish, as Pa accused them of being, and Martha Jane wonders if anything her parents told her is true. So far, nothing they said or showed her has prepared her for life on her own.

She's soon saved seventeen dollars, nearly the amount she'd planned for freeing her siblings. The money's hard-earned, though, and she's not sure she can shelter and feed two children, as well as herself. Saul and his wife may be generous, but with their own two children they have little to spare, so bringing the others here won't be possible. Nor can she expect to live rent-free forever, as the generosity of strangers can be a shaky, changeable thing.

Still, Martha Jane worries Lena could end up a sister wife among Mormons, if left where she is. Her brother might end up wanting several wives, instead of loving one. At least, she comforts herself, if she goes back for them someday, they won't always feel abandoned. In the meantime, maybe they'll work their way closer to heaven, the Mormon way; as for Martha Jane, she already sees how easy it is to fall along the way home to God, even on those days when she's genuinely trying to do right.

She pines for them, and the cold, dark lonesome hits her hard after a month without Lena and Lige. She has nobody now and wonders if she'll ever be part of a family. But when she takes a little whiskey and sets aside her guilt, it's a relief to only be responsible for herself. That's hard enough.

Whiskey keeps her body warm and her worries at bay, but it's expensive. She learns to put up her hair, dress like a lady, sit quietly in the saloon, and wait for a nice man to buy her a drink. As she sips the burning liquid, she pretends to listen to him and laughs at his jokes. In her heart, though, she waits for the better part, that sense of something immense like God or, at least, the rush of warm feelings about Him. Not the sort of father-god who'd sell his children. Not a mother who forgets her daughter. Someone she can trust.

After a few shots, it comes, that warm breath in her hair and something like a whisper saying, *Fear the judgment of no man. Martha Jane belongs to me, and she is loved.*

While today's generous businessman creeps his hand under the table out of sight, Martha Jane's heart cracks open, and tears flood her eyes. The grace. The glory, so bright. She feels light as an angel and looks back to see if she's sprouted wings. If only she could feel the same when praying or in church as she feels with whiskey, she could be a decent girl, a real Christian after all. She could be sure of the God who hides.

But after the two additional shots the man presses to her lips, everything spins, and the girl runs outside sobbing, vomiting in the street. The businessman holds her arm until she's finished, then leads her up a flight of stairs, not to heaven, but to a room.

He answers her yes, she's an angel, a sweetheart, a porcelain doll. He puts his hands everywhere at once. Backing away, she falls down on the bed, and as he tears her dress she thrashes to roll away, but the room tilts. Martha Jane tumbles down and around in one place, into herself, and she finds herself to be a deep, black well.

The next morning, she's alone in the hotel room in a soft, clean bed, but she's sick and ashamed of something she can't remember. The man's long gone, but three silver dollars shine on the bedside table. She has a powerful thirst, and she'd cry, but she can't make tears. After drinking until her belly's a hard lump, and then washing herself at the porcelain pitcher and bowl, Martha rewraps herself in the soft, wrinkled sheets.

Her body stings and aches in wrong places.

Eyeing the bedside coins, she hates the silver for what it means. Because of what it makes her, more like Ma than she meant to be. But if she gives the money to Lena and Lige, then it won't be wrong. It'll be a work of mercy, a sin turned to good, to save somebody else.

Besides, no girl can be a true daughter of sin when she's only twelve years and four days old.

She blinks and whispers to the lady in the painting above the bed, "I'm just a child."

Martha's fresh, hot tears run down as she promises the good, warm God who loves her, the one who comes to her in the whiskey, she'll never let it happen again.

CHAPTER NINE
SPLITTING

Martha Jane marches up the farmhouse porch and raps on the door, twenty dollars tucked in her belt and her knees knocking together with the enormity of her choice. This time, nobody's dropping the weight on her. She's decided to be a mother, to claim her family, and it scares her nearly to death. She's resigned to leaving the baby sisters where they are, but Lena and Lige will grow up with Martha Jane. It's another promise she's made to God.

When her brother and sister answer the door, Martha Jane deepens her voice to sound confident. "Come on," she orders. "We're getting out of here."

Lena's been crying, and Martha asks what happened.

"Ma switched me for leaving suds in the corners after I washed the floor."

"She's not your ma, and that's foolishness I'd never hit you for," Martha sputters. "You come with me. I'm your family."

Lige shakes his head. "It's rough out there, Martha Jane. We can't make it."

He doesn't know the half of it. Martha Jane shivers but puts on a brave face. "Sure we can, together."

The back door slams, and Eben's voice rises, calling for his wife.

"Now," Martha Jane whispers, poking her thumb toward the road.

"I gotta get my things," Lena argues, heading up the stairs.

"Meet me behind the roses—fifteen minutes." Martha Jane backs away from Eben's nearer voice.

"I got nothing to pack. I'll come now." Lige bumps his shoulder against Martha Jane's as they hurry across the lawn. "I sure as hell missed you, sister. And I'm not gonna be Mormon, not even to get my own star someday."

Martha shakes her head. "What the hell would you do with a planet?"

Lige shrugs. "It's like Christians believing in heaven, I guess."

"That's a stretch, too," she mumbles. "But maybe we can make a little one on earth, us three."

Lena eases the screen door shut and scurries out, toting a pillowcase full of clothes.

Martha nods and hugs her, moving her along behind some trees. "Sister," she chokes out, relieved, and shifts the burden to her own shoulders. "Let's get something to eat," she says, eager to prove her care for them.

She leads them to a little café, where they stuff themselves with roast beef, potatoes, and gravy.

Lige belches, and Lena giggles. "You gonna whip him for that?"

"Hell, no." Martha chuckles. "I'm gonna top him." She croaks out an even deeper one, to the frowning disapproval of the gentleman one table over.

Martha stacks coins on the table for the bill, with a tip for the serving girl.

Lige wipes gravy on his sleeve and sighs. "Martha Jane, maybe I was wrong."

She walks them to the alley shed she's furnished as a little home, with crates for tables, cast-off rockers, and a cracked iron stove she's patched with dark clay.

"It's like a doll's house," Lena murmurs, setting down her bundle on a corner pallet.

"I'll find work," Lige offers, grinning. "I learned from Eben how to work in an orchard and how to bale hay."

"That'll be good. Whatever you can do. You two settle in, while I go work, too."

As she closes the little shed door, Martha Jane feels proud. She wishes her father could see it; she's the better man.

Two blocks from the shed, somebody sneaks up behind and tickles her ribs. She whirls with a punch, then laughs to find Ralph's crossed eyes above her.

"King Ralph! I figured you skipped town."

He shakes his head. "Just looking for greener pastures, but they was brown." He eyes her boots, not so lovely now. "Things gone hard for you, girl?"

"I find my way," she answers, smoothing her skirt and lifting her chin. "I got my brother and sister back from the Mormons. Got them a little place, too."

"How you do that?"

"Different kinds of work," she says, waving details away. Taking three rubber balls from her pocket, she tosses them into a juggled waterfall.

Ralph nods, jutting out a lip. "Hmm. People pitch pennies for that?"

"Nickels and dimes, mostly," she brags. "Once I got a dollar."

"You gonna need more than nickels and dimes, to keep two children."

She nods and sighs. "I'll do it."

Ralph looks her up and down and says, "You almost looking pretty, so grown."

"Don't hurt yourself, tossing such big compliments," Martha retorts.

"I'm not kidding. Some man might pay good money to kiss you, love you up a little."

"I don't want that," she says, pushing away that bad night in the hotel.

"A little poke ain't nothin'," Ralph says. "And I can get you clean fellows, nice ones who won't hurt you. No dirty miners or ruffians, I swear."

Martha Jane raises her voice. "I won't sell myself."

Ralph's cocky grin flattens. "And here I thought you'd be grateful, after all I done for you." He glances at her boots and shrugs, muttering, "I lost my job because of you."

Martha Jane shrugs, admitting to herself she owes him. "Well, anything but that."

Ralph backs away, cold. "No more favors for you, Missy. Your name is mud."

Angry, she's ready to let him go, but it niggles at her as he walks away. She has no other friend in the world, and he did risk his livelihood for her. Him calling her a liar is more than she can stand. It's one thing to wind up a stretcher, to make people laugh, but it's another for folks to say your word's no good.

"Wait!" She digs down for the words, then regrets each one as it leaves her mouth. "You swear he won't be mean?" *Dear Lord,* she thinks, *she's stepping on hell's cellar door now.*

Ralph forgives in an instant and hurries back, running a hand through his striped hair. "I got a real gentleman set aside for you, Martha Jane." He steps closer and kisses the top of her head. "You're a good sort. I knew I could count on you. The way this works, you get seventy-five percent after expenses, and I get twenty-five, for picking the best customers."

"Only this one, because I owe you," she objects. "There won't be any others; this ain't a business partnership." Martha unclasps her clammy hands and dries them on her skirt, then breathes deeply to slow down her heart.

Walking home, she tells herself that, in a roundabout way,

she's doing this for Lena and Lige, not just for Ralph. She won't spend it on herself but will feed her family. And this way, nobody can say Martha Jane Cannary's a liar.

Like Pa always said, your word is your bond.

The gentleman Ralph sends up to the hotel room is as promised, respectful and clean, but Martha Jane still feels dirty afterwards. When the man leaves, he claims he paid Ralph already. Closing the door behind him, Martha stands wrapped in a quilt and rests her head on the door.

"It wasn't so bad," she tells herself, making a beeline for the washstand. But it was, and she's lower than a skunk. Not to mention, she lied to God. Again.

Ralph deducts the price of the room and his percentage, leaving Calamity seventy-five cents for her trouble. She wants to cuss him, hit him, or otherwise cause him some damage he won't soon forget. Instead, she forces a smile and says, "I'm done with you, Ralph. If I'm to be a scarlet woman, I'll take my own chances from now on."

Ralph shrugs. "Well, you ain't hardly a woman, or scarlet, neither. But I earned my share, Martha Jane. It's what a pimp's for, to protect a girl and manage things."

"I'll manage without one, then," she says, hardening her voice and turning her back on him. She sees him now. He's no friend, just a schemer who wants to profit off her.

The cold lonesome settles in again, and she stiffens her shoulders against her shame. Worse, she feels she was a fool for trusting Ralph. Maybe there's no such thing as a friend, but only family after all. She has precious little of that.

Dabbing sweat from her forehead with her sleeve, she feels the coins weigh down the pocket where she stowed her juggling balls. To cheer herself, and to feel more like the girl she was, she stands on a street corner and tosses them, one, two, three, keeping them airborne in high curves while singing, "Oh, Susannah." Two well-dressed men drop coins at her feet, a better morning's work, untainted. She tries not to think of that other deal and vows to put it behind her.

How Lige heard of it, Martha would never know, but he's fit to be tied when she returns to their shack with apples, bread, and cheese for her family's supper.

"You're as bad as Ma," he cries, knocking the food from her hands, to roll across the dirt floor.

She stammers, "What?"

"Don't lie!" he shouts. "I know you went with that man."

His eyes scare her into telling the truth. "I made a bad deal," she whispers, trembling. "It wasn't what I wanted!"

Lige won't listen but storms out, leaving Martha Jane and Lena in tears. Lena pats her shoulder and says, "I can't have you sinning for me."

When Martha Jane tears open the loaf for her little sister, Lena won't take it from her hand.

Martha Jane's eyes are dry, but still red, when Lige returns, but she's not prepared. He rushes around the shed, repacking the pillowcase Lena had emptied a few hours earlier.

"We're going back to Eben and Mary. Mary's kind to Lena, mostly, and I can head out on my own in a year or so. I'll light out for the mines up north, where there's new gold strikes."

Lena nods, says it's not so bad there, that Mary doesn't let Eben whip her much. And there's always food.

Martha Jane tries to argue, but Lige won't let her speak.

"We won't be the cause for your whoring, and you burning in hell," Lige blurts out, blushing.

Martha Jane hangs her head. "I could still do it the honest way, I swear. I'm sorry I failed you. I just love you, need you . . ."

"You didn't fail; you did more than you shoulda," Lena

murmurs, "but it was the wrong kind of love."

Martha Jane can't believe there's any such thing. What shouldn't a person do, to save her loved ones, anyway? Sick over losing them again, she lashes out at her sister. "So you think you're better than me, now?"

"No," Lige interrupts, leaning between the sisters. "Maybe worse, because you did it on account of us."

Martha Jane hugs herself and shudders. "I meant to protect you."

Lige dashes away tears and sets his jaw. "You can't, because you're just a kid, too. Not as grown as you think."

"I can take care of myself," Martha retorts.

"But not us," Lige insists, taking Lena's arm. "We're going back, Martha Jane. I'm not gonna stand by while my sister becomes a . . ."

"Whore?" Martha Jane grimaces around the word she's thought but never said out loud.

"A . . . lost girl. Maybe if we go, you'll be saved."

Martha Jane cringes under the raised whip of religion. Sorrow floods her, and she waves Lena and Lige out the door, pretending rage. "Go on, then. Give up on our family." Her eyes brim with tears she won't let them see. She's near to breaking to pieces under her failure, but worse, she's weak with relief to finally set down the burden, the responsibility of care.

As they walk away, she whispers after them, "It ain't your fault. Not one damned bit."

When her brother and sister turn the corner and pass out of sight, she walks the opposite direction to the saloon. It's all she can hope for, that God might wait for her there, even now.

CHAPTER TEN
HELL ON WHEELS

1869

Great Salt Lake City clenches like a fist pounding her chest with the constant reminder, the hard ache of failing her brother and sisters inescapable here. How can she reconcile herself to failing the folks she loves?

In this, Brigham Young's paradise, godly people press in, each one making Martha Jane feel low about herself since she's become what the kindest would call a fair but frail girl or a soiled dove. She can't help but feel changed beneath her skin, and seems there's no turning back, now that Lige and Lena know what she's done.

Sin is a terrible weight, she thinks, *and there's no dropping it once it hangs itself around your neck. Even if you'd like to set it down, folks won't let you.* She wonders whether Ma felt this way when people watched and whispered as she passed, and whether she ever stopped caring.

Once she's made up her mind, Martha considers how best to travel. She follows a bullwhacker from tavern to store, then on to his tent under a tree outside the city. He walks without staggering, still sober at the end of the day, and when she approaches his campsite, instead of shooing her away, he offers her a tin plate of beans.

As she accepts it, he rumbles, "What you eyeing me for, girl?"

The tone of his voice, hoarse but gentle, eases her. She detects no menace there, so she admits, "I need me a ride to Fort Bridger."

He shakes his head and narrows his eyes. "Fort Bridger ain't no place for a little gal. No good would come of it."

"I've got no home. Nobody. I can find work there, washing, cleaning, or cooking." Martha resists wrinkling her nose at the burnt beans. They smell and taste awful but fill her growling, hollow core.

The old man nods, then. "Sure enough there's call for those things at the fort. Maybe I can find you a family to look out for you."

"I don't need anybody," she argues, and the man grunts, then shovels in his own beans with a bent spoon. Speaking with his mouth full, he adds, "Well, I'll get you there safe." Grunting again, he tosses his coffee dregs into the dying fire. When she's finished her food, he gives her a smoky-smelling blanket and invites her to settle under his wagon for the night.

Minutes after he retires to his tent, snores rip the evening sky. Rolling herself in the blanket below him and tamping down the grass, Martha wishes she could fall asleep as fast as this man, whose name she forgot to ask.

The next day, she learns his baptized name is Red, not a nickname for anything, but after the Bible's Red Sea. He has a headful of stories, but not one is from the Bible. Martha matches him tale for tale, and as they roll into Fort Bridger, he tells her she's more than paid her way, with entertainment.

"That journey never felt to go so fast. You got the gift of gab, and a big imagination," Red pronounces, easing down off the wagon seat and handing over her little bundle. "I could see those ropes fraying, clear as day, while your Pa lowered your wagon down that Wyoming cliff, coming west." He reaches out as if to pat her cheek, sees her cringe, then jams his hand into his pocket, instead. "You're a good girl, Miss Martha Jane Cannary. Stay that way, and don't trust the wrong folks."

Good? How does he not notice what she is? Martha wonders, then feels grateful the stain of sin isn't as dark on her as she feared. Maybe she still is, or could become again, good.

Red walks her into the store, where he holds a hushed conversation with the sutler, who sits on a scuffed pickle barrel. The younger man peers at Martha and nods.

"See here," Red announces when it's settled, "Mr. Sand runs a little laundry out back. He could use your help. Would that suit you, girl?"

"Sure, Red," she agrees, sizing up the sutler. He's short, with legs that don't reach the floor from the top of the barrel, and his blue eyes light up a face plain as a tin pan. He seems young to be running a store but appears kind enough. "I thank you. You've been good to me, Red, and I won't forget it."

Red waves away her gratitude and selects a tobacco pouch, tossing it on the counter beside the till. "I'll have me some jerky. Add on whatever this gal wants to eat."

Martha points to a basket of bread and a round of cheese. "Just a hard roll with a wedge of that, please."

Grinning up at Red, she says, "I'll pay you back someday."

"You set me in one of your tall tales, make me live forever, and we'll call it even."

Martha Jane grins and agrees. It's hard to see Red go, because he made her feel safe and not so lonely. As he leaves the store, Martha's hands tremble, and her heart chills. Here she is again, bound to a stranger. But over the next few days, the sutler proves to be as gentle and plain as his face. He works her hard but sets up a cot for her in the back room, where she can lock herself in and feel safe at night.

She's not sure why she itches to run. She's well fed and has a roof overhead, but the fort feels nothing like a home. The soldiers cussing and walking free make her wish for a different life. She's restless and twice nearly walks into the soldiers' saloon for some fun, but knows it'll be the end of her job with the sutler. He's a Mormon, too. Kind, fair, and very strict, he's not inclined to put up with any nonsense.

Religious folks can sure put a crimp in your wire.

She overhears two soldiers discussing Piedmont, a wild little town not far from the fort. Overcome by restlessness, Martha Jane ties her belongings in a bundle and tosses it over her shoulder. Not a hundred yards down the road, she already feels better.

But then she notices the sad Shoshone who walk the trail with her. Haunted by stories Pa told, she's afraid of them, but they slide their eyes away from the little white girl beneath their notice. Like a dog being ignored, Martha Jane has to be seen, so she offers a Shoshone boy a crumble of cheese. He smells it and makes a face, then offers Martha a flat, greasy stick of meat. She tastes it, surprised by the sweet and savory blend of chokecherries and smoke.

"Good," she says, nodding, and the boy pops the cheese into his mouth. He twists a wry face again but doesn't spit out her gift.

Thinking she may have found a friend, Martha's hurt when the boy walks off without a word. *Maybe he's like me,* she reasons, *lonesome, but too proud to admit it.* Then she sees him run to a cluster of children and a frowning, blanketed woman who narrows her eyes at Martha Jane. *Even that boy has a family,* she thinks. Stiff with resentment, Martha almost throws the last bite of pemmican on the ground but thinks better of it. Today, hunger's nearer than any friend.

She picks up her walking pace and then waves down a family in a wagon, to reach Piedmont by nightfall. It won't do to sleep out in the open alone, with Indians around. As the wagon passes that Shoshone boy, she doesn't look back or wave from her high seat.

Five beehive-shaped kilns hump tall outside Piedmont, and Martha takes them for Mormon structures, given that those believers hold the beehive to be a sign of their hard work and community. When she says so, the driver explains those kilns have no Mormon meaning. They've provided charcoal for trains since Piedmont first became a hell-on-wheels (pardon his language) town for the up-and-coming railroad. The town still chars and supplies it, along with water the trains require.

"Everything revolves about the railroad now," he tells her. "Someday folks won't go anywhere by horse or wagon, that they could go by train."

As he speaks, an incoming train puts out a frightful, shuddering attack on Martha's senses. Blowing smoke and steam, screeching, thumping, stinking, and roaring into the station, its vibrations rumble up through her feet, into her heart. Her eyes burn and stream from the smoke, so she dries them on her sleeve, but she can't stop looking. Fascinated, she swears that, once she finds work, she'll save all her money for tickets to ride that grand monster, maybe as far as another world.

The kind sutler at Fort Bridger had mentioned friends of his in this town, the Altons, so at the Piedmont general store, Martha Jane inquires about them.

"Ed's a laborer, and Emma runs a boarding house," the man behind the counter tells her. "They got a little boy, name of Charlie."

"I'm looking for a position," Martha Jane says, spinning it as she speaks, "maybe to take care of children, cook, and clean."

"They'd be a good family," he says, judging her grubby hands and dusty dress. "There's plenty of work to be done in that house. She won't put up with any trouble, though, and she likes things clean."

"I sure could use some soap and water, sir, after that dusty road," she says with a shrug, apologizing. "But I got no trouble to give," she promises, folding her hands and thinking of Lena, mimicking her sister's best angel face. "I'm a good, church-going girl, orphaned when my folks got killed by Indians, coming west."

Red was right, she thinks. When she needs to, Martha can spin quite a yarn.

Sizing up what the storekeeper delivered to her door, Emma Alton squints, hesitates, and then agrees to give the girl a chance: room and board in exchange for child care, not only for her own boy, but also for the boarders, as well as cooking and laundry. Martha Jane will earn ten cents a week in spending money if she works hard, which, by the girl's quick calculation, won't get her very far on any train. Martha Jane agrees anyway. She's tired, hungry, and glad for a roof as nice as this clapboard house can offer, for now.

After two days she wonders, though, whether she truly prefers a house to the open road.

She tells Mrs. Alton she's fifteen, despite just passing her thirteenth birthday in May. No sense letting on what a child she still is, when she's already responsible for herself. Do-gooders make up your mind for you, if you tell them the truth, and Martha Jane's sure Mrs. Alton is one of those, dyed in the wool.

It irks Martha Jane when the woman tries to mother her: yanking back on her shoulders to make her stand up straight and insisting she press knife-sharp pleats into every skirt and blouse. She makes Martha Jane pronounce every word distinctly, the way a lady would. Mrs. Alton is relentless in her rules, always watching, and Martha finds it the hardest thing she's ever done, to abide in her household.

She soon figures out she's the only girl in town without a mother or father, the only woman dangling like a fraying, loose end of rope—that is, other than those few in tents outside town, the kind you don't mention. There's respectability in the Alton house, so Martha tries hard. She cleans and cares for Charlie, as well as all the other boarders' children. Nights, she falls asleep with little time to wonder about her life, but through her open window she hears music and dancing from across town.

The music tickles and nibbles at her, so finally she slips out that same bedroom window, carrying her shoes so they won't thump on the shingles. Shimmying down a trellis of dusty, autumn-drying roses, she hurries down the street in the dark, past the best of Piedmont's houses.

Crossing the main avenue, she finds golden light, piano and fiddle music, and men's laughter spilling from several open doors onto the boardwalks. Spitting on her palm and smoothing down her hair, she glances at her gaslit reflection in a store window and takes a deep breath. She's been good so far, keeping Mrs. Alton's rules, but a powerful thirst for fun has her feet itching for rhythm. With a light heart, she steps through a yellow-lit saloon door.

Because so few unattached girls live in Piedmont, Martha Jane's eager feet get little rest, scuffing and whirling through shottisches, reels, waltzes, and squares with at least a dozen partners. She drinks whatever's offered and finds her heart lightening, head spinning, and burdens falling away.

Too soon, the eastern sky pearls gray and pink, and Martha Jane's dance partners slow down, most nodding off with their heads on tables, or staggering home. Hurrying back to Mrs. Alton's boarding house, the girl climbs the bowing trellis and into her bed before breakfast.

Her puffed, scratchy eyelids, throbbing head, and cotton mouth from the whiskey make her chores more difficult, but now she knows how to survive this hard life. There's always a party somewhere, and a young girl like Martha Jane will never want for companions. Dancing with the fellows sure makes life worth living. A girl can't live on work alone.

The soldiers, miners, laborers, and cowboys give Martha much to think on. She envies how free men are, staying out all hours and then coming and going as they please all day. Meanwhile, their women, the wives and daughters, stay lonesome at home. Then there are the girls they pay for pleasure. Martha wants a free life but won't sell herself again. Best to go among those men dressed as they are, as free in every way.

After her second week of sneaking-out nights, Martha Jane dresses in Mr. Alton's old cotton shirt and some trousers a boarder left behind. She gathers loose fabric with a belt she's cut from an old bridle. Unable to see her full image in the book-sized mirror hanging beside her attic bed, she glimpses enough of herself to like the effect. Tying her hair back in a knot, she settles her old floppy hat and tucks up the loose wisps that soften her face. Her heart pounds as she wonders whether the saloon boys will recognize her. And will they still want to dance?

They know her right away and still seek her as a partner. One fellow offers her a bite off his plug of tobacco and shows her how to tuck it next to her gum. He says she's even prettier in trousers than she was in a dress. Exhilarated, she kisses him on the cheek but then punches his shoulder to keep him from getting the wrong idea. He laughs and backs away. Martha Jane gets so worked up, with a nickel of her earnings she buys herself a drink to calm down. It's the last one she pays for, that night.

Reeling home, dizzy and tired, Martha loses her euphoria when Mrs. Alton meets her, arms crossed, at the trellis. Beyond words in her disappointment and anger, the woman slaps Martha Jane's face and locks the girl in her attic room, pronouncing her punishment. There'll be no food for a day, and Martha Jane's to spend her time repentant, in prayer.

Still wearing her men's clothing, Martha falls on her little bed, repentant only for getting caught. Glory, it was a beautiful night. The fellows really liked her, even in men's clothes, and maybe more than before. They didn't hush their smutty jokes around her but let her listen in, one of the boys. Falling asleep, she dreams of men smiling, holding her close, and toasting their trouser-sporting queen of the dance.

By the time Mrs. Alton releases her, Martha Jane's decided she'd best simmer down, or she'll be on the road again. She avoids the saloons for a few weeks but aches for the attention, music, and fun. Winter brings a mixed comfort and torment; as it sets in hard and fast, she's less tempted to run around cold, icy streets in the dark, yet more bored than ever.

Frustrated and lonesome, Martha Jane pulls faces at Mrs. Alton when the woman turns her back, sending Charlie into fits of giggles. She reminds herself everybody has to work sometimes, but she pines to become a woman, grown and free. Come that fine day, she'll ride a train over the Territories to see it all.

On a damp May morning in 1869, Martha Jane's in town picking out potatoes and apples for Mrs. Alton, when a hubbub in the street distracts her. Piedmont's usually quiet, but this morning it teems with hundreds of men shouldering through. Behind the rhythmic ring of metal on hot metal at the smithy, and deeper than the steady rumble-rattle of wagons, thuds a feverish bass. A mob gathers and pulses in the street. Boots stomp the boardwalks and ground, and disgruntled men growl, deep as a hymn the devil would sing.

A boy in knickers and a sooty shirt stops when she asks him about the fuss. He explains the men are railroad workers, suppliers, tie cutters, and wood haulers for the Union Pacific, whose transcontinental line these very men extended to Promontory Summit. They've heard Mr. Thomas Clark Durant, the vice president of the company who held back their hard-earned wages, will pass through today on a special train to claim glory for their work at the junction of the eastward and westward tracks. Word is, the rioters would block him from attending his ceremony, unless he pays.

Martha dives into the crowd, caught up in the simmering fluids of violence. She recognizes some faces from the saloons, but today those men are hot with resentment and blind to Martha Jane. Still, she moves with them, shoved and sometimes half carried by their close, hard-muscled bodies and thrilled to be part of a cause, an energy so much greater than herself. Her heart beats fast, and she shouts with them—"Hold the train!"—and raises her fist with theirs. She's their partner in this dance, too.

The determined men forge a wall of protest on the tracks as a train whistle wails to the east. Some workers, fearing the corporate train won't yield to mere flesh, carry and stack leftover railroad ties across the shining rails, while boys toss old chairs, scraps of lumber, and chunks of cement on top, to fortify the construction.

"If the cheating bastards won't stop," Martha Jane hears one swear, "they'll derail."

With chuffs and rumbles, the oncoming engine approaches, sounding its whistle in fast, short bursts. The locomotive's more than a point on the horizon now, its weight and momentum more solid than flesh. Yet the human wall, finding its own mass and courage in union, surges forward like a mudslide. Near enough for them to see the cowcatcher, the stack, and the sunlight flashing off its polished trim, the engine rushes toward the station. The men shout louder and press together, bracing for the onslaught of steel.

Lordy, Martha thinks, standing among them, *that train's not half a mile away and won't stop in time; it will surely run us down.*

She closes her eyes and swallows, then forces herself to look, so as not to miss this fierce moment of her life or her own death. Her gut clenches, and she grabs a man's sleeve. He looks down at her and frowns but then steadies her to keep her from being trampled when another man almost knocks her down.

"Miss, it ain't safe for you here," he says, blinking and straining his neck to see over the caps and hats.

"I'm standing with you fellows!" she shouts. Her chest swells with pride to be one of only a few women in the crowd.

"Well, you got grit," he shouts back. "And we're gonna make that bastard pay."

Martha nods, then breaks his grip to shove between two tall workers to see. There, with the huge machine bearing down, she hears the brakes finally clamp and shriek. The train slows but still barrels forward to plow or scrape the mob off the tracks. Will it stop in time? Martha Jane feels her arms and legs tremble, as rails send vibrations through her shoes.

The men rally, with more bringing torches to light the stack of pitch-soaked rails. Flames leap and braid in the wind. Finally, as the cowcatcher nudges the bonfire in its way, the train grinds to a halt, and its whistle yields with a whine.

The mob spills on either side of the locomotive, casting stones they pluck from the siding. Clusters of men circle, beating fists and railroad ties on both sides of the gleaming passenger car, where Durant and other U.P. officials ride and hide in luxury. The train's barely rolled to a standstill when a handful of men surge between the cars to uncouple Durant's. With gritted teeth, the strength of rage, and a team of oxen, they roll the car onto a spur of track. With lengths of logging chain, the workers lock Durant's vehicle to the very rails they laid for him.

After half an hour, an anxious ambassador waves a white handkerchief and steps down from the train. He raises hands to quiet the crowd, then announces he's to telegraph the Union

Pacific with their concerns, if they will let him pass. At first, the angry men refuse, fearing it's a ruse—he'll call in soldiers to subdue them! The rioters exclaim Durant himself must appear, to personally hand over the gold, which he surely carries on the train.

The ambassador, sweating through his silk brocade vest and white shirt, stutters that Mr. Durant must have corporate authorization before he can do anything. "Believe it or not, men, he's employed, as you are."

This brings a roar of scoffing and more oaths Martha Jane's never heard, which she stores in memory for later use. A man to her right suggests they take control of the telegraph office, to interrupt any stunt the ambassador might pull, once inside. One to her left unholsters a six-shooter for enforcement and steps next to the sweating little man.

The boiling crowd eventually agrees to let the ambassador pass with a few armed escorts, while hundreds remain beside the rumbling locomotive to prevent it taking on coal or water.

Martha's heart pounds. She's not clinging to anyone for safety now but takes a wide stance, shoving back at any man who'd topple her in his enthusiasm. For reasons she can't explain, she breaks into shouts, tears, and then laughter, again and again. She's never seen people band together so powerfully in such great number. This thrill's deeper, more invigorating than whiskey or dance.

Damn, if she could get with a bunch of stouthearted fellows like this every day of her life, they could change the world.

As the black, gleaming engine puffs and idles, the men mill like ants, holding it in place with insufficient chains and the fragile threat of their own bodies, risked. It occurs to Martha Jane that the worst thing for Union Pacific would be to run down hundreds of its own men, spilling blood en route to their crowning celebration. As a local newspaper man jots notes and photographs the scene with his big box camera, it also strikes her—a newspaper, or all newspapers together, can change the actions of powerful men, by holding them accountable.

Folks believe what they read. Martha Jane doesn't know how to make sense of words on paper, but she recognizes the power of what's printed. *If only,* she thinks, *I could get myself in those papers, maybe my life would change, too.*

Interrupting the girl's thought, the Union Pacific lackey—the very lamb whose superiors threw him to the wolves—exits the telegraph building waving a piece of paper. "I got a message from the U.P. for Mr. Durant!" he cries, sweating, nodding, and grinning his way through the crowd and back to the passenger car.

As the men suspected, Durant holds both cash and gold in his car, and from these he's agreed to pay part of what they're owed, with the balance to follow on the next train. The ambassador, more at ease now, sets up a rough table on the ground near Durant's railroad car for the disbursement, despite the crowd's demand for Durant himself to count out their coins. Agreeably disagreeing, he urges the calming crowd into a wavering line.

From a book provided to him by one of the Piedmont managers, who glares over the ambassador's shoulder to verify the numbers, the little man counts out half of each worker's wage and swears on his mother's life that the rest is forthcoming. It's enough of a win for the day, so the men, eager to take home or drink up what they've gained, clear the tracks and recouple Mr. Durant's car to the train. Others load coal and siphon water to the locomotive tank.

As the U.P. vice president's convoy pulls out of the station, the men peer up at the car's reflective windows. They don't expect to see that coward Durant's face, and more than a few wonder if they'll truly receive the balance of their pay. But, some of them mutter, that sure was something, wasn't it? They congratulate one another, slapping shoulders, shaking hands, and finally noticing their powerful thirst. Some reach out for Martha's hand, too, and smile at the girl among them.

Forgetting Mrs. Alton's apples and potatoes, Martha Jane joins the saloon party, toasting the brave men who brought down the railroad to claim what's theirs. She feels a part of the change. She's tasted and shared the power of men.

When Martha Jane wanders home, Mrs. Alton bites her lip, studies the girl, and shakes her head, muttering, "I can't do this much longer. By the good Lord above, I can't."

In June, at her wits' end with the incorrigible girl, Emma Alton orders Martha Jane to pack her things and leave.

* * * * *

PART TWO
1870s, BEING A MAN

* * * * *

CHAPTER ELEVEN
MINER'S DELIGHT

1872

She takes on work that lasts until the mothers, aunts, or grand-mothers who hired her tire of her swearing and rebellion. Martha Jane learns the signs that she's worn out her welcome: pursed lips, deep sighs, and a pulsing vein in the temple. There's also that certain look in the would-be mothers' eyes. Not the first one, which is warm and loving and hopeful of a young girl she might call "daughter," a child who will grow up Christian and reflect the mother's best qualities. A girl to love, to keep.

But after the first few days, Martha Jane tires of trying. She falls back into being herself, and the discipline comes down with a slap, swat, or switch on her bare legs. Sometimes there's a beating with a stick or a paddle, and Martha struggles not to strike back. She understands it's the way of the world; children can be beaten but can't raise a hand to an adult. It's the first rule of family life, and it confounds the girl.

That last look in a would-be mother's eyes is always like ice or a door slamming shut.

Seeing that look, Martha Jane rarely waits for the words. She ties her clothes in a bundle and sneaks down the service stairs to the back door. Alton, Gallagher, and other family names that hang over houses, over Martha Jane's memories—these are the names of failed attempts at home.

How could a girl find anything but joy in a town they call

95

Miner's Delight? This is what she asks herself as she leaves family behind her for a fresh start. She can't be anyone's daughter, it's clear, so she'll draw a straight line out of girlhood into womanhood.

She admits to herself, she's simply unlovable. Her own mother was never warm to her, and Pa tried to give her away. The families who rejected her had other children they loved just fine, so there must be a critical fault in Martha Jane.

In Miner's Delight, Martha Jane finds something close to family love, the affection of men who'll put arms around her and buy her drinks. She's not quite ready for what the men want, but with nothing else to sustain her and no other comforts, she flirts and lets the men kiss her, sometimes. If they press her too hard, she slips away at the last moment, leaving them angry or confused. When they accuse her, she tells them she didn't know, that she's only thirteen. Now her real age is her defense, the way she calls those men back into their right minds. Sometimes it works. Other times, the light in their eyes just burns hotter, and she has to beg another man to defend her honor. That thrill mixes with the liquor the men give her, exciting and tiring the girl. Starved for attention, she plays the dangerous game, getting as much as she can without giving back.

Work isn't hard to find in the mining town. She rubs hard black bars of soap into dirty flannel underwear, work shirts, and denim trousers in an iron kettle over a fire, then wrings them out until her chapped hands bleed. She works for the men who are too mineral-crazy to clean for themselves, and they put bread in her mouth.

She has a knack for cooking. Hard-working men love her flapjacks, johnnycakes, and slow-roasted pig. Two old men propose marriage on the texture of her sourdough bread alone, but she can't abide their whiskers and sulfurous odors, not for all the gold dust they hoard.

With what she earns, Martha Jane buys and sets up a spacious tent near a glacially fed stream, for access to fresh water. The hard work tears and builds her muscles, strengthening her each day. When men in the saloons get out of line, she's ready and strong enough to throw a punch in her own defense. Soon her reputation and boundaries are clear among the miners; Martha Jane Cannary is no easy girl, but she'll take you for all the drinks she can get. And look out for her roundhouse!

At James Kime's hotel, she finds better shelter and indoor work, just in time for winter. Mr. Kime keeps a clean place, with no funny business, so Martha works hard for him, cleaning and cooking. In return, she enjoys a nice room with a real feather mattress, a mirror, and a washbasin on a filigreed stand. She struggles to be good, to keep the good things she's gained.

Yet, as her heart echoes empty, and the cold, dark lonesome chills her mind, whiskey becomes her daily comfort. At first, she keeps a bottle in her room, but she misses her latest friends and soon ventures into the saloons.

A few of the bartenders in town look out for her, steering men away when she's had too much, then letting her sleep off her drunks in their storage rooms, instead of turning her out into the dangerous streets. She often awakens forgetful of the night before but none the worse for wear under their paternal protection. One proprietor, a rosy-cheeked fellow named Ted, warns her she'll fall into trouble, drinking so much. When he cuts her off after two drinks, she cusses him and staggers to another establishment but finally wanders back to Ted for a place to sleep.

Women are so scarce, and men so poor at taking care of themselves, that Martha learns from trial and error how to nurse them, too. Some of the sick and injured men, not on their first bloody go-round, talk her through what to do. Busted lips and heads from fights, fevers, cuts, and broken bones abound. With no doctor to teach her, Martha Jane learns to stitch, poultice, and dose. Needles and thread, a razor, a tiny crochet hook, and a bottle of laudanum line her bedroom shelf, at hand, but her favorite treatment maneuver is to wedge her foot in a man's armpit and jerk hard on his arm until it slides and pops, resetting a dislocated shoulder. She fails the first two times she tries it but learns not to let the patient's agony unnerve her. Same with digging bullets out of wounds with her crochet hook or pocket knife and yanking rotten teeth with pliers. She learns to pretend she's sure of herself and deaf in both ears, to take care of men. They may damn you to hell while you treat them, but they love you afterward.

After nursing a dozen or so men back to health, Martha Jane earns affection in the camp. Some of the men call her an angel, without smirking.

When four men carry John Borner into Kime's hotel on a blanket stretcher, the injured man hollers for a doctor. When Martha Jane comes to him, he scoffs at her and insists on an educated medical man qualified to set his bone.

Martha narrows her eyes at him and shrugs. Tells him to haul himself onto a donkey and try his luck in Atlantic City, if he's so particular. She turns then, gathers up her skirt, and heads up the stairs.

Muttering, *"Gott in Himmel,"* he calls her back. "You ever done set a leg before?"

"I figure it's something like setting an arm," she snaps, shrugging again.

John Borner rolls his eyes at the ceiling and pants, the pain popping sweat beads across his forehead. *"Ach,* fine," he agrees, motioning to his friends to carry him up the stairs behind the disheveled girl, his only hope.

Martha Jane sets and splints Borner's leg, devoting her spare time to Borner's demands for four weeks; he needs his pisspot dumped, his blankets tucked, his eggs over easy, and his coffee hot. He preaches about everything, from politics to religion to the year's expected rainfall, all with complete certainty.

The first time Martha Jane cusses in front of him, he hardens his opinion of her. "So you're that kind," he sneers, shaking his head. "No good Christian."

Stung, she acts like she doesn't care. "Jesus wouldn't see you throwing stones, now would he?"

"Surely he would speak the truth," John argues, his blue eyes sparking. "You are a child. Don't pretend to know the mind of *Gott.*"

"Ain't that what you're doing?" She glares back at him, and, to her surprise, he bursts into laughter.

"You are a feisty one," he grumps around his smile. "But you be careful, or you'll burn *em Höllenfeuer.*"

"You mean in hell? This ain't it here?" Martha raises her eyebrows and puffs out her cheeks. "I got to ask. What is such a fine Christian man doing in Miner's Delight?" For all his lecturing, John Borner hasn't said much about himself.

Turns out he's a transporter en route to Great Salt Lake City. He claims he's charged with finding a worker and companion for the wife of Fort Washakie's Indian agent, which now he's delayed in doing. Martha wonders if it's a job she could do.

John Borner must guess her mind, because he scowls under his handlebar mustache and shakes his head. "I bring James Patten a quiet, God-fearing girl, or he will never trust me for more important work."

"So, you're looking for somebody just like me," Martha teases, pressing a hand to her bosom until John reddens and squirms on his mattress.

"Just kidding you," she says with a chuckle, but then she offers another idea. "I know a good girl—my sister. We're as different as night and day, with me being the one you'd call night."

"Bring her here," Borner says. "I'll decide."

Martha explains Lena's in Great Salt Lake City with their brother, Lige. "I know you'll approve. Maybe when you bring Lena back, you could bring Lige, too," she suggests. Since coming to Miner's Delight, Martha Jane's had no word from her family, and as she can't write, neither has she posted any letter with her address. Truth is, she wasn't sure they'd care.

John Borner agrees to interview Lena, once his leg's healed enough for travel. For her sister's sake, Martha Jane plops extra chunks of ham and chicken into Borner's soup and stifles her curses whenever he's near enough to overhear. He still disapproves of her but seems willing to bring Lena and Lige. Martha still hopes to save Lena from being somebody's plural wife. As Martha Jane imagines the day she'll hug her brother and sister again, her chest feels like it'll burst, and glad shivers tickle her spine.

Two months later, John Borner carts both Lena and Lige to Miner's Delight in his fancy wagon, but he's decided he likes Lena too much to deliver her to the Indian agent's family. He woos the girl with hair ribbons, hard candies, and daisy bouquets. To keep her pure, he finds her a position in another boarding house, far from Martha Jane's influence, and pledges to marry her when she comes of age in two years. Lena starts to wear her hair up in fancy styles. She lengthens her skirts to prove she's a woman, now.

John Borner enlists Lige to work for him as he sets up his new farm and builds a house for Lena in Lander. His future secured, he comes and goes as he pleases, with Lige following him like a whipped dog, out of Miner's Delight.

Martha Jane's cold lonesome comes back with a vengeance after her all-too-brief reunion with her brother and sister. John Borner bamboozled her, first promising to restore what was hers, and then keeping it all to himself. With his little pig eyes and guttural German that Lena finds so mature, Martha Jane considers Borner worse than the devil himself.

She comforts herself as she scratches burnt bacon bits out of a cast-iron skillet. Maybe it's just as well. Courted by John, Lena's changed into a highfalutin' stranger. She sticks her nose in the air, slathers creams on her chubby pink hands, and wears lace gloves, all the time believing what he tells her, that she's born to be a lady, his pure bride. She sniffs nosegays and picks through the French chocolates he presses into her hands. Little brat takes a bite out of each one, so Martha Jane won't take any.

When Martha Jane warns her sister that John Borner's a tough old German, a man like any other, and he'll work her like a plow horse on his homestead, Lena sputters. Without taking a breath, she spills what she really thinks of the big sister who sold herself, smokes cigars, and drinks all night in saloons with men.

Martha knew it, but hearing it again hurts like the kick of a mule.

Lige, on the other hand, is still his good-natured self. As far as she can tell, he doesn't hold Martha Jane's desperate sins against her, but because he sees a future with John, he steers wide of his oldest sister, too.

Martha tries to reconcile, bringing a handful of hair ribbons for Lena, but her sister quotes from the Bible, admonishing Martha Jane to get on the holy road. "Until you repent, you can't be coming around to see me," she explains. "John says you're a bad influence."

"Damn it, I did those rotten things for you."

"No!" Lena's blue eyes widen and flash. "You can't push your sins on me."

Lena's never had to fend for herself, not yet, and Martha Jane feels sorrowful for the untested girl. "The ground's hard when you fall, sister. I hope you never get thrown."

Martha Jane wants to be angry but resigns herself. If Lena's determined to prove her holiness by looking down on the one who saved her, there's nothing Martha Jane can do.

It puts a bitterness in her mouth and an ache in her heart to feel her family turn away again. Knowing no other way to ease the pain, Martha Jane dances, drinks, and howls at the moon with her wild boys. They see good in her, grow to love her as a sister, and tell her so.

After a decent interval of about a year, John and Lena marry. As Borner absconds with her family for good, moving them lock, stock, and barrel to Lander, Martha stifles her tears and gives a jaunty wave with her hat. Hitching up her trousers, she looks up her friends in the saloon and dives into a three-day binge she won't remember.

Lena, John, and Lige can all go to *Höllenfeuer*. Maybe, in spite of their holy pretensions and fine manners, she'll one day reunite with them there.

CHAPTER TWELVE
HOG RANCH

1875, Fort Laramie

The handsome officer growls, "Hell, no, I ain't buyin' you a drink." He sneers and shrugs. On his blue-uniformed shoulder, back-combed, shining locks fall like water. He calls her camp-following trash and says, "Get the hell away before yer French pox gets on me."

Martha blinks and talks back louder than he did. She pounds her fist on the plank bar and calls him a whoreson, self-righteous son of a bitch. She faces the other end of the bar, sniffing, lifting her chin and the corners of her mouth as if he hasn't nicked her feelings.

It comes with the territory, she tells herself. Men in saloons ain't always the most well-mannered, after all. This fellow maybe got religion, but if so, he's some hypocrite, leaning on the plank bar, leering at those other flounced girls.

She taps and slides her coin on the wood and calls for another, gripping the fat glass while the round, cheerful bartender with a damp, red face splashes in cloudy, amber relief. He always has a kind word for the girls and now he stage-whispers to Martha Jane, "Some fella's got a too-high opinion of himself." Then he shrugs, and with that easy gesture he persuades her to let the insult run off, like rainwater into a barrel.

Martha Jane smiles back, licks salty beads of sweat off her upper lip, then tosses down the liquid fire. Just feeling that burn, she gets a lift. The knots between her shoulders loosen.

Knowing well enough her many faults, she's never said she was a schoolma'am. But, she wonders, why the hell are some people so mean? If they have so many virtues, why ain't charity one of them? And, as for herself, why does it still sting? She ought to have a thicker skin after all this time.

For nineteen years, folks have looked down on her. Before she was old enough to do wrong, even when she took over being mother and begged door to door to fill her siblings' bellies, strangers judged Martha Jane to be of low character. Judgment didn't fall by way of her own sin back then. It was a stain leeched off her mother.

Martha gathers up her petticoats and skirt as she chooses a seat at a table across from a kinder-looking companion, a fellow with the moniker Teddy Blue. He nods and smiles at her, but he's three sheets to the wind already, now at ten o'clock in the morning. His eyes don't seem to want to focus together, and his head lolls. Even though she just met him, Martha Jane can tell he's a good fellow, kind and true and safe to sit alongside. A comfort to ease Martha Jane's memories of her mother.

Back in Missouri and Virginia City, Charlotte Cannary was known as a loose woman and a secessionist, a "Secesh," while the folks who stayed true to the Union mocked her red petticoats and cigars. Was it Charlotte's fault then, when Martha's father fell from grace to gamble away all they had? Eve catches blame for Adam's sin and so on, down through all time. Then there's that old saying about the sins of the fathers coming down on the children. But people make it so. God can't be that cruel, to damn children on account of their sinful parents.

Martha Jane doesn't like to pity herself or blame others for her problems. People ought to tend their own fires. She can't lay her troubles back on Charlotte, so she dismisses that woman from her mind, sniffs, and licks the last drops of whiskey from her glass.

Her back's turned to that officer, but she feels his disgust radiate like heat off a stove. Maybe worse, he's already forgotten her. She could fix his flint with one punch; she'd do all right. He's not so tall, and he's two drinks ahead of her, so he'd be easy to knock off balance. But taking him down that way wouldn't feel like winning, not after the first minute, anyway.

Every time a man adds her up like she's a simple sum, it hurts. But what does any man know, or any woman either, about Martha Jane? She's young, but she already knows how each human heart is a mystery, unknown even to itself.

She eyes the players guarding their creased, fanned cards at the next table. Their bids, cussing, and clicking wooden chips cheer her a little, but she doesn't drift over to play. She spent her last coin on that shot.

The low, dark mournfulness ices her belly. Instead of fighting it this time, she lets it take her, half believing she's as bad as people say. She can't remember not feeling guilty. She's cavorted some in her time, cutting up didoes with the fellows, but it's harmless fun. Men act the same, and nobody gives them the eye. She's never hurt a soul, she reminds herself, but that never kept folks from talking down to her.

And, God help her, she may be something, but she ain't a painted cat.

Another thing—it's too easy to get on the wrong side of good people, even outside the saloon. Wear a man's clothes the way she does for chores and horseback riding, and they say you're no lady, that you're even breaking the law. Helluva thing. Wear a velvet dress with sparkles, they say you look cheap. Go with a man you ain't hitched to, they call you a daughter of sin. Don't sit in church, they damn you to hell. Enjoy your whiskey, you're a falling-down, hopeless drunk. Dare to run out of money, you're no-account. Be hungry, and you must deserve to starve.

Unless you get religion. Then there's soap and bread and soup enough to share, along with kindness and foot-dragging tunes about the whiteness of your soul. Holy folks will lift you up and give you the right to look down, like their terrible paintings of God frowning on those unfortunates still in the gutter, where you were before. But at what cost? Insufferable sermons, judgmental pastors and priests. Black dresses with collars that'd choke you in this heat. And those hymns! How they plod, lest you dance. There'll be none of that.

How could there be heaven without dancing? Who'd even want to stop by?

It comes to her then, in a heart-rumble and mental flash, like lightning under a blue cloud—if a girl doesn't know who she is or where she belongs, some man will make up her mind. He'll put legs on a mean story until it walks on its own, and, before she feels it happening, she'll believe what she hears. That opinion will squeeze like a corset, forcing its shape until it feels true, forever, for better or for worse. A girl's supposed to cinch herself up from then on, to fit inside that story.

Martha Jane takes a breath so deep her own corset pinches, then huffs the air out. Mutters, "Such is the way of the world, and yet here I am." Sweat trickles down between her shoulder blades. A fly circles her head. She pulls out the hatpins that scratch her scalp, lifts off her hat, and sets it on the table, fluffing up the flattened cabbage rose. She combs her fingers over her tender skin, up to her bun, and wipes her damp brow with the back of her hand.

The bartender walks over with another shot. She shakes her head and says, "Got no coin," but he replies, "For your troubles. On the house." She places her warm hand gently over his cool, freckled one as he pours. Wants to kiss him, she's so grateful. But he walks away, expecting nothing in return, and her heart swells to find grace in so dingy a room. As she sips it, the whiskey tingles, numbing her lips before it burns a line to her gut.

Teddy flops his head down on his crossed hands and lets out a soft snore. His hat topples off, and Martha sets it beside her own. Like a married couple, her flowered one and his battered Stetson sit side by side.

Martha Jane sighs, casting back one last glance at the cocky soldier at the bar. He seems farther away and out of focus now.

She creases her brow and cracks her neck. People say she's bound for hell, and maybe so, but she vows she'll go her own route. She asks no odds of anybody, and she'll kick against their version of how she lives.

Like a worm in an apple, her own story niggles in her mind, both the good scenes and the bad. Half-drunk, daydreaming, she considers how much better that story could be. Folks will surely talk, but she need not bend to the word around town. Instead, she'll grab hold of her own story while still dancing and doing as she pleases.

She wiggles inside her corset, closes her eyes, and imagines unlacing what's done up too tight, while aching for a deeper breath.

Just let those holier-than-thou gossips think they've figured out the ending of Martha Jane's story; she'll top them with a twist they never saw coming. In her own words, not theirs. Picturing that, she drifts and smiles.

Keeping back only one of her dresses, Martha Jane sells her womanly trappings to a hog ranch girl. She lets go the gewgaws and lip rouge and those cheap necklaces the boys offered, to win her. The lot brings less than she hoped, only a few coins and a few flakes of gold. From studying on the game in the saloon, she knows the rules for faro, so she'll need that satin dress to wear while dealing. She shoves the gown to the bottom of her rucksack, though, with its not-so-pleasant, rustling rules of who she pretended to be, while wearing it.

The soldier boys always liked her when she dressed up; they'd come on gentle and sweet and call her lovely. She knows she isn't. Martha Jane's seen herself in a mirror and knows her appearance holds all the charm of a pigsty fence. But because she liked their sweet talk or their stories, she'd go with them, sometimes, to dance or kiss or cuddle, and afterwards, they'd leave a little money behind. They never called her anything dirty and never shunned her in the muddy street. She'd been nice to them, and they were grateful, so they helped her out the way friends do.

As easy and free and clear as it seemed, living that way got to be like a chalk line drawn on slate, easily smudged. Folks look down on such friendships, so Martha Jane figures she'd best set aside that life, now. It seems a monstrous change to consider, but she sets her mind to it.

That handsome, rude officer did her a favor, showing she can't play up what men first encourage and then condemn. She can't be a fun girl who likes a good time, or a sweet, comforting pal for the soldiers and for traders. She can't seem remotely like the hog ranch girls, her now-and-then friends. She's never judged them, and she cares about each one: Grace with the heart tattoo, Margot with the parakeet she keeps in a basket, and Estelle with one lazy eye.

Martha walks over to their cribs and, with a lump in her throat, waits to say goodbye to every girl. She lies, saying she's had enough of the West and will head back to Missouri, where her mother still lives.

Martha Jane has to draw a hard line, from now on. She's determined.

In the new story that begins now, Martha Jane isn't easy to

bed, judge, or forget. She isn't desperate. She has all the time in the world. If she gets hungry, she'll do a man's work, fight for or steal what she needs the way a man does, or she'll starve.

She sees the problem clearly now. Trying too hard to be womanly, applying graces and charms to convince men to supply what she needs—that's where she went wrong. Then it seemed she had to choose between being a lady or a prostitute. In those lean days, to feed Lena and Lige, and recently, to feed herself, she couldn't always afford to be a lady.

Martha Jane murmurs to herself, "When you ask the wrong question, you get the wrong answer." She finally asked herself, why not be a man? The answer surprises even her.

So, after saying goodbye to the hog-ranch girls, Martha Jane steals a Bowie blade from a dozing private and saws off her hair at her ears, tossing the long, dark locks into a bush for birds to nest with. She musses what's left, and the breeze blows through it. Hacking it even shorter, she feels light and free. Hair was always a weight and chore: curling, pinning, twisting, and knotting. *No wonder,* she thinks, *men accomplish so much without it.*

She collects the soldiers' cast-off linen shirts and woolen trousers for her clothing. Already threadbare, they tear easily but make her invisible. She pitches a patched, discarded tent on the side of the camp opposite her old friends, the followers, so they're less likely to see and recognize her. Martha Jane rubs a little dirt on the parts of her face where a beard could be. With her strong jawbone, she figures folks will easily take her for a boy.

Proving her right, a soldier notices her shivering and says, "Here, buddy, take my old coat." It's thin but serves. She lies awake nights, hollow with hunger, imagining how to survive among men, how to prove herself. She tells herself not to fear being wrong, that she need only be brave.

Screwing up her nerve, she stomps into the fort store and

asks for work. Says she's new to these parts and will do laundry, sweep, organize shelves, carry coal and wood, and cook for the post factor. He takes her at face value and readily calls her "Jack," the name she offered in her introduction.

In a few weeks, she's earned enough coin to buy buckskins and replaces her worn-out pants and shirts. Lumpy, yet comfortable, the leather shirt and trousers flow wide over her breasts and broad hips. Flattening her curves into angles and lines, and too thick for any man to push or pinch through, the buckskin hides her sex and protects it. Martha Jane feels safer and imagines this is how a knight must've felt, fully armored.

The leather blocks the cold Wyoming wind as well, and after a few rains they shrink to fit, without her old corset's constriction. She buckles her waist and laces on heavy boots, the kind that kick with authority. With the proceeds from her bartered baubles and dresses, kept all this time, she buys two Colt six-shooters to wear at her belt.

When she walks among the troops dressed as a man, it's funny how few soldiers notice or care, even if they suspect she isn't male. She enjoys playing her dumb charade, though, so she spits, cusses, drops her voice a few notes, and keeps up her dirt beard shadow. She senses most men take her to be a teenage boy, and this delights her. Being free in the camp returns her to a better place and time—riding west on horseback with Cilus and shooting rabbits with that Henry repeater, while Ma, her babies, and family troubles trailed behind.

It's so simple, Martha thinks. Why didn't she see it before? Leaving behind your old self is easy as cutting off hair.

Fort Laramie's troops gladly shuck their petty responsibilities, letting her chop wood, deliver messages, and haul water. She lightens their duties, allowing them more time to play cards and sleep. Built tall and strong, she can handle their work, which further reinforces her strength; Martha Jane's hard labor stokes the fires of liberation, forging her masculinity.

One day, an officer needing manpower in a tight spot hands over a bullwhip to Martha Jane. She gladly follows his order, up onto a buckboard to whack a team of oxen sonsabitches through a bog. The next day, she marshals that stubborn team through a gully thick with aspen and pine. She swears louder and better than the other teamsters, and the soldiers gather around, chuckling, to see the young kid manhandle the massive beasts. The ones who know she's a woman grin, shake their heads, and quietly forgive her womanhood. Impressed, they would never unmask her, and soon they all but forget she's pretending, so when an axle busts on her wagon, they don't say it was her fault, that she's female and weak. They blame luck, as they would for themselves. They claim and name her, lifting their glasses to christen her "Calamity."

She holds her head up and strides longer, feeling the buckskin trousers chafe and callous, even as they protect and veil the soft places she'd once too freely given away. Her body is her own creation and responsibility. When her monthlies come, she pads herself with rags, but nobody can see her secret, through the leathers. There's no shame in her; Martha Jane glories in being innocent again, a woman-man born in Eden.

In Martha Jane's wild garden, she hears the voice of gunfire. Shooting again, as she did with Cilus, is a hell of a lot of fun and ushers her into deeper camaraderie with the soldiers. As she once practiced with the wandering Mormon boys outside their camp, she sets up tin cans on stumps. This time she wagers for drinks, that she can outshoot her competition. Soon she's able to beat them, but she still knows to let the fellows win at least two out of three.

She picks up a wide-brimmed Stetson somebody lost along the trail and bends the chewed-up brim so it swoops down over one eye, for a boyish, jaunty look. She learns how to gamble and how to be a good sport when she loses. She buys her pals drinks and beats them at cards enough that they like and respect her, so they teach her how to cuss longer and better, with style. How to chew tobacco, and how to hold her liquor. Soon she's matching them, drink for drink.

Martha Jane watches how men can decide another man's weak if he's too nice, and how they push each other to the brink. She figures out when to double down and when to let a fellow save face. Studying fists and footwork, she imagines how to stand her ground. Her shoulders and arms thicken, and she looks every man in the eye. She punches a few ornery fellows to prove she can take care of herself; they don't bother her again. She earns her place at the bar, and the admiring men learn she can whip her weight in wild cats.

She is new.

The cold lonesome inside her heart persists. As deep gray as her mother's eyes, Martha Jane's sorrow sounds to her like her father's whine when he'd wander home, sick and sorry. It's Lige sauntering away, leaving her as if she doesn't matter, and it's Lena calling her the worst kind of sinner. Martha Jane can't escape it but has a few drinks to make herself cherk. After three shots of whiskey, she can smile and laugh and believe she's Calamity.

While drunk, she's not little Martha Jane pounding doors for crusts of bread with crying, snot-nosed, starving brothers and sisters tugging her apron. She's not dragging a dead brother, not scraping a hole to bury him in frozen ground.

She sleeps alone. Her solitude feels like a line she's scraped in the dirt with her boot heel, one she's scared to kick over, to erase. She won't be what Lena called her, even if it means she sleeps and lives alone.

She saves a brown-and-white fice pup from a garbage pile,

squirming among his dead littermates, as she had done. He's barely the size of a sausage, so she soaks a rag in milk, dribbles it on his little split lips, and nurses him to strength. She names him Henry, after the gun and the horse and good memories, pulling meaning from the past to hold today. She tucks the pup into her shirt pocket, next to her heart. When nobody's watching, she cradles Henry like a baby, and, when he gets teeth, she feeds him bits of meat she's already chewed.

Once he's big enough, Martha Jane's dog follows her in and out of the puncheon-floored saloon tents and over trampled ground, loyal to her hand, her word, her heel. On horseback, she totes him in a gunny sack tied to the pommel, with a hole in the weave where he can peer out. While Martha Jane drives oxen, Henry huddles on the platform at her feet. Every day she combs and picks fleas from his short coat, and every night Henry warms her bedroll. He even learns to dance on his hind legs, for love of her smile. More often than not, it's his red tongue that tickles and wakes her in the morning, easing her out of her whiskey dreams.

CHAPTER THIRTEEN
NEWTON-JENNEY

1875

There's something about a blue uniform that tempts Martha Jane to take a risk, so when the expedition is forming up to go to the Black Hills, she slips in among the troops. In Company E, Third Cavalry, a young officer flirts with her, asks her to come along with him, that he'll hide her on the way. She tells him there'll be no funny business between them, so he says she'll have to just slap him if he keeps trying. He seems a good sort, teasing her that way, so she agrees to a ruse. He bribes the fort tailor to measure her for a fine blue uniform, to outfit her for the Newton-Jenney Black Hills expedition.

She loves the soft weave, the cut, the navy wool, and the gold buttons. She stands taller and breathes more easily, as that uniform bonds her with the others. Walking among the barracks, she lifts her chin and nods to soldiers, who nod back. Whenever anybody needs a hand, she puts herself to work, and, as the newest private, she cooks, mends uniforms, and washes clothes for her superiors. She takes special care of her sergeant benefactor, holding him at arm's length, though, swatting his hand when he tries to slide it between her body and her belt.

"It's conduct unbecoming," she jokes, "and I can't risk my rank." She's quick with the phrases she overhears around the officers. When her love-sotted sergeant quits her in frustration, she tags along with a group of newer boys.

A young buck private offers to hide her. It's cool at night, so she follows him to warmth and safety. Glad not to sleep out in the open, she lies next to him as he snores. He laughs at her jokes, but she wonders why such a handsome young man doesn't touch her at all.

She notices how the boy seems glad, or maybe relieved, and blushes like a girl when jealous soldiers josh him for getting what they'd like to take from Martha Jane. She's heard about boys who like boys and how hard it is for them to fit in among men. She sees how he appraises and admires the other men, too. Yet she's offered him a kind of protection in exchange for his, and the arrangement suits her fine.

So she plays at loving him, at painting him a man in front of the others. His friends seem nice enough, but she thinks they might turn mean if they knew who he really is. She ponders this, realizing the power she holds over her pretty boy, but her heart is tender. She'd never betray him, and she hopes he's as faithful to her.

Looking at him across the smoky fire that burns her eyes, she hopes neither of them slips or gets caught.

Her rabbit stew, bacon, and bawdy jokes win over his friends. She's like no girl they've ever seen, one they can't easily hurt. When they get fevers, she makes special broth and spoons it in their mouths, singing softly the way their mothers did. She changes bandages, lances boils, and doctors them more gently than the camp surgeon, who's prone to leeches and vile turpentine concoctions.

When she salutes officers and goes undetected, her brother privates stifle their chuckles behind fists and whisper, "Calam's at it again." Standing in formation, she copies the fellow ahead of her, and it doesn't seem so hard. She loves the drills and the unison. The crack of the weapons firing and the rhythm of their boots thudding the ground raise the hairs on her neck. She's fitting in well, but then something, she's not sure what, gives her away. When she's called in front of the others, she hopes her pretty boy didn't betray her.

An officer grabs her sleeve and pulls her forward. Martha Jane shudders with desperate, low shame, to be called out of line and named a camp follower in front of her brothers in arms. She blushes and then hates herself for appearing guilty. The officer yells, calling her dirty names while her so-called friends and her pretty boy study the ground, silent. Not a word of the officer's accusations feels true. She's put her past so far behind her, it's as if some other girl did those vile things. The truth means nothing, though, and people will believe the worst possible thing about a woman.

Enraged, she stuffs it down. Her only hope is to shrink into herself and become forgettable, so she covers her face, swallows oaths, and murmurs apologies to that officer. As the guard halfheartedly escorts her out of camp, she slips into a grove, to shuck her beloved uniform for her buckskins. She changes her color, her shape, and her story again. Now, she imagines and instructs herself, she'll be a trader, trapper, or Indian fighter. Stuffing her loose curls in her battered hat, Martha Jane rubs another layer of dirt on her face. Only soldiers work to stay clean, and she's not one of them now.

A stroke of good fortune befalls her as she steps from the bushes—a bullwhacker in the wagon train keels over, too drunk to drive his team. From where she stands alongside the trail, with her rucksack over one shoulder and Henry in his peephole sack over the other, she scrambles up to claim the stalled wagon. Taking the long reins, she gives a reassuring wave to the officer who strolls by. He's the same one who pulled her out of her company, but he doesn't recognize her now. He never truly saw her to begin with.

As the expedition pulls out of Fort Laramie, Martha tugs her hat brim low, clears her throat, deepens her voice, and hollers,

"Gee, haw," and, "Goddamn you sorry sonsabitches," cracking her whip like rifle shots until her oxen lumber forward to bump their noses on the wagon box ahead. Once the train is moving, the billowing dust and shouts are better than a veil. She's nobody anybody could name.

Her heart pounds, her eyes burn, and she chokes on dust. Within an hour, her shoulders are on fire. The whip seems to weigh a hundred pounds. She drives standing for a while, then with each knee bent while sitting, shifting her weight on the bone-jarring seat; she'll have bruises on her butt bones, for sure. Her head pounds. Her neck stiffens, then cracks in relief.

Oxen truly are the hardest-headed beasts on earth, she muses, and, if they weren't so strong and their meat wasn't so stringy, they'd soon be stew. She musters up new profanities, twisting vile combinations of timeworn oaths that keep her amused and the oxen moving. She wonders how far it is to the Black Hills. Hours? Miles? Days? Regardless, with God having provided her a place in the expedition, Martha Jane won't give it up, so she hacks mud and spits it off the side of her wagon, then wipes her streaming eyes on her leather sleeve.

Her dry lips crack and seep blood. She finds the fallen bull-whacker's jar of liquor rolling on the boards beside Henry's sack and drinks deeply of the cheap alcohol. It crosses her eyes but wets her whistle, clears her pipes, and lifts her spirits, too. She sings about Blue-Eyed Jenny and tells herself, if she's lucky, she may not choke to death on dust. Her arms may not rip free of her shoulders. Indeed, she may survive death by oxen to die this very day pierced by a Sioux or Cheyenne arrow, and that story get printed in newspapers back East. A grand adventure featuring . . . What is it the boys call her? Calamity Jane.

She grins to herself, feeling sweat trickle between her buckskin-flattened breasts. To boost her energy, she bites some tobacco off a plug and lets it soften between her cheek and gum.

"Henry," she mutters, "my flea-bitten friend, it's a glorious day to be a man."

She's checking the oxen's foamy nostrils for blood and slopping water buckets for their thirst when a hand on her shoulder startles Martha Jane. Some man must be picking up her shape or an unconscious gesture that gave away her sex. Thinking he can touch her, he could cost her the set she's earned on that buckboard.

She balls up a fist and hauls back, whirling to face the man.

He raises his hands and cries, "Sis, it's me, Lige!"

She whoops and slams into him with a hug. Ruffles his hair and notices she's outgrown him, both wide and tall. His jeans are torn and crusted with mud, but he's wearing a gray frock coat that's not so old. A beet-red linsey shirt with no collar and few buttons hangs on him, three sizes too big. He's fair the same way Cilus was, but Lige wouldn't remember the brother who died before he was born. Every time Martha sees Lige, she sees both. It's almost like getting her lost brother back, only to lose him afresh.

She gulps and smiles, then pats her Bowie knife and says, "You oughtn't sneak up on a body that way."

"You're all decked out, ain't you," Lige says, taking in her guns and knife. "You set to fight Indians?"

"Indians never hurt me at all," she answers. "It's white men I got to look out for."

"I took you for a boy, at first."

"Good," she says, laughing. "Goddamn, it's good to see you. You look hungry, though. That tight old Kraut Borner starving you?" Martha shoots a line of tobacco juice to splatter by an ox's hoof.

Lige shrugs, but when his sister pulls a chunk of bread from her rucksack, he tears off big bites with his teeth, struggling to swallow what he's barely chewed.

"Slow down, there's plenty. Here, drink some of this," she says, handing him what's left in the mason jar.

After feeding Lige and the oxen, Martha sets up her tent and slips back into uniform. She likes how the breeze breathes through the fabric, but she likes even more how it feels to fit in with the company. It's like being a finger on a hand or a drop of water in a sea. Belonging is a kind of forgetting and a remedy for fear.

Lige tells her she looks fine in that color, trim, well-fed, and fit. She's so happy, he's nearly convinced to enlist, but he figures he'd get court-martialed the first week, and he'd rather not get shot.

"I got a problem with authority," he says, grinning and hitching up his grubby jeans.

A man with round, black glasses and a gray bowler hat minces along, leading a low-slung mule, while trying to balance on his own shoulder his bulky, wood-and-accordion camera. His burden's blunt, brass-coned lens glints in the sun like a diamond or a shooting star. He sets it up, unfolding a tripod under it to steady it in the sparse grass, then inquires if she might be Calamity Jane.

She glances at Lige and shrugs.

Bowler Hat says he's heard about her. Sweat runs down in his eyes, and he dabs it with a silk handkerchief. The citified fellow shifts foot to foot as one eye twitches, like a wink, and in an oily, put-on French accent claims his name is Guerain. He's polite to her though, more than most folks are, and asks if she would *s'il vous plait* pose for him, for the papers.

"Stretch out there, *mademoiselle*," he says, waving one arm like a dancer. "On those stones by French Creek."

"Like this?" She climbs up, reclines, tips back her hat, crosses her legs, and squints at the wooden box.

"A girl soldier," he exclaims. *"Extraordinaire."*

"I ain't a soldier, Frenchy," she argues. "I'm a goddamned legend—Calamity Jane."

Lige snickers and dusts his cloth cap by smacking it on his thigh. He whispers, "There's my Martha Jane."

The corner of her mouth twitches just as the photographer says, "Don't move." He counts, and she tries not to blink as he freezes her in grays.

CHAPTER FOURTEEN
HER STORY

This should've happened.

I hunker down with the soldiers, all the boys in blue firing and reloading fast as they can, cussing when rifles jam, ducking when they see arrows cutting curves through the sky as if they are the sun wheeling over. I'm behind the wagon wheel, biting my lip and firing my Henry repeater five, six times without hesitating, blue smoke snaking up into the cold air. Reloading from the ammunition on my belt. Ducking when arrows slice the air to my left, zinging past the corner of the wagon box. Jumping when bullets tear through the aspen leaves, thud into the ground. Nearly pissing myself.

Those Sioux are fearsome with their face paint black 'round their eyes like raccoon masks and glorious with feathers tied to strands of their hair. Whooping, trilling for each soldier they drop. Popping their heads out now and then to sight their nocked arrows and rifles on us, one by one. Eyes gleaming like hot coals. Some of them fire gunshots out from those trees, too.

I wonder if these are the same braves who shot down that family in the wagon just days ago, where the plain trails into the Hills. Or are they the ones the Army's been chasing down, to herd like cattle? White people ain't supposed to be here, but neither are they. This territory's chock full of gold, or so Custer says, and that's what this expedition is set to prove. Official and for the government, we are an exception to the rule, a break in the treaty that's to hold us white people out of harm's way.

It rushes through my mind—maybe they're angry we're on their

121

holy mountains, what I heard called Ȟe Sápa. But maybe we're angry they shoot us down when we ain't looking. A bullet splinters the wagon tongue. I blink. Got to concentrate. Right and wrong might be a matter for discussion if we survive, but not in this hour.

Here, now, it's whizzing bullets and arcing arrows like rain. Air thick with dread. Dry mouth, hard to swallow, acid churning up out of my stomach, taste buds nasty with fear. Hair tingling on end, alert for the crush of a tomahawk, then a sharp bone blade slicing through the scalp. Blood seeping dark red, brain matter oozing like gray jam, same as what crowned the days-old bodies we found with crows and turkey vultures coiling like twisted wire above, unfurling down, settling, wings wide, and hoping for a feast. The gingham bonnet, the calico skirt, the spilled snowy flour, the green-black flies buzzing, and the old man's trampled hat.

Dear God, I am terrified. Dare not show it, though, to these enlisted men whose respect means everything to me, who feed and hide me in their ranks. I won't betray their trust or the risks they take by hightailing it, by becoming the weak, scared-shitless woman they figure I am inside.

So when the sergeant to my right cries out, "Hail Mary!" and grabs his arm, and blood rushes through his gloved fingers, I catch my breath, set down my Henry, and crawl to him where he's crouched. I yank off my bandanna and knot it 'round him so the blood slows, and he nods at me.

"Goddamn," he mutters, sweat like dew on his black-stubbled lip and his voice cracking like a boy's. "How can I shoot my rifle with one arm? These savages will scalp me yet." So I unholster and hand him my six-shooter without joshing him for forgetting his own sidearm, and him an officer. I don't look him in the eye, either.

The fellows ten yards ahead of us stand up together, as if on a count of three. Two stop arrows straightaway, one with his chest and the other with his eye. My stomach cinches up as if it's my own body pierced. Those shot fall backwards limb by limb and joint by joint, bodies coming unstitched, arms thrown out wide in astonishment even though they stood up in front of a screaming, yipping horde armed with notched feathers and steel. As if they didn't decide, and death is ever a surprise. The other three fire as fast as they can into the brush where the arrows and bullets slice through, and the torrent of feathered sticks thins to only many, then a few here and there. Gunfire relieves. The standing boys shot true.

My heart pounds in my chest, my ears, my eyes. My vision blurs from the sweat trickling down, and I rub it off with my cotton cuff, eyes tearing up, stinging, blinking. I need to see what's coming, study on that line of trees where the Sioux hide. Not safe yet. I can't swallow, my mouth sticky and a lump in my throat the size of a tobacco plug. When I try to spit, it barely wets my bottom lip.

Another band of good fellows, mostly buck privates, kneel, shoot, stand, and rush the bushes, taking turns giving cover. They bust into the undergrowth like elk or deer crashing in rut, whooping and beating the leaves and branches, thrashing for Sioux. They find not a one. The painted, feathered marksmen and bowmen have slipped beyond our outrage and retribution. Silent, just the way they surely came to take our unlucky caravan scouts. The boys walk out grinning anyway, as if they won.

I stand up and resettle my cockeyed hat, then reach down and grab that sergeant by his good arm, to pull him up. He's a big man, but not as tall as me. His knees straighten and lock, but he sways. I wonder if he ever got shot before, but I don't ask. I almost say, "Glad that's you, not me," but he might not find it funny as I do. He squints one eye, mutters thanks, and gives me a strange look, as if questioning what he sees. He hands back my six-shooter, and I slide it home.

I turn away as if my Henry is the most interesting gun in the world, buffing my sweat and black dirt off its butt stock and long barrel with my buckskin sleeve. "Gotta fetch my oxen, somewhere down that ridge," I mumble, dropping my voice as low as it can fall. Sniffing and spitting what I can gather up now, I leave him wonder-

ing but, if I'm lucky, too grateful to think on me for long. When I glance back, he's calling his men. Shaking his head over the ones cut down, scattered like broken dolls.

This surely should've happened, just the way I'll tell it from now on.

So even though I came on the scene just now to stand in the ruin where a clean glove was dropped yesterday and now crumples, clotted with thick blood, even though I am a day late and a dollar short, as they say, I see and hear and smell the way it happened, the battle I missed. In my nerves lifting to the edge of my skin, my nose wrinkling at the stinks of shit and vomit, and my tongue bitter with the tart black gunpowder sifting from this broke-down wagon's shot-up casks, here I stand in grass pressed flat by the struggles of men. I smell the green, the earth's own blood, spilling out of stems busted by terror and pain. Here I should've been kneeling, peering between spokes and beneath the tilted bed, firing back, and lending a hand to that grateful officer who bled out there, where he lays.

Instead, I'm following the scouts with the rest of the troops. Walking with our heads bowed, cussing the foul heathens, and begging heaven to open for these brave men. As we dig the graves, untouched as cowards.

CHAPTER FIFTEEN
DEADWOOD PARADE

1876

She wonders if it's only a rumor, that he's ridden into Fort Laramie.

Martha Jane scrapes the dung off her boots on the iron outside the door and peers in, her eyes adjusting from noon sun to dim saloon. The half plug of tobacco softens in her mouth, and she feels the first lift it gives her, like breeze under a hawk's wing. Beyond that doorway, men stand still as trees in mist.

She squints, studies, and singles out one stranger. Tall, lean. Could be him. Hard to know from the newspaper sketches she's seen. She takes a last breath of woodsmoke and steps into the different fog of cigars and sweat, where she feels a strange comfort in the low rumbles of men. Her heart beats faster, and she lifts her chin. Throwing back her shoulders, she pulls down the brim of her hat, shifts her weight back on her heels, and hooks a thumb in each front pocket.

At the bar, she glances sidelong at his profile. It has to be. Yes, Wild Bill Hickok is a fine-looking man, even beyond the gossips' estimation, beating the pants off those rough newspaper sketches. Deep-blue shirt with a red adornment, a red sash, and two Navy Colt pistols with handles turned forward, for a twist draw. He moves inside his shirt like the cat that rubbed against her leg on the boardwalk this morning. She wishes he would. Henry paws at her leg and whines, and she shushes him to *sit, boy.*

Wild Bill glances over at the dog, not at her.

He smells as good as he looks, like sweet, spicy hair pomade, leather, and dust. He sets down his shot glass and signals for another, rolling a sidelong look at Martha Jane. He raises one eyebrow.

"You must be that Calamity Jane I heard about."

She smiles. "I can't guess you heard anything good." She takes another whiff of his hair grease and chuckles to herself at the vanity of men. This vice never surprises her in women, but always in the stronger sex. Why do they bother to pomade their hair or scent their bodies? The complete world, with its wealth and power and all its women, is already theirs, requiring no special effort. Especially for one built like him. Filling out that shirt the way boulders bulge out of mountainsides. Land sakes.

"A drink for Calamity Jane," Bill Hickok calls to the bartender.

Martha Jane stops the slid glass and raises it in thanks, swallows her whiskey, and blinks. Wild Bill has an air that makes her want to cinch up a corset to fit into her faro-dealing bodice and skirt, but rumor has it this man just married a pretty circus gal named Agnes. Martha knows herself to be no pretty little thing, not much of a thing at all, folded up in greasy buckskins like a trapper, and two weeks since her last bath, to boot.

There's no chance for love, but maybe he'll play a little.

His fingers are long, with little dark hairs like wires between the rocky, swollen joints. They look strong, but flexible and younger than his face. She considers the stories, how Bill's as good with a knife as he is with those twin Colts. She tries to remember what folks say, how many men he's killed. Her eyes wander to his cheeks, his eyes, his mouth. She wouldn't mind kissing those lips, feeling those hands on her, but there's something even better in his gray eyes, an intelligence and humor she'd rather lock in friendship. Even better than teasing, kissing, and surely losing would be to settle in beside him. Listen to him talk about himself, another thing she's heard he likes to do.

So, instead of flirting, she asks him if he wants to play cards, something he's sure to say "Yes" to. Her heart beats faster, and she bites her bottom lip to keep from smiling, when he does.

Wild Bill's heading up a party to the Deadwood gold fields, so she reckons to tag along. At Fort Laramie, Bill introduces her as Calamity Jane to his pals Charlie and Steve Utter, good chaps who like to drink and bite cigars and whirl the schottische. They enjoy her stretchers, egg her on when she gets wild, and keep her glass full. They're dreaming of a Deadwood strike, too. They'll make fine companions.

Just thinking of riding out of Fort Laramie, she feels a quickening, a catch in her chest at the idea of being somebody new in somewhere better, so she whistles for her dog Henry, who's wandered off to sniff a hitching post. Martha Jane bundles her clothes and saddles the broken-down bay she bought in a rush from the livery. The nag needs to carry her a couple hundred miles, so Martha hopes she's stronger than she looks.

Martha eyes Wild Bill's stallion tied there and tells herself, someday she'll cut a fine figure, with a mount like that. Come that day, people will look up, admiring, and not just joking, when she comes and goes. They won't look at her the way they look at the painted ladies, her friends Madam Mustache and Dirty Em—as if Martha Jane, or any woman tagging along with this motley band, could only be sex for sale. Someday they'll see her for the legend she's set out to be. The gal Bill sees, Calamity Jane.

That'll come. For now, just riding with Wild Bill Hickok, a man so elegant and so fine, is enough, almost as good as being a legend herself.

And it is a glorious day. The black pines stud the hills like whiskers, and the clouds graze over in flocks of white, yellow, and gray. Sky so blue it hurts your eyes, makes you want to believe in heaven.

She finds Bill, Charlie, and Steve in front of the mercantile, kneeing the bluff out of their horses to cinch and saddle them. Securing their cargo with rope, tightening their creaking straps. While she waits, she liquors up, sipping from the flask she tucks in her leathers. As the sun peeks over Old Bedlam Bachelor Officers Quarters, Wild Bill spurs his horse, spins him, and starts north. Following him like a left hand, she nickers to her bay, narrows her eyes, and plunges into the famous man's dust.

How the Deadwood crowd knew the thirty wagons were coming, Martha Jane can only guess, but she's glad they gathered. Hats fly up and tumble down as Wild Bill rides in, and men shout, pressing in and punching the air with fists to celebrate him.

Colorado Charlie Utter tells Martha Jane the shouts are as much about the ladies he's carting in behind them, as about Bill. Madame Mustache, Dirty Em, and their gals wave hankies as if they're noble ladies in a hansom cab, meanwhile bouncing and hanging on to their pitching oxcart seats. Tugging down lacy bodices, they lean over the miners, blowing kisses wild.

Steve Utter reins his horse closer to Jane and calls out, "We're nothin' but Bill's lackeys, but that ain't so bad!"

"Hell, second fiddle's fine by me! Least we're making music!" Martha Jane calls back. She figures nobody will make out her rough edges or see her face through the dust of the working girls' transport, or in the shadow of Wild Bill. Then somebody hollers, "Hey, is that there Calamity Jane?"

The world swooshes and slips like water around her. She grips the reins and straightens in her saddle, smiling in the direction of that voice. She shivers as if she just found her own skin, after all this lifetime of not feeling her own edges.

"Damn right!" She draws her Colt and fires it into the air. Men whoop and pat her side-stepping horse's flanks.

They know her. Like a shot of whiskey, something like love rushes to her head, spinning her further into something new. Something that runs ahead of words, into story.

From that day on, if they even knew that girl from before, every last man, woman, or child forgets there ever was a Martha Jane Cannary. They only want Calamity now, the wild woman of the West. Dime novels change her size and shape, give her untold beauty, and cast her into wild adventures. The past filters away like mud from a sluice box, leaving only her say-so and her new name. She's never had a real home, but now her address is the whole wild West.

She begs, she borrows, and sometimes she even pays back. The Utter boys and White-Eye Anderson tell Martha Jane she could get work sooner, if she'd clean up and buy herself some female clothes. Taking their offered money, she bathes in the creek with perfumed soap, then goes shopping. Dressed in her best, she dances, hustles drinks, tends bar, and closes down the saloons. Along with the fellows she rode in with, she makes new friends every time she turns around.

Wild Bill eyes her, not quite approving, but grudgingly admits it. At least now she looks like a woman, and the stench is gone.

The whiskey's rotgut but does what she needs it to. Eases her, makes her brave, helps her forget the cold lonesome. When Martha Jane drinks, she's everybody's sister, daughter, and wife.

Newspaper men pick up Calamity's antics and write her

down. Not much of what's printed is true, but she doesn't mind. Their lies are a welcome wind, blowing away a sad girl's footprints.

Besides, Martha Jane tells herself with a wry smile, for anything they accuse her of, she's likely done worse. There's no explaining the whys of anything about herself, so she won't stoop to argue with anyone's version of her life. Like riding a horse, it's better to nudge a tale one step forward on the trail, instead of trying to whip it backwards.

Eavesdropping outside a store one day, she overhears a yarn about herself robbing a bank. It's a flattering, wild, bald-faced lie, and it quickens her pulse, making her stand taller and throw back her shoulders in a deep laugh as she lights her cigar. Being somebody worth talking about is like leaping over a canyon, to land on something solid.

Hearing Charlie and Steve read back to her off the newspapers her deeds and misdeeds, she dreams up more adventures she'd like to claim. She spins and resells her own yarns in saloons and on the boardwalks, even stopping strangers on the trail while she leans back in her creaking saddle, bloviating with a wide grin. She crosses her heart and swears her homespun tales are the God's honest truth.

Well, God's got a sense of humor, you know.

She likes to see the shadow of doubt, then the light when her listener chuckles and almost believes. At that moment she knows they'll pass it on, and who knows? Maybe some just-off-the-stagecoach newspaper man with a pencil, scribbling notes, will catch her new story.

With Wild Bill, Charlie, and Steve, those first two weeks in Deadwood spin like a child's top, fast in one place. She considers it the best time of her life, with people knowing her wherever she goes. Joy thumps and drenches her heart like whiskey, to finally have her say, to write herself into being with nary a pen or paper. Without even being able to read or write, she's an author. Through the stories, she now and again breaks free of the sad, cold lonesome, that pain that's dogged her since Virginia City, or, if she's truthful, since before she can remember.

Hundreds of words, some of them her own, carry her out of her cold, dead edges, beyond Deadwood and back to Fort Laramie. From there, they speed north, west, and east over telegraph wires, humming above the mountains, buttes, and tall grass plains to Virginia City, San Francisco, and New York. There her story presses down thousands of times as ink, in shapes she couldn't decipher and caricatures she wouldn't recognize.

But to Martha Jane, being captured by the press is magic, myth, and mystery, the stuff of change. Like dying, only without the pain, to be born again.

Martha Jane tells herself she's wilder, harder, and prettier than she is. She begins to believe herself to be the adventurer, the rebel, and the woman she foretold at French Creek. She believes in Calamity Jane.

CHAPTER SIXTEEN
A BULLET AND A BUTCHER KNIFE

1876

But then the world stands still; the top wobbles and falls.

She claims she was there, that it was none other than Calamity Jane who rounded up Jack McCall with a butcher knife so that coward could face execution. It didn't happen that way. Not even close. But if she can't be part of Wild Bill's ongoing life story because of his murder, she'll at least tell herself into his ending. People snicker when she mentions Bill, though, knowing their hero barely tolerated her during their two weeks in Deadwood. Now she's a byword, a joke, and a reminder of Deadwood's sordid tragedy, if people acknowledge her at all.

At the oddest times, Martha Jane catches herself crying: while sudsing her underthings in a tub, cracking an egg into a cast-iron skillet, or hearing a woodpecker *rat-a-tat* on a lodgepole pine. It hits her while watching yellow aspen-leaf discs flutter off spindly branches, playing hide-the-quarter with a little kid on the street, or sawing a plug of tobacco with her Bowie knife.

She hikes up to Bill's grave, kicking her dark skirts aside with scuffed boots, bubbling over tears both angry and sad. Stumbling from drink or the need for it, she stands over the broken dirt drying in the sun. Most days, she or one of the dancing girls sets out for Bill's glory their string-tied, wilting bouquets: Indian paintbrush, strawflowers, bluebells. Kicking aside yesterday's dead ones, light and dry as straw, to be forgotten like everything that blooms.

Martha Jane doesn't indulge in poker as often, without Bill in the room. When she has, the last few months, she's suffered a losing streak. Instead, she works as a dancer in lumber-and-canvas hurdy-gurdy tents. She gets her drinks for free, plus a percentage of what her partners buy.

Al Swearengen's tent is the biggest, with the worst reputation and the most money to be made, so Martha Jane works there when she can. She's a fine dancer, giving her partners a run for their money and a powerful thirst, good for business. Al's hired a fiddle, a guitar, and an accordion to keep the dancers moving. Whirling on a never-ending whiskey high, Martha Jane loves the work. Fights break out ten times a night, and she's not averse to piling on, adding her fists to the mix.

She's having a hell of a time, as long as she doesn't stop and think of all she's lost.

In the spring of 1877, Swearengen opens his new Gem Variety Theater to replace his narrow boxing hall, The Cricket. He ran girls there, too, working them in the alley behind the fights. Now his girls are more sophisticated, asking high-class prices for pokes in rooms with doors that actually shut.

Al's a mean sonofabitch who'd sooner punch or slap the girls than look at them. Even his own wife he runs as a prostitute and then beats her when she balks or disagrees. The longer Martha Jane knows him, the more she fears his unpredictable rage, and she wishes for other work. But when she dances or tends bar anywhere else, Al's men trail, threaten, and escort her back to the Gem, where they say she belongs.

She comes back to tell Swearengen she won't whore for him or for anyone else. He slaps her and says she'll follow his orders, but lucky for her, she's too ugly to sell for sex.

"Hell, you'll scare them into the priesthood with that face. Tend bar and dance. Put your hair up half over your face, paint on some lips, and wear a corset to push up your titties. Give these men something they can stand to look at."

She balls up her fist and sasses him, only to find herself facing the wallpaper and bleeding from her lip.

"Good thing you won't be putting that mouth on anybody," Al laughs, then reminds her to be behind the bar at five, dressed to kill. Or be killed.

For Martha Jane, Deadwood's a different town without Wild Bill, not so much a legend-in-the-making as a cesspool to be drained. So much so, it surprises her to see children there. Most of them are as wild as she was at that age, scrapping for themselves while their fathers dig, sluice, and gamble. God only knows where their mothers are.

Seeing the little ones hungry, she buys them bread and cheese. She teaches them the vanishing coin trick she used to support herself, not so many years ago. Making sure each one has a quarter to perform with, she sets them near the saloons to ply their new trade. One boy, she teaches to juggle pine cones, walnuts, or stones from the ground. He learns fast, and she feels proud of him. The little scavengers meet her every afternoon before five, before she goes into the Gem. If they haven't made enough to buy any supper, she makes up the difference.

Licking a thumb to swipe smudges off their chins and feeling their soft hands tug at her arms and dress, Martha Jane imagines she might find a good man and settle down. Maybe have a few kids of her own. She could be a good mother, if she put all this behind her.

Al doesn't own her; he's just using her for a while.

CHAPTER SEVENTEEN
LIFE AFTER HICKOK

1877, Sherman, Wyoming

She let them blow air into the story during that long year after the murder, when newspaper reporters were so voracious for Wild Bill stories, they'd print any truth or lie. She let those money-grubbers claim and publish it, that she and Bill had been lovers. She didn't deny the stories, but they'd never shared a bed, just memories, whiskey, laughs, and dog-eared decks of cards.

She'd loved him, sure. Still does. Everybody loved and loves William Hickok: men, women, and children. Even the folks who hated him roasted that ardor over fires of love—not the least among them was the bastard who shot him in the back, for having been scorned. He, maybe more than anyone, put his whole heart into Hickok. Only the beloved suffer murder, after all, and only those who pine will fire the gun.

Yes, those who inspire passion get run down, shot, and remembered. Sensing this, Martha Jane has a sad, odd sense of safety, thick and gray as wool on a sheep. She's told and retold, handled and moved, even laughed at, but seldom loved.

She misses Wild Bill's sunshine on her face, so she keeps telling that lie about going after Jack McCall with a meat cleaver, bringing the scoundrel to the law for the hanging he deserved but wouldn't suffer until after that second trial, in Yankton. She orates herself as the hero, despite the fact she was dead drunk at the time, trapped in a fevered dream. And then, when she finally woke up to hear Bill was dead, she found herself too sick to walk, let alone chase down McCall.

But if she must continue to live without Wild Bill, she'll tell herself into his last chapter, carrying out in story the love or justice that should have saved him, but couldn't. Martha Jane's heart breaking and McCall's body swinging from a rope—these events change nothing.

As for painting herself as the heroine, Martha Jane believes Wild Bill might grumble but wouldn't truly mind. What's the harm in a beautiful lie, a story of friendship to the end? The gist, if not the plot, is true. And Wild Bill's legend is secure, while hers is ever in doubt.

On occasion, as whiskey laps at her brain, and she opens herself to desire, Martha Jane wishes she and Bill had found, or at least used, each other that way. It would be a memory to clasp in the dark stretches once fenced by his laugh, his scowl, his casual indifference. She wonders what kind of lover Bill was to other women, even to his Agnes. Hard, lusty, and fast? Slow, tender, and easy? Or was he distracted, looking over his shoulder the whole time, the way he did at the poker table?

All Martha Jane can picture, when she imagines him out of his clothes and above her, is water circling in a mountain pool, while from his lips, a clear moist breath quenching her thirst. But she mocks herself for this hankering. She tells herself the real Bill she knew over drinks and cards is memory enough: a friend or, at least, a man who allowed her a seat at his table.

Sometimes she despairs of love. Those few men took her for money, back when she was a bony rag scraping together food for the babies, but she's never yet held a man she wanted. A few times, she's startled awake, mid-dream and alone in her blankets, arched and breathing fast for a shadow determined and strong enough to make her soft. One with a gentle voice and a tender heart who'd kiss her, then run his hands under her buckskins or up her gartered leg to find what she keeps hidden. A gentleman who'd ask first, who'd never insult her with a sweaty coin.

Awakening, she loses her phantom lover and rummages through her pack to choke down a gulp from her flask. Running her callused fingers through her tangled hair, she berates herself for the folly of hope, for moistening under a dream. She tells herself nobody wants her that way, and nobody will. Al's right about her face. She's a sorry excuse for a woman.

She's been used a little, maybe even misused, since she was a girl in Fort Laramie, and even more since she ran off from Deadwood to get away from Swearengen. Waking up sore and confused after blackout nights of drinking in whatever town, she's felt vaguely ashamed and couldn't remember who, when, or if she'd even said "Yes." Feeling she couldn't have consented but also knowing most men wouldn't care if she hadn't. She's heavy with shame, cussing herself for sliding away into drink, leaving herself exposed.

Feeling the whiskey's ease, she pulls her thin blanket close and listens to the breeze lift, *whuff,* and drop her tent walls overhead, backlit gray by the moon. She melts down and cries a little, then tells herself nothing bad happened with that last man, for what little it meant, and there's no harm done. Still, she misses what she can't remember and regrets what she didn't give.

Tonight, thinking about the love that streams over the world without touching her, she feels threadbare and chilled. She's been worn and cast off like a ripped shirt, but not loved. She's tough and bawdy, flippant with a coarse joke, and ready with a laugh, but her heart remains untouched and, oddly, that of an unsullied virgin yet. Martha Jane waits inside Calamity as if still twelve years old. She's the snow six inches below the glacier's crust, exposed only by a scouring wind, waiting for April's sun.

So when love thumps her like a bar-fight bottle over her head, Martha Jane can't make sense of it at first. George Cosgrove is nobody new. He'd ridden into Deadwood with Hickok and the Utters, no valiant knight, just one of the crowd. He's a big man, muscular and slow. He has no poker face and loses at cards, with luck as lousy as Martha's own. A kind fellow, he talks softly and likes to dance, but he's never the first man to ask her. He lets the other fellows pair up with her first and bides his time for the slow dances, then holds her up when she's tired or has had a few too many. He sees her home twice when she can't see straight, without taking advantage of her, unlike some others. A patient sort, he sits next to her at cards, giving her slow smiles. But for Martha Jane, George is only a blur when Bill sits across from her at the table.

After they bury Bill, Martha swims from bottle to bottle. From ruminating, then telling and retelling sorrowful things, she comes to believe them: her love was true, she'll never love another, and Bill would have grown to love her, too.

After finally quitting Swearengen, but while still ducking his henchmen, she finds work as a bartender in a hurdy-gurdy tent. Two nights later, she's fired for sneaking drinks from the stock, crying too much, and making the customers sad.

She goes back to doing laundry during the day, which is excruciating, because daylight hours find her too sober to stand herself. Martha Jane's self-pitying tears fall unnoticed into the suds. At night, she deals faro with a placid face, so that in the game's frenzy, not one player notices her tears slipping down. She's making a spectacle of herself, but she doesn't care. After she packs up the faro table each night, she dives under the whiskey for safety from the deadly world that would cut down

Bill Hickok, the strongest, dearest, and best. How then can lesser beings like herself survive? Martha Jane mourns for Agnes, the widow she'll never meet, and for herself, the wife she'll never be. No other man will measure up to Bill or be worth the trouble.

With a fistful of wilted wildflowers, George Cosgrove appears at her tent flap and interrupts her tearful binges with clumsy words of love. At the No. 5 Saloon, he shifts his hand from her waist to her hip when they dance, then slides it lower. He pulls her close and breathes down into her hair during the "When 'Tis Moonlight Waltz." She notices how her head tucks under his chin, just so, as if they fit. His gentle, contained brute force calls her out of drink and grief. To test him, she leans in and lets him bear some weight. He doesn't let her fall. He makes her laugh with a joke about a cowboy and a dog.

He rides to her tent in the mornings, and they take long rides through the Hills, following deer and antelope trails. Climbing rocky hillsides on horseback, they attain ridges to look down on the world. Strangely, unexpectedly sober, she breathes in the pine and spruce and hears the flutter of aspens. He strokes Henry's ears with a gentleness that stirs her. He shoots better than she does, and yet he's confident enough to admire her skill. She softens to his company, and his voice soothes her old state, what she calls her cold lonesome. Her heart warms when he prepares broken-yolked eggs and charred bacon over a smoky, open fire, and she's never tasted food so good. She snuggles against him in their bedrolls inside the tent, where they sleep fully clothed.

He calls her Maggie. She likes the new nickname when George says it. Any other man, she'd punch in the nose for changing or deciding her that way, but George is good and kind, and she thinks, *maybe this comfort is love. Maybe I'm not meant to be alone.* He seems like one she could center on, forsaking all others. And when he finally unlaces her buckskins on a river bank, she gladly says "Yes," because he's the first one who means anything. He calls her "Wife," and in return she calls him "Husband."

When the other boys in the saloons come on sweet-talking, hot with need and offers of drinks, now she tells them, "I'm Maggie Cosgrove now. No business on the side."

Maybe it's because she's trying to stay sober, or because Swearengen's men glare at her from all corners, but even through the haze of romance, Deadwood's stench gags Martha Jane now. She wonders why she stays. Her beloved, ragtag street children sense they're no longer her first love, and, because she's with George, they avoid her. The new romance is showing some wear; after their first few euphoric months, Martha Jane and George have settled in like two horses harnessed together. Deadwood's gloom and the weight of their poverty strain the make-believe marriage, so the hard-bitten lovers sell most of what they have, which isn't much, then bundle the rest on their horses. Riding to Sherman, Wyoming, they tell each other things will be better, or at least newer, there.

Things turn out not to be, so the weary couple pack off to Rapid City to pan gold. George expects a fortune, and, when he can't make a strike, he cools to her as if emasculated. His pride injured, he backs off as Martha Jane encourages other men's attentions.

After knowing George for a few months, she sees him more clearly now; like the mica in the granite hillsides, her man is shiny but thin. Martha Jane's love for George cools further when an enthusiastic suitor named Jim flames up beside her. George turns surly and won't fight Jim for her, so Martha Jane hides her dented heart and follows Jim, because a girl has to feel wanted, at least. Even Al's girls at the Gem feel desired. Jim says it at least three times a day to her and everyone else in the bar; it's something truly fine to love up, and be loved by, Calamity Jane. George's love seems pale beside Jim's florid pride.

Jim's a flashy spender, a heavy drinker, and an all-the-chips gambler. He runs through money fast, but Martha Jane doesn't hold that against her new man because she drinks up a lot of cash, herself. But when Jim talks to reporters about her and their love affair, she listens in and begins to doubt his motives. The dime novels make her out to be a hundred different things, and she cringes, feeling her story twist out of her control. Now Jim adds on his own tall tales about her. When Martha Jane chides him, Jim tells her it shouldn't matter, as long as people are talking about Calamity Jane. She's famous! And, by the way, isn't it fine how drinks are on the house wherever they go?

With the cacophony of other people's words about her, Martha can't find inside herself the blood or the bone of her story. Feeling shapeless, lifeless, and directionless, she drinks until she passes out, losing hours and days at a stretch. She craves the reeling freedom she finds in her first few drinks and, then, how everything seems funny. She likes how, with a bottle in her hand, she can fill up her own legend. But she senses her life force ebbing. She's sickly and losing weight, so she tries to drink less while pretending to be more drunk than she is, so folks will like her and gather to hear her stories.

Too suddenly sober, she finds herself trembling and queasy, with a watery sense of weakness in her gut, arms, and legs. She hates to think she's become a true drunk, like her mother. If she'd stayed with George, her first love, she wouldn't be drinking so much; he was better for her. She feels tenderhearted when she remembers him and weeps over her hands of poker, even missing her turn to ante up. Wild Bill was only a fantasy, but George was real. He's a U.S. marshall in Deadwood now, a good man, too good for the likes of her. He didn't even look her way when she drifted back to see him, for old times' sake.

She wakes up beside Jim feeling sorry, longing for sweet, gentle George. She kicks herself for taking up with anybody, because she was getting along fine, before, but now she has a love-shaped cavern inside her, and it echoes empty, even with Jim snoring so near.

Best to swear off all men, like the whiskey. Martha Jane's not strong enough, but Calamity Jane's a hard one, a fighter, a stone. She doesn't need a man.

Martha Jane gathers up her clothes while Jim's still asleep and rides her horse to Sturgis. She works there in a dance hall setting up drinks and doing laundry. Doing her best to wean off the alcohol, her best isn't very good. When she loses that honest job, the only women's work she could find, she outfits herself in her buckskins for men's work: carting liquor and supplies between towns, hauling barrels of water, and cutting wood.

Total strangers point and chuckle, commenting, "Isn't that Calamity Jane?" Delighted to see her, all the same they fault her for crossing that line—pulling on trousers and callusing her hands. One man in a velvet vest passes her behind the lumberyard where she labors and chortles, "For God's sake, can't you act like a lady?"

"Sure as hell, I could, and lady enough to make you drop your drawers. But sooner or later I'd starve," she tells him, biting down on her cigar and hoisting a maul to her shoulder. "Because you men are fickle sonsabitches!"

Finding her muscles burning, hardening inside her sleeves, Martha revels in the sweat and the pain. The sun caresses her back, and her good dog Henry pants in the shade, near as a whistle and ready to come. These are the good things in life, things no man can take from her.

She forgot for a while and let herself get soft, but it won't happen again. Sure, it was a natural mistake for a girl of twenty-two. She tells herself she'll not forget again, not for any man. Love feels solid when you fall against it, but it won't hold you up. She's got to depend on herself, alone.

CHAPTER EIGHTEEN
FALLEN ANGELS

1878

Al Swearengen won't leave her be. She danced for him at the Gem, some months back, and he holds that over her, along with his fists. As if he did her a favor, he claims she owes him for his having given her a job, and for her abruptly leaving his employ.

"Haul your ass to Nebraska, Martha Jane, and bring me ten girls. It'll take that many to replace such a fine woman as you," he says, but his dark eyes glitter like obsidian, mocking her. Less than an hour ago, he called her "dogface." Said a fellow'd have to tie a bag over her head to stand poking her, but maybe he should anyway, to collect on her debt. Martha Jane flees the saloon before he can wrench her arm and shove her upstairs into his, or some other fellow's, bed.

She'd give just about anything, just not that, to buy back the virtue she's spent. At the Gem, she's already slipping coins and wallets out of drunk dancers' pockets and double-charging for drinks, because a girl has to eat. Since she's returned to Deadwood to forget about George and Jim, at least she's kept her misbehavior down to dancing and stealing, not like the girls who won't pass up the extra money for a roll upstairs in the brothel rooms. She feels her virtue on thin ice, though. Martha Jane hates to think what Al might make her do yet, so she follows his last order and rents a wagon to drive to Sidney. Al Swearengen's a big man in Deadwood, too big. He could have her killed, or worse.

To ease her conscience, in Nebraska she only talks up girls who are half-starved, assuring them there's a better life for them in Deadwood with Al Swearengen. That all they'll have to do is dance and sing for pretty dresses, clean rooms, and soft beds to sleep in, not to mention three square meals a day. *Not to mention*, Martha thinks, *because they won't happen*. The rest is mostly true, except for the "only dancing and singing" part. Martha Jane cusses her lying self under her breath and feels sorry for the skinny, desperate girls she loads into the wagon. More than half'll end up whoring, she figures. Probably all.

She sips whiskey and holds her tongue, though, letting the filthy, sorry girls rock in silence in the buckboard. Finally, her conscience pricks her like a grabbed cactus, and she hollers back, "Just don't argue with Al. Think of him like a father you got to obey, and he won't hit you much."

Hearing this, one girl starts to cry and says she wants to go home to her mother. Martha Jane eyes her and says, "Sure, if you think she'll be glad to see you, you now being what you are." It's cruel, and Martha feels shitty for saying it, but she knows it's the truth; this particular girl's already gone too far for any Christian mother to welcome her home. The child surely knows it, too, so she settles back, snuffling, and pulls her shawl over her tiny breasts. Martha feels damned. She should let the child go back to clean living, but she's scared, and Al said ten. Ten girls, the price of freedom.

She tells herself she's not truly ruining them; they've already made their choices, and, if there's a virgin among them, Martha will eat her hat. The girls' eyes are cold dead already, so Martha Jane comforts herself. She believes they can't go much lower, and Al Swearengen may save them from dying in some gutter.

It's no kindness, she knows, but pure and simple white slavery, to work at the Gem. No fancy words or logic lighten Martha Jane's conscience, so she staunches her guilt with whiskey.

Al racks up high-interest debts, charging for things a girl never ate, drank, or wore, and she ends up owing him more than she can earn. But if Martha Jane gives Al these ten pretty, young hens, maybe he'll let her flap free of his coop.

In Deadwood, when Martha Jane files the bleary, raggedy girls into the hotel lobby, Al says they're hardly what he was looking for, but they'll have to do. Skin and bones, full of fleas, and dumber than a bag of hammers, the whole lot. For her delivery, Al pays Martha Jane nothing, not even reimbursing her for the wagon. He admits their account's settled, at least until he says it isn't. That's Al, keeping grip on a girl's wrist, to yank her back.

Martha Jane watches the girls file up the carpeted stairs. Some weep, while others gape at the velvets, the paintings, and the shining wood floor. The madam tells them they stink like hogshit, then growls down at Martha Jane. "You could have at least cleaned up the merchandise!"

After turning her back on Al and his new girls, Martha feels her spirits plunge so deep, she craves a drink to drown her guilt, far from the Gem. This may be the worst thing she's ever done, and there's no undoing it now. She hopes those girls are clever enough to escape Al Swearengen, cleverer than Martha Jane.

A street preacher perches on a splintered box, barely outside the wagon and horse traffic. He hollers 'til he's red in the face and sweat soaks his collar. Martha Jane's impressed. As an aspiring, working performer herself, she can admire that level of devotion and stage presence, even if his message is lost on her.

He sings, in a tremulous but sweet tenor, "Amazing Grace." She's so moved, Martha Jane hums along with a tear in her eye. It's a comfort to think of sweet grace trickling over wretches like herself. Then the preacher sounds a new pitch on his mouth harp and begins one she's never heard, a song about a story.

Moving nearer, Martha Jane pulls a long draw off her whiskey bottle and settles on a barrel outside the mercantile. The sun flares in her eyes, and she weeps at the boyish voice singing "I Love to Tell the Story." It's about Jesus, most likely. Preachers hardly sing about anything else, but this one's also about love and telling. Martha Jane concentrates, catching the tune enough to hum along.

The last verse is a corker, and she commits it to memory. It renews her belief in repeating old stories, because they matter. Every person's story is unique and important.

Long after the preacher climbs down off his box and the crowd drifts away, Martha's singing that tune.

> *I love to tell the story, for those who know it best,*
> *Seem hungering and thirsting to hear it like the rest.*
> *And when in scenes of glory, I sing a new, new song,*
> *'Twill be the old, old story that I have loved so long.*

Damn, those words are almost pretty enough to revive Martha Jane's hopes for her own scene of glory. But even if the scene is to be denied her at her final judgment, her present story, not her eventual glory, is the point of the preacher's song, as Martha Jane understands it. She's gathered thousands of stories, after all, glory upon glory in themselves. She wonders, taken together do they form one greater story, her scenes and memories and even the parts she's made up, her bald-faced lies forged with her life's true events?

The whiskey warms her as she closes her eyes and leans back against the mercantile's split-log walls. Her muscles soften in sweet release.

I love to tell the story. Spinning her own tale is her first love now, so people will see and remember her, sure, but also so they'll recall this moment and this place she feels slipping past her like a breeze. Martha Jane takes a deep breath, her chest filling with the moment. She absorbs the stinks of manure and sweat, and then the perfume of fresh-hewn pine. There's some passing lady's lilac soap, the fatty scent of bacon frying, a whiff of shit, and those odors of men: machine oil, pomade, and tobacco smoke. She celebrates ordinary music in the jingle of wagon chains, the scraping whine of a saw at the mill, and the ring of horseshoes on stone. A dog's bark, a man's vile oath at something or somebody he can't change, a child's laugh, and a mother calling her own child, maybe that very one, home.

The smells, the sights, the sounds, the fights. The joy and sorrow, the loves and hates of her life. Martha considers the preacher's song and what it means about why she's here, dropped alone and smack in the middle of it all. She smiles to herself.

The story is the thing. And by God, whether He be hard or merciful in the end, Martha Jane will fold it together, telling it all. Her way.

The Chinese fall to the smallpox first, so among the whites there's little concern; it's said to be a disease of filthy races. The Christian folks of Deadwood feel proper, clean, well-to-do, and above the scourge.

Not two weeks later, two local white miners and a cowboy from Texas come down with the spots, fevers, and delirium. Hundreds fall ill like decks of cards scattered in the wind. The town sets up quarantine tents in one quarter, but it's too late. Sick men sprawl on the ground between the crowded cots, without enough blankets for all. The sufferers cry out for mother, for sister, for wife.

Martha Jane hears them from her corner shack. She's running out of money for rent or whiskey, so she's unusually sober, with a profound headache. She wanders to the quarantine tent, pulls up a flap, and peers in. It's a pitiful sight. Men thrash, close as logs on a lumber truck, their bodies crusted with filth and running sores. The stink is even more potent than her own body odor, which, she grants, is surely considerable, with three months having passed since her last bath.

She swallows hard, crouches down, and scratches Henry behind the ears as she considers the situation. She's grown weary of her routine—the senseless drinking and rowdy nights are a blur. She's lightheaded from hunger but hardens herself to her own empty belly, to turn her heart to these abandoned men. If there's any good in her, if she's anything more than a white slaver or a drunk, she senses now's the time to prove it. She steps into the tent.

There's only so much she can do. She scavenges a big black kettle, boils water, and throws in a plucked chicken nabbed from some unsuspecting citizen's coop. She adds some shriveled onions and boils it all into a broth. Knocking on church doors, she begs for clean rags and volunteers but returns only with the rags, which she dips in boiling water to wash the sufferers. She guesses it might feel better to die clean.

Martha Jane's never thought her singing voice was much, but this audience is too weak to complain. When she croons "Goodbye Liza Jane" and "There is a Green Hill Far Away," the men open their eyes, blink in the canvas-filtered light, moan, and reach for her hand. She croons that one verse of the preacher's song from memory, too, pouring extra soul into it. When she's exhausted her song repertoire, she follows with her accounts of scouting with Custer and fighting Indians. She offers her voice, in truth and in lies. The men love every note and word.

One feverish fellow weeps and calls her an angel.

"You'll soon enough realize your mistake, dear boy," she murmurs and dabs his cracked, blistered lips with bear grease.

Martha Jane stays, sleeping on the plank floor. A few aproned women drift in to play at being nurse, their clean hair caught up in bleached kerchiefs. They swoon after a few hours, dab perfumed hankies under their noses, and excuse themselves to tend their husbands and fathers. They don't know how to bear it, Martha understands. Coming from high places, they get dizzy when they look down. But for Martha Jane, this tent is better than most places she's slept. After the first day, the blood and shit and stinks don't unsettle her much.

She changes men's trousers and long johns when they soil themselves, then boils the laundry behind the tent. She clips the wet laundry onto cords to flap dry in the breeze. After two days of this, dressing and undressing her patients, she knocks on more doors to beg for old sheets. Stripping her patients, she keeps the men naked, cool, and easier to clean until their fevers pass and they can lift themselves onto chamber pots. This lewd adaptation to the realities of nursing and Martha Jane's matter-of-fact demeanor about it drive out her last helper, an older woman who sings about Jesus on the cross but can't set eyes on the nakedness of a dying man.

How the hell? It's downright ridiculous, and Martha Jane yells after the fleeing saint, "Good riddance, you self-righteous biddy." She bites her cigar, which wafts a sweet odor into her face, and resigns herself to the heavy lifting.

There's a skill to nursing, and Martha Jane figures it out. She learns how to tell from the clarity of his eyes whether a man will hold down his broth or spew it back. She mixes bear grease, beef tallow, and menthol into salves. When a Chinese physician stops by the tent, he offers medicinal herbs and advice, then stays to help her. He tells her she has good instincts, a quick mind, and a healer's heart.

Martha Jane swallows hard and cuts her eyes away. Instincts, maybe she has those, but a quick mind? Nobody ever accused her of that. She only knows when somebody's suffering, she can't turn away; of all her sins, that would be most grievous. Even trading girls to Al Swearengen might be argued as a lesser transgression, as those girls might benefit from a hot meal or two. But to let a man suffer and die alone, well—it stops her heart to think it. Martha Jane senses a mystery, that being so close to suffering may be something holy, or some sort of opportunity. Take that thief on the cross—didn't Jesus speak to him?

Yet whenever Martha Jane steps out of the tent for some fresh air, to light a new cigar, and to roll the kinks out of her neck, she sees Deadwood's finer citizens walking the long way around the quarantine quarter. Like horses with blinders, they stare ahead and cover their mouths with hankies as they keep their distance.

It riles her, so sometimes she hollers, "Hey, Mr. Banker, and Missus Feather Plume Hat! Spare a dollar for the sick and dying?" Sometimes she shames them enough that they flinch and toss a coin toward her feet. By the time Martha Jane recovers their guilt offerings, the tossers have rounded the corner, safe from her haranguing.

At least, she thinks, *there'll be beef in today's broth.*

Men die every day, crying, shitting, and calling women's names. The first few break her apart, and her tears splatter dark spots on their burial canvases, as she stitches them in. When the wagons arrive to carry the men to their unmarked, communal graves, she has to bend over, hands on her knees, to gather breath, courage, and strength enough to heave the bodies into the back. She's losing this fight, one man at a time. But then Henry comes and licks her face, jumps up and yips, finally turning in a circle on his hind legs, offering a trick she taught him.

"All right," she murmurs to the dog, "I can do it one more time." Sighing, she offers Henry a leftover crumble of that

151

morning's bacon for his trouble, for cheering her. Back inside the tent, she tells herself they won't all die. "Not this one," she vows, wringing out a rag and turning her love, her song, and her story to a different patient.

"You will not die," she pronounces, "not if I get to decide."

The moans and cries and snores rise and surround her in a chorus of misery. She bites her lip and studies the man-child under the sheet. If not for the running sores, his writhing, and his fever-split lips, he could be one of those fine white statues in Greece, nearly a god. He could be Cilus or Lige.

Again, she sings her verse.

Forgetting Calamity for a while, she gets through the tremors and panic to find a new and gentle way. Taking care of the smallpox patients lets her lose herself; it eases her thirst and quenches the cold lonesome, even without her usual flow of whiskey. They need her. And as the ones who survive look at her with adoring eyes, she finds love she never knew, love of and from humanity. Her weak patients return gratitude, clasp hands, and call down blessings. She helps them to their feet and walks them along the boardwalks until they are strong enough to leave her.

One day, as she exercises a boy half her age, her dog Henry darts after a rat and into the street, then into the path of a barreling stage. Leaving her patient gawking in front of the Gem, Martha Jane stumbles into the street, kneels, and gathers up her pup, whose neck was broken by the gilded wheel. Too shocked to cry, she cradles his soft body for hours in a saloon's soft afternoon shade. Finally, as evening falls, she carries him to where Wild Bill is buried.

She's been upright as a ponderosa pine, bearing death after death: miners, cowboys, even abandoned children ravaged by disease. The smallpox was her sworn enemy, and she fought it hard, with few tears. But this little death cracks her open, and all the other deaths hit her like a roundhouse punch. The guilty and the innocent together, the human and the beast—everyone falls.

Death yawns at Martha Jane, insolent and bored.

She howls beside Bill's grave, cradling the dog as images flash on her squeezed-shut eyelids. Cilus's rolled-back eyes, her mother's spotted face, her father's blue lips, and Wild Bill's slack jaw. So many precious dead, and Martha Jane falls into the space they left inside her.

As the sun sets, one of the girls she sold to Al scuffs up to Martha Jane and pats her shoulder, gathers up her satin skirt, and crouches to save her. "Now, now."

"I'm so sorry," Martha Jane sobs, kissing the limp, cooling body in her arms, then raising a hand to touch the girl's cheek. "For all of it, I am."

The girl convinces her to hand over her pet and urges Martha Jane to dig a grave. "My pa is a preacher, so I know a little prayer," the girl offers, shrugging. "Pa would say a dog ain't got a soul, but you and I know better."

"After what I did to you," Martha wonders, feeling dazed at the brilliance of the sun on her face.

"You didn't do nothing," the girl argues, bending to kiss Henry's head. "I was a bad, lost thing before ever you found me. And now I got a home."

"This is no home," Martha whispers. "This is the gateway to hell."

Martha Jane stabs at the rocky ground with a sharp stick until there's a hole big enough for her friend. Tears and snot stream down her face as she lets go of the first pure love she ever knew, the only being who was loyal to her.

After handing over Henry to Martha Jane, the girl straightens, folds her hands, and sing-songs the prayer she promised.

An angel with a radiant face,
Above a cradle bent to look,
Seemed his own image there to trace,
As in the waters of a brook.

"Dear child! who me resemblest so,"
It whispered, "come, oh come with me!
Happy together let us go,
The earth unworthy is of thee!"

The frail dove's voice fills Martha Jane with little comfort, but more shame for having sold such a child to Swearengen. Surely this is her punishment, to lose her little pet. And there will be hell, to follow.

When the verse is done, together they cover Henry with dry dirt and stones. The girl pats Martha Jane's hard shoulder, then brushes her hands clean and walks, head down, back to the Gem.

Martha trudges alone to her quarantine tent, where half a dozen men in damp sheets writhe and whimper her name.

Degraded and ashamed, Martha breaks down and can only tend her patients with whiskey's fortification. Just a nip for strength, she promises herself, and then a few swallows for forgetting. In the whiskey's spin, she finds ease and restless sleep in her cold, empty blanket.

A few weeks later, as her last patient boards a train to somewhere else, Martha Jane stands alone in the quarantine tent. She can still see the bodies outlined on the pallets, and their spirits, with her dead ones in that same company, hovering over; it's a terrible haunting and more sorrow than she can bear. Feeling her good works as nothing, she walks alone to the nearest saloon, still pained by, and looking away from, the empty space beside her boot.

Once the quarantine tent comes down and the threat of contagion is past, the citizens brag about their Deadwood heroine. Their own angel of mercy, Calamity Jane. She accepts their toasts and drinks the shots they slide down the bar as if she deserves them. It's part of her story now, but it doesn't reconcile her to herself. She shrugs away the adulation, uneasily fearing the truth, that she's damned already. Destined to be alone for eternity, a dead dog in dry ground.

★ ★ ★ ★ ★

Part Three
1880s, The Bad Mother

★ ★ ★ ★ ★

CHAPTER NINETEEN
MONEY BY THE BED

1880

July is a billow of yellow dust at Fort Pierre. Martha Jane chokes on the bits of earth that won't stay out of the air, churned up by mules and horses and soldiers crisscrossing the plains. The Chicago and Northwestern railroad camps stir another kind of flurry; handsome, hardworking men stomp, rush, and linger with their musky, sweaty odors and jingling pocket change. Their rough laughter draws Martha Jane to East Pierre, where dance halls and saloons ring with shouts, curses, and piano music.

Martha Jane is a bee to flowers with the droves of men, and they, hungry for even a hint of feminine graces, josh and tease her. She dresses to please them and opens her own saloon that offers faro, drinks, food, and music. Flouncing her skirts, she pours drinks, whirls on the dance floor, and reminds them what they miss now or never had at home. She brings in good, clean girls to sit at the tables and dance. Martha Jane stays sober as proprietor, to serve and then to keep order when the Bowies and six-shooters appear. Big enough to wrestle troublemakers, she earns respect and enough coin to break even.

In the mornings she cooks for the miserable men who never left, offering light sourdough biscuits to settle their whiskey-soured stomachs. Calam's dingy place is like home to them, only better; a fellow can spit on the floor, knock over a bottle, and piss off the porch. He can even sing at the top of his voice, knowing she'll join in.

When the men flare up over bad hands at poker, too much drink, or hot-flung curses and spill outdoors to shoot each other down in the street, Martha rushes in to staunch the blood, wrap a bandage, and soothe the pain. Her raucous, tender heart moves with pity, sorrowing over the hot-burning jealousies and violence of men. She chides them for the ways they bind and break each other in the usual course of things. In her brown eyes, they see a mother, a ready gal, a pal, and a saint. Seeing herself through their eyes, she becomes more than she was without them—a deeper, more loving Calamity Jane, even in her misery. She tries to be a better woman.

But after a few weeks of sobriety, the better version of Martha Jane can't bear the unbearable ache, that old cold lonesome that inches, glacier-like, through her chest. The good things she wants to believe about herself can't be true, so in her discouragement she sets out to disprove them. Closing her saloon's welcoming doors, she sheds her satin and dons her buckskins to make the rounds of East Pierre. She corners bleary-eyed listeners and further stretches her stories, adding more Indian fights, cavalry charges, and bloody escapes. With the liquor as inspiration, she crafts and increases herself inside the legend she would be.

With her hat on the bar, she drinks down to the floor men twice her size. She laughs and nudges them with her boot, then sings with the ones still standing. *It is good,* she thinks—the sweet, whiskey-soaked camaraderie of menfolk, so simple and pure. Even their disgust is sweeter than women's scorn, and it's a softer shame she finds in masculine eyes. Men will even muster a grudging affection for a girl who will drink, dance, and lie down: they'll adore one who can beat them at cards. And when men aren't stringing one another up into trees, firing guns, or throwing punches, Martha Jane finds them so easy to be with, so ready to laugh.

As Calamity Jane carries on, the satin-ruffled, cooing saloon doves lean in and look on, wondering at that woman's double nature. Her ruffled shirtwaists and filthy buckskins drop and switch faster than molting feathers. Then as to her personality, her coy wildness and tender masculinity confound their definitions. Wishing to be that free, to cross lines the way she does, the working girls study her and wonder: Is it possible for a woman to choose who to be? Even to choose that forbidden thing, to become a man?

Head aching and mouth nasty with old-whiskey cotton, Martha winces at the way sunlight pierces her eyes with shards.

She was dreaming again about Charlotte. Yawning, Martha studies the veins like blue swollen rivers on the backs of her hands, the fingernails shaped like pale tombstones, and the middle fingers curving, leaning out against the bare ring fingers with little crescents of space, between. Ma's hands were the same.

How much am I like her? she wonders. The thirst for liquor is the same. But that other thing, the quick warming in her belly and the weakness in her knees for a man who whispers to her, is lately as strong as her need for drink. Was it the same for Ma? It seemed she was only and ever out for the money, that men were a business for her, even with Papa. Martha Jane flushes, remembering her mother's sharp voice behind the hanging quilt that hid their mattress from the kids. "What will you give me?" she'd quarrel, and only years later did Martha Jane understand her father's pleas and the bargaining, that sex was for profit in Charlotte Cannary's bed.

Martha Jane can't remember being held or coddled. Ma was greasy, hard, and cold as a cast-iron skillet off the fire. Did she love her children? She sold herself and claimed it was for them;

Charlotte would tear open and hand over stale loaves buttered only with her complaints of how she suffered for her children. Breaking the crust with her teeth, Martha Jane couldn't look her mother in the eye, for shame.

Before the girl knew what one was, her mother called Martha Jane a child of sin. The first time, the woman whistled her daughter back like a dog, then cuffed her and accused the seven-year-old of swinging her hips, looking for trouble. Charlotte prophesied that day, calling Martha hot blooded and destined for hell. So it can give Martha a twisted sense of satisfaction to this day to go with a man, proving her mother right, even as she takes a swing at the dead mother who convinced an innocent girl she was bad. *Take that, and that. See what you made me? Just like you.*

It's because of you, Martha thinks sometimes, picturing Charlotte's bitter face as she kisses, undresses, and sinks down into pleasure with whomever he is that night. More often, she thinks to taunt and blame her mother in the morning, when Martha Jane spots the coins on the floor or bedside table. Martha Jane never asks for payment, but some of the men leave it anyway. She lays down a woman, hungry for love and touch, but wakes up to find that the men with their money tell her who she is. For a while, she hates them for it. But the men are too precious somehow, living and breathing and holding her close, so she calls on far-off, dead Charlotte to atone. It's a peculiar comfort to speak her mother's name, to imagine that woman near enough to curse.

But while the anyones snore beside her, Martha Jane knows better. Her mother didn't put her in this bed, and, when Martha Jane can't sleep, she drinks to stifle the voice in her that argues "No, it's you deciding," because that voice is her own. It alone tells Martha Jane the hard truth, while the angry mother silently falls to dust in her Montana pauper's grave.

The Deadwood newspaper implied as much, so now folks believe she'd been drinking when she fell down the stairs in Pierre. And so she had been, along with everybody else, to celebrate the railroad's completion with a poor man's ball, drinks, and dancing. Railroad executives even honored their hirelings with a real band: fiddles, brass horns, guitars, squeeze boxes, and drums. Outside the hall, November winds swirled snowflakes around the window panes to drift on the sills. Inside, red faces glistened with joy, liquor, and sweat. Caught up in laughter beyond words, Martha Jane whirled in the center of it all, then slipped off a top step.

Her busted leg also busted up the party. The injury's been slowing her down for a few weeks, so the men bring food and liquor to ease her recovery. Sitting alongside her floor pallet, they entertain her with tales of insults, hot tempers, and winning hands. Men's gossip is grand, much better than news women choose to dish: who punched hardest, who reached for his gun first, who's true blue, and who'll likely stab you in the back. The speculation is endless and fierce.

True friends, she calls these men and then wonders if friendship isn't the highest form of love, at least next to a dog's devotion. As men wander in and out to sit with her, scuffing their hobnailed boots on the wood floor, spitting, and hawing, Martha Jane feels their appreciation. She once nursed them, and now they gladly return the favor. It warms her to be loved in her convalescence but also to be sustained by the bottles they keep at hand. The doctor told her she'd need six weeks to mend the femur, but after two she hops downstairs, using Charlie Utter as a crutch. At the bar, she raises her glass to the boys, her dear companions. They cheer.

She can't read the print, but people pass on the latest news. The newspapers have taken pity on her since her fall. Calling her an ornament of society and a tender plant, they wish her the best of health. One reporter wrote she's their treasure, and she smiles to hear such a thing about herself read aloud and spread across the region.

As soon as Martha Jane's leg can bear her weight, the old itch to wander returns. With the railroad pouring goods and well-dressed folks into Pierre, that town doesn't seem either wild or west enough, so she dons her best traveling dress and boards a stage to the next town.

At a new saloon she calls for a double shot of Thistle Dew, then drapes her travel-dusty arm around a hard-muscled, kindly fellow who looks young enough for fun. When the glass slides to her and cools her hand, she sips and asks that boy-man what he knows about love. She whispers that she's hungry for a companion, after too long abed with only her broken leg. She's lonesome, and would he like to be tonight's husband? Would he be gentle, generous, and kind to Calamity Jane?

When his eyes widen and he pulls her close, she feels herself at home. Smelling of cloves, he breathes a darling word into her neck and kisses her lips. She almost asks him the name of this town but decides the particular *where* and *who* don't hold any secret or substance.

What matters is to never be alone.

CHAPTER TWENTY
CHILD OF THE KING

1881–1882

Frank King comes on slow as a February thaw. He pretends not to watch her from across the street, while she struts and spins her revolver into and out of its holster and brags with the cowboys. Today she's dressed like a lady, with her holster belt swagged below her embroidered bodice and her guns positioned like iron jewelry against her velvet skirt. She's the best of both, she figures, woman and man. She's proud of the way the corset pushes up her breasts, plumping them toward the neckline, and she can tell from the way passing women huff and look away, there's at least one thing about Martha Jane their glancing husbands don't mind.

Her face may have all the charms of an adobe wall, or so that miner in Boulder hollered across the hotel lobby. She didn't dispute it then, and she won't now, but she blinks away his harsh words and recalls instead the *crunch* and her own satisfaction as she broke and bloodied his nose. Some men need to be reminded how to talk to a lady.

Frank King keeps looking, so Martha Jane consoles herself; Calamity Jane may not be pretty, but she has other things men can't get enough of—adventure, spirit, and a body that doesn't disappoint.

Maybe he's sizing her up for hire. It's a temptation, to earn a few dollars that way, although she's tried to give it up. Another fifty dollars or so, and Martha Jane could set up her own place again here in Miles City. She could hire a few girls and let them do the sex work, while she'd cook, launder, and madam the brood.

She glances back to see Frank King, who's spiffed up in a red cotton shirt and new leather chaps, now looking her in the eye, instead of down lower. As if he sees past her costume and performance, clear into her, and she senses he's judging her character. Irritated by his arrogance, she calls across the street, "What're you gaping at, Slick?"

He grins, raises an eyebrow, and lights a cigar, puffing gray rings in a row over his head like haloes before he walks back into the restaurant.

"Son of a bitch," she mutters, shrugging him off and stepping into the First Chance saloon. She accepts a half-drunk beer from a dusty ranch hand there, but the well-dressed man across the street niggles at her. Frank King is something other than ordinary for this town, and folks have been jawing about him. He's a road agent, a rancher, a railroad speculator, or a wanted man, depending on whom you ask.

Whatever he's guilty of, Frank King shines like a new penny dropped in this grimy town, so fresh and clean he makes Martha Jane feel dirty and wrong. She itches for a bath, but her own coins slip through her fingers. It's dear, the cost of easing her thirst and keeping down the shakes, and so is a dunk at Rosie's Bathing Saloon above the hotel, where a girl can sink down in a hot tub for a good soak and scrub. Martha Jane's been settling for a daily splash in the livery horse trough; it seemed enough until today, but now she suspects that stench is her own.

Martha Jane fingers the oil and grit in her hair and decides to wheedle a dollar from the better-smelling fellow seated beside her at the bar, so she can clean up. She promises this cowboy nothing, but she'll surely need to dodge him later. He has an awfully hopeful look as she gathers his loose change, but she can't say what she's thinking; she'd never gussy up for a common fellow like him. It's Frank King she's preparing for.

"Thanks, Dusty." She smirks, patting his leather-vested back. She likes to make up nicknames for people instead of trying to remember their real ones, and people don't seem to mind.

Whatever His Name Is pinches her backside through the velvet, but she bites her tongue and sways her hips to encourage him. If he suspects he's been bamboozled, he might grab his donation back from where she dropped it, between her breasts.

She imagines his eyes following her as she crosses the street, but she doesn't look back. Maybe if he keeps drinking, he'll forget her adobe face. She winces and pushes away the insult again.

While she soaks, she questions Rosie, who reports what she's heard, that Frank King's a well-to-do rancher here in Yellowstone Valley with his own spread about twenty miles from town. He's looking for a good companion, maybe even a wife.

"Where'd you hear that?"

Rosie purses her lips and looks indignant. "Every man's looking, and this one don't even got a wife already, to shuck before bedding the next one."

Martha Jane studies her pale limbs under the cooling, gray water. At twenty-seven, she's still fresh enough, she figures. Cleaned up, with a dab of toilet water behind each ear, she might be what Frank King's hankering for.

Rosie offers to brush the dust out of Martha Jane's skirt and bodice, for another nickel.

"How about for a dime you let me borrow one of yours?" Martha knows like attracts like, and she'd best look finer than usual, to hold Frank's eye.

Rosie purses her lips, considering.

Martha Jane combs her fingers through her squeaky, wet hair. "How'd King afford to buy a ranch?"

"Had himself a good poker run a year ago, in Billings."

A gambling man. Martha Jane bites her lip, cups a handful of suds, and calculates the risk. Big losses probably, like with Pa, but big wins can get you rich quick. "Rosie, how about that dress?"

"Well, I got a red duchesse satin might be long enough. You're a tall one. Just don't flex those arm muscles and split the lace sleeves. You got such mannish shoulders."

Martha lifts her arms out of the water and does just that, showing off her muscles. "I'm a strong gal, for sure, but I'll go easy on your dress. Can I rent it for a week?"

Rosie sighs. Baths aren't selling yet, on Tuesday. "How about fifteen cents?"

Martha Jane stands, drips, and shivers as Rosie tucks a lavender-scented towel around her lanky frame. "Well, I ain't got that much now, but if all goes well, I'll get it by Friday."

"So you and me are gambling now." Rosie shrugs. "I got too big around the middle for that dress, anyway—too many fried pies. You pay me Friday, it's yours for good."

Martha towels her hair, then opens her hands for the scented oil Rosie pours into them. She rubs it in, sweet as almonds.

While Rosie combs the oil through her long brown curls, Martha Jane closes her eyes and sighs. She could get used to being taken care of. Maybe Frank is the one. Good looks. Money. And if she hits the jackpot, he'll even be kind.

She'll need to settle down her tough act and play up her ladylike ways. Frank probably won't want a hell-raiser, not outside the bedroom, anyway. In there, she can be a wildcat, but on his arm she'll be charming as Rosie. Martha looks back at that smaller, more delicate woman in the mirror, admiring how her hands flutter up and down like birds when she talks. Martha Jane should try that. It's downright enticing.

"You got a sweet way about you, Rosie," Martha Jane

murmurs, her sleepy eyes closing. "I wish I could act like you all the time, and I'd surely have a good man of my own."

"You think so," Rosie answers, leaning over her shoulder and resting fingertips on Martha Jane's cheek. "But nobody's sleeping next to me now. Men don't know what they want. When a woman's soft, they want hard edges. When she's tough, they want a flower. Don't make yourself crazy, Martha Jane Cannary. Just be who you are, and wait for the man who sees you."

Martha opens her eyes and looks again back at Rosie. *That's well and good,* she thinks, *if you have good in you to find.* She reaches up and squeezes Rosie's hand. "Thanks, honey. Let's hope Frank King desires a cactus flower, thorns and all."

"Well, good luck," Rosie says, gathering and wadding towels as Martha Jane slips into the whispering satin. "I declare, Martha. Red is certainly your color. You positively glow in that dress, like I never did."

"It's the color of sin, after all," Martha joshes. "Sorry I took so long. I'll be out of here soon as I pin up my hair."

Rosie shrugs. "The rush comes on Saturday, and nobody's paid for your used water. No hurry. You might as well take that matching red hat with the feather off the stand. My gift."

Martha blinks back tears as Rosie leaves. What a better world it would be, if all folks were kind as Rosie. She vows to repay the sweet girl for the dress and her kindness, once Frank antes up.

Coming down the stairs, she looks both ways to avoid Whatever His Name Is, in case he's waiting.

Frank King keeps his eyes on her like she's a vaudeville show and Cleopatra, together. He laughs when she cusses in a stage whisper, and then he smiles around his cigar when she taps her lips with gloved fingers and apologizes to everyone at the table for her slip of the tongue. He orders cidery Stone Fences made with AA whiskey for her to drink and then laughs at her raucous jokes. He even lights cigars for her, too.

Upstairs in his hotel suite, he unwraps her like a gift. She turns loose the dirty talk she'd toned down earlier, then rolls him like a grizzly bear until he pants, splays over the sheets, and whispers, "God almighty, what was that?"

In a word, Martha Jane styles herself to be Frank King's perfect wife. It's easier than she thought it'd be, because Frank is kind, generous, and an adventurer in bed. On top of that, she truly likes him.

So she's not angry when she finds he's not as rich as Rosie had reported. Her tender feelings kick in when he takes her to his little ranch house. It's simple clapboard with rough pine floors, but, with Frank beside her, it feels like her home. And, she tells herself, it even has glass-paned windows, for curtains, and a brand-new potbelly stove.

Four months later, Martha Jane's waist pops a seam on Rosie's red dress. She remembers then, she never paid for it but figures it's too late now. With a baby coming, she'd best stay close to home. Just going to see Rosie might draw her into the taverns and set Martha Jane off into a ripping good time.

Frank seems happy about the baby, and Martha Jane vows she'll settle down. Isn't this what she's always wanted, a family of her own?

Frank misses the bustle of town, so they ride in on his wagon to hear saloon bands play on weekends. They dance a little, and Martha Jane takes her whiskey punch neat, with extra sugar for the baby. Even though she still loves and fancies Frank, the gambling, hooting cowboys seem to be having more fun than she and Frank are. Watching from their corner table, she'd give her right arm to deal a few hands of faro, to feel those boys' tension and joy up close.

Settling down is awfully hard work, even when Frank's

around to encourage her, and being pregnant makes her feel as bloated as a rising sourdough loaf. No matter how much she sleeps, Martha Jane's tired. During her long days at home without Frank, far-off pianos tinkle and boom in her head but can't drown out the lowing calves and chirruping crickets. The ranch silence calls her demons to sing, and she craves dancing music, any noise loud enough to cover her old cold lonesome.

Frank loves her up fine when he's home, but he sells cattle across Montana and Wyoming. He's gone for days at a time. Without her husband close at hand to remind her what she's about, Martha Jane struggles to do the right thing. She fears she's not cut out to be a wife. Maybe Charlotte was right about the devil in Martha Jane. Just thinking about Ma dries out Martha Jane's mouth and sets her fingers twitching for a bottle. Too bad she poured out her firewood-pile-hidden stash in a flash of good intentions.

Too sober, she agonizes. What if she proves to be as irresponsible and cold as Charlotte? What if she fails Frank? Why'd he pick Calamity Jane to settle down with, anyway? The man must be crazy.

Going off the bottle so suddenly brings on the shakes and the sweats. She vomits so hard, she fears she'll lose the baby but tries to tough it out. When Frank comes home to find her in bed, he suggests she take just a teaspoon of whiskey in some milk, to ease her body down, so she does that. Hardly ever does she take an extra dose. She won't be Charlotte Cannary, she tells herself. She'll take care of her baby, even before birth.

Work helps. From Martha Jane's lingering in bed, her muscles have softened, but she feels stronger in mind. While she gathers wood, the sun strokes her skin. A breeze tickles the back of her neck as she senses her own change of season and the life ripening inside her.

Seeing her on her feet, Frank leaves her to pursue his business again. She misses him something awful but decides she'll chop and split an entire winter's firewood before he returns. That way the three of them will be warm as piled pups when the baby comes. It should arrive in December, by her calculation. *A Christmas baby,* she thinks, stroking her mound of belly.

After a few weeks sober she appreciates how, without the whiskey, she feels agile and strong. The falling-down bruises on her arms and legs fade from blue to brown to yellow. When he passes through, Frank's grateful for her change. He nuzzles her hair, puts his arms around her, and pats where his baby's hidden. Best of all, he swears she'll be a damned fine mother.

She smiles for him and withholds the truth of herself. Healthier than she's ever been, she's still defenseless against the night terrors that paralyze her in the dark and linger to haunt her daylight hours. From some black hole inside herself, specters of rats teem, starving children wail, and rough hands grope while she struggles and stares, unable to move or scream.

In the months leading to her confinement, Martha Jane remembers the few pioneer women she spotted along the trail west. Peering out of their soddies or their rough-hewn cabins, they shaded their eyes and held down their skirts against the unrelenting winds. Their faces, even when young, bore wrinkles from the prairie sun—to Martha Jane's astonishment, even those women emerging from sod houses appeared clean. She remembers wishing Charlotte had possessed their work ethic and dignity. Now that she's older, Martha Jane wonders whether those pioneers were dignified or merely resigned.

To scare the devil from her idle hands, Martha Jane stitches together a white apron and embroiders it with Indian basket-flowers, those little sunsets that blaze yellow in the center, then flash out to orange and red. She's never attempted handiwork, and the results are rough, but she's pleased when she ties it on and smooths the colors over her baby belly. Peering into the little shard of mirror she's propped on her dresser, Martha Jane wets and tucks her hair into a neat, pinned bun, the way those pioneer women wore theirs. She sets her mouth into a tender, determined smile.

She can be that good, strong sort of woman if she tries.

When the first clotted snowflakes spiral down to stick on her cabin windows, Martha Jane cuts two layers of flannel into shapes of a tiny person, front and back, for a gown. Once stitched together, the garment is obviously too small, so she burns her failure, stabbing it with a poker so it's consumed before Frank can see. She tries again, this time cutting the shapes larger. As she stitches them together, she ponders the upcoming birth, wishing she'd at least attended one other woman, to know what to expect. Her hands tremble, and she pricks her fingers and thumbs, staining the flannel with red. Poor baby, wearing such rags. She hopes Frank will be so proud of his child and so concerned with appearances, he'll insist on buying store-bought baby things.

The birth is a shock, a revelation that severs Martha Jane from the woman she was before. Delivering alone while Frank's in town, she feels herself wrung out and split wide. She cries out against the bearing down that grips her as if she's possessed, her own body working against her will, and her desperate urges to quit her childbed and run. If only she could! She bleeds and breathes as hard as a running mare until finally come the hot sliding, the hollow relief, and the enraged tears she'll never admit.

From between her legs, she gathers the slippery infant into her arms and severs the cord with her Bowie knife. A boy, ten fingers and toes. A mop of hair the color of Frank's, and a nose eerily like her own. After drying and warming her child in a

173

scrap of flannel, she awkwardly presses her nipple to the newborn's lips. Born knowing, he latches on, spreading tingles and heat through her chest.

So this is what she's for.

After, with blood running out of her and the baby boy swaddled in her arms, her heart's exposed. Little Calamity's torn away a piece of her flesh and spirit, carrying her into the world further than she wants to go. Martha Jane pictures building a fence or wall around the cabin, to protect them both from intruders and to prevent her losing him.

Maternal love stretches her heart, to fit him in it, but hardens its exterior like a shell. She thought herself brave before, but that was mere bravado. In this trembling passion, Martha Jane knows she'd kill to protect this baby.

When Frank comes home, stinking of whiskey and perfume after a whole night gone, and reaches for the boy, Martha Jane reins herself in. Instead of baring her teeth at him to snarl and snap, she forces something like a smile and swallows down her accusation, the "where-the-hell-have-you-been." With a deep breath, she beats back instinct and parts the flannel to reveal her miracle, her son. She blinks and bites her tongue when Frank crows out his accomplishment, but she can't credit the liquored-up braggart, this Johnny-come-lately, with any part in the miracle God and Martha Jane have wrought.

The baby nuzzles, nibbles, and sucks away Martha Jane's edges. The sweet, slightly sour scent of her milk sustains her, too. She tells herself this boy will grow up strong, shoot straight, and be her story long after she's gone. But he's retelling her, too, giving her a new meaning in the present. Little Calamity's fist curling and his soft nails scratching her breast—these ordinary touches are signs from God that Martha Jane's sins are forgiven. She is beloved and loving, beyond the need or esteem of any man.

Frank hovers beside the bed but she blocks out the man, any advice he would offer, and any right he would claim. Feeling her devotion shift off and away, Frank grows churlish, claiming she never loved him right, and never enough. Has she forgotten who's the King around here? She's holding that baby too much, then in the wrong position, and now she's letting his head flop.

Martha Jane rolls her eyes at him. Insulted, Frank turns mean and tells she's dumb as a cow, and that fat. She glares until he mumbles, "Sorry, but you act like that baby's your whole damned world."

She tries to care and searches for the words. As if talking to a little brother, she explains she's still his woman and always will be, but she's worn out from the birth. She'll love him up as soon as she can. Martha Jane's not sure she means a word of it.

He teases her from across the room as he sips whiskey. Sloshing the bottle in her direction, he's a tempter. *Worse,* she thinks, *he's the devil himself.* Imagine, asking her, when she's worked so hard to sober up, if she's ready for a snort. It's as if Charlotte's ghost has come to haunt her here.

Martha Jane forces a laugh and tells both Frank and Charlotte to go to hell.

He insists he'll go where he pleases, with any woman he likes, if she won't see to his needs.

She remembers the perfume stink he just brought home, knowing his need's not been simmering long. She wonders why she doesn't care about his cheating, or anything else, for that matter. Only the baby breathing, latching on to her.

He's not a baby, she tells him, and he can wait. He stumbles to the bed and gropes her, grabbing and demanding sex. She slaps back and cusses a blue streak, reminding him of things any man should know: her fresh wounds and blood, and her need for time to heal. What kind of man badgers a woman still in her birthing bed? It's only been a week. Is he a beast?

He blushes, falters, and storms out, slamming the door. His boots scrape on the ice, buckles and bells jingle on a harness, and the horse snorts as Frank saddles up. She tells herself, good riddance, but Martha Jane's chest tightens to the rhythm and momentum of another man riding away.

To comfort herself, she raises the swaddled baby above her lap and lets his windings fall. His tulip lips purse and his tiny toes spread. The dark stump of umbilical cord that once bound them together is dry, about to fall away. Martha Jane tells herself this sign doesn't matter; no earthly thing can separate her from her newborn love.

Frank stays away for a week to punish her. She tells herself she doesn't care, that he's useless as a nipple on a bull.

Alone in her lumpy bed, Martha Jane dozes, sitting up only to change and feed Little Calamity. When hunger or thirst become unbearable, she shuffles to the sideboard for some bread and old cheese, or to the stagnant water bucket beside the door, for a drink. She rinses her rags and dirty diapers, then hangs them on a cord next to the stove, which she stokes from a dwindling woodpile on the cabin's back wall. Missing Frank's episodic thoughtfulness, she tells herself he's proven false and doesn't consider her needs at all. So much for the love of a man.

Still, mother and child wind together in their own rhythmic world. Sleep, nurse, clean, and gaze into one another's eyes, only to begin the elemental circle again. The agony of the birth and her life before, these seem to Martha Jane merely dreams, now nearly lost to forgetting. She learns how to pin a diaper so it stays, how to make her little one belch, and how to settle his colicky fits. For once she's glad she was the little mother to her siblings, for what she learned.

In the baby's third week, Martha Jane awakens from a dream

of hot coals burning her breast. Little Calamity is red, listless with fever, and rigid in her arms. Coughing and wheezing, he weakens and goes limp in fewer hours than it took him to be born.

She squeezes her wide brown nipple to dribble milk for him, but he won't accept her salvation. The blue-white pearls dry on his slack lips and curdle on his chin. Kissing his damp hair, she feels the chill grow as Little Calamity's will to live dissolves.

She swaddles him in another layer and holds him to her heart. "My God, my God," she whispers, her tears streaming down. "Take me for my many sins, but leave the boy. Throw your fire down on me, alone, and I will gladly roast in hell."

From beyond the plaster ceiling comes only silence.

Martha Jane has long feared the cold lonesome would kill her, but it's come for her baby first. That same morning, it circles, flaps down, and devours her mind.

When Frank, only half-sober, staggers home two days later, he must wrestle the tiny shape from her arms. Martha Jane scratches his face, then follows him into the snow, barefooted and wearing only a soiled nightgown. He walks her into the house and forces her into a coat and boots, but the tussle leaves him panting and weak, muttering, "God damn, god damn this world." Following him outside again, she stands blank and mute as he thaws a hole in the ground with hot coals from their stove. The frozen grass singes and smokes, smudging their faces and stinging their noses and eyes. Later, while Frank digs into the softened ground, Martha Jane sings the hymn that little prostitute sang over her dog, Henry. From that song of angels she repeats the only verse she remembers until finally Frank breaks down, shouting at her to stop, for God's sake, stop.

Blinking, she falls silent. As if half awakening, she abruptly notices the gray sky, the smoke-stained snow, and the dark hole in the ground. She walks away. She doesn't know what she's doing, only that if she stays that hole will swallow everything that matters. Stuffing all she can carry into a carpet bag, she leaves Frank to all that's dead and gone.

The horse is still saddled, miserable in their lean-to barn. Martha Jane's still so weak from the birth, lying-in, and sorrow, it takes three tries to heave herself into the saddle. Once mounted, she sits, dazed, not knowing where to go. Finally, with arms and legs and face trembling, she rides away.

Slack and pale, he watches her take the only horse he didn't just lose at cards. He calls out to her with the word *love*, then stoops to study the flannel bundle on the ground. Pinching his nose between thumb and finger, he spits, cusses, and stabs the earth again.

Down the road in Miles City, Martha Jane throws back four shots as fast as the bartender can uncork, glug, and slide them to her. She chokes as if drowning, forcing the liquor down. Finally, she feels a movement in her chest as if a heart beats there. She tips the bartender and buys four burlap-wrapped bottles of whiskey for the road.

You have to be careful, she thinks as she secures her saddlebags, *or all can be lost, dried up like a drop of milk.*

She's not sure why or where she's going; there may be no safe destination, no home for her outside a bottle. Given what's ruptured and torn loose, and with that ravenous cold lonesome pecking the edges of her sanity, Martha Jane senses only this— she'd best not stand still.

CHAPTER TWENTY-ONE
HOPE OF FIRE

The fast white river's edges thaw into slush like lace, but the wind is a knife. Looking at the setting sun painting the high rocks orange, I climb uphill from the river. It ain't gonna be warm when I get there, but I got to go higher.

Twigs pop and bent branches swish back when I stomp by. I'm alone but not. Over me, you float like a snowflake dances in the air. I can't feel anything but you, Little Calamity, the way a dragging match feels flame.

On the breeze a shush of pine needles or is it a sob? Baby, don't cry. I didn't lay you in the ground. That was your hard-hearted pa, but maybe he loved you, in his way. I don't know what love is. I only know my need of you.

When I close my eyes, I see and hear your lips click in that nursing pucker, sucking while your blue-marble eyes move back and forth behind your purple-tinted eyelids, skin thin as paper, you my book and my Bible pages. You root for your fist, then grunt, turn, and latch on my white breast's saucer nipple. Pinching with hard gums, you hurt me before easing me, pulling my cup of milk shed for you. Our needs meet where skin heats skin. My need, to be emptied. Yours, to be filled.

Even standing here in the snow that seeps in my busted boot, I feel the tingling, hot sweet letting down, the release when you sucked life-milk through me. I see drops like pearls shining in the corners of your mouth. Lord, I wish for those terrible cramps you cranked in my belly to make me bleed harder. You were the sweetest weight in my arms, drooping, dozing with your belly round as a sourdough loaf, risen.

Stay. Follow me through this crusted snow and I'll break through for both of us. The pines drop white fingerlengths of powder, surprising my neck. I catch my breath. Did you feel that? Sure, you did. You are me.

I pull up my collar but ignore my hat riding my back, bouncing on its lanyard. I set out this morning ungloved, bare-headed as a child, as if guardian angels do line this trail, watching for fools. But I know better. Nobody's guarding anybody.

I press my hard, dead fingers to my bleeding lips and suck them warm, but I feel your mouth, not mine.

Come along. I miss you, but missing ain't the word. It ain't gut-deep or pointed enough. I clutch and cramp for you. You were in—no, you were—my body, but now I'm a husk.

Stay. My breath puffs out like ghosts that fly, and cold air rushes in, scours my lungs like sand scours a burnt pot. Snow soaks and freezes my sock-wool into teeth. I don't build a fire, I'll lose some toes. There's matches and char cloth in my chest pocket. That snow-dragged juniper bough shows some brown dry needles, but being warm, even the hope of fire, is a thing I don't deserve. Not after what I done. Or like I heard a priest say, for what I failed to do.

My cheek is tearful-wet, soft, and warm but then crackles hard with a new skin, ice.

No fire because of this, too: the stink of sulfur, spark, yellow pop, and flare would startle you. I picture your heaven a quiet, cold place, as cold as your body got in my arms. I figure there's only chipped-ice stars for light, but no flames, burning, or smoke. It must be clear as water, where you are.

The sun is setting. What I wouldn't do to feel the weight of you again, your hard turning and feet climbing my ribs. I hunker here in the snow, lean against this boulder, and study the last orange strip of sun thinning itself over the whiskery mountain. My breath clouds and freezes my eyelashes. I could go blind and still see you. I could die here and be with you by morning. So short a time and this gun in my holster arguing with me to shoot, to shoot, but I argue back, my hands are like stone. My heart thuds slow in my ears. To live or to die, I'm frozen between, a yellow-belly coward.

The moon swings high like a fancy rich woman sashaying to a dance, trailing a white scarf cloud. Beautiful, but she can't feel anything. She acts like nobody died, nobody should care. I turn my blame on her. Heartless bitch was there the night you died and did nothing. If I could feel my fingers, I'd shoot her, drag her down, and bury her. But you might be so hungry now you'd choose her for suckling. You might forget me.

The match drags, and hope like a smoky flare comes when I spot your first star in the high, purple west. Star bright, first star I see tonight. I tell the star my whole wish, your name, but the word falls like a chunk of snow beside my boot, too heavy for you now. No more wishes in the world, I guess, but I'm stubborn. I croak a lullabye through my bleeding lips, like a trap.

Freezing without your heat, I tell myself I still believe, but when I close my eyes, I can't see you. My dried-up dugs are empty and flat as that flying bitch moon I hate as much as I love you. She has you now.

I wait all night, even after she drags you down in the west, to keep.

By morning, the cold lonesome scrapes my soul raw. I can hardly stand or move, but in my hard sleep a mercy of snow blanketed me, so I didn't die. Who knew the devil could be kind?

Ignoring the guns that could ease me into your night, I let you go. I kneel and strike a real match. The sulfur burns my nostrils, and the first blue flame turns as yellow as the coward I am. I cup the match, light and blow on the glowing char cloth, then coax the tinder. Finally, juniper catches and pops into a smoky fire, making me cough. Bowed down beside what I ain't got a right to, I shudder. Light shatters down through the pine needles when I look up, like to blind me.

Uncorking a bottle, I guzzle and choke. Then more burn and belch until I don't see the wisp of hair that coiled around my finger or your granite eyes. Until I can't feel your soft fingernails, fierce as a whore's but as desperate as true love, clawing my breasts for milk.

CHAPTER TWENTY-TWO
COWBOY AND INDIANS

1883

Teddy Blue puts an arm around her and leans in to say she's the best gal friend he ever had. He toasts their friendship, rekindled six days ago.

"A man needs a woman. Not just for a poke, mind you, although that's a fine thing. But to listen to him, to hear his troubles."

"Like a mother?" Martha Jane teases, ruffling his hair. Teddy's a good sort, one you can count on. She likes him too much to have ever taken him to bed; she'd hate to gamble him on love. Now, since Little Calamity, she's sealed off and not much inclined to sport. Just the thought of using her body that way gets tangled with memories of the birth, the nursing, and a baby lost. She won't get pregnant again.

She longs to tell Teddy about her lost baby boy, to see some genuine pity or at least some reflected sorrow in his eyes, but the story clogs her throat. She forces a jovial note. "Or maybe I'm like your sister? Same way Wild Bill saw me."

"No, no, you got me wrong." He chuckles and tosses back the last of his drink. Teddy's been tired and thirsty since his long cattle drive from Texas to Yellowstone.

She orders another round. He digs in his trouser pocket and comes up empty but swears he'll pay her back.

"Hell, no, you won't. It's on me."

"I am a man of my word."

183

She smiles at him, wondering if there is one on earth.

But Teddy Blue Abbott is as genuine as they come, not one of those remittance man cowboys funded by a rich daddy back home. He's a real cow puncher whose father first ranched, and now farms, near Lincoln, Nebraska. His old man sent Teddy on his first trail ride when the boy was ten. Scrawny as a grasshopper and with eyes nearly as big, young Teddy knew his father meant to toughen him up or kill him, and the old man didn't care much either way. When the Nebraska farmers ran the herds and cattlemen out, Teddy's father gave up ranching, while Teddy followed the cattle through the years and over the range, to here in Montana.

He explains, to Martha Jane's delight, how cowboys came to be called cow punchers. Not long ago, Lincoln was the far north point on the Texas cattle drives, the place they loaded cattle onto railroad cars. Now that point is here in Miles City, Montana, but back in Texas the cowboys figured out how to "punch" fallen cattle with their prods through the slatted shipping car walls to get the animals on their feet again.

Martha Jane could almost kiss Teddy Blue for the way he explains things to her, as if he expects her to understand. He makes things clear without talking down. Few men talk to any woman, let alone Martha Jane, as if she's smart. It's a rare dignity Teddy offers to her, and Martha Jane doesn't say it, but she's pledged her everlasting friendship in return.

She's proud to be seen with such a man, too, as it's good for her image. Teddy cuts a fine figure in his high-crowned, white Stetson, his bright cotton shirts in red, yellow, and blue, and his Oregon-sewn, checkered pants. Despite his typical, Texas-slump shoulders, curved by riding horseback, his sun-hardened face, ready smile, and dark handlebar mustache render him handsome.

To Martha Jane, Teddy always behaves as a gentleman and

even tips his hat when he sees her. When he does get a wild hair, he finds a dove to pay; he doesn't whiskey-slump onto Martha Jane to use her for free, the way some men try to do.

Teddy Blue elevates Martha Jane's behavior—not altogether or for the long term, but noticeably so. When Teddy's in town, Martha Jane twists, curls, and pins her hair and picks out cleaner, nicer dresses because Teddy notices and tells her she looks fine.

He doesn't mind when she dresses like a man, either. He does tease her, that if she'd dressed like that on the trail when he was a boy, the cowboys would've stampeded into the brush in shock, as if they'd seen an elephant. For her good taste in men's wear, he admires her fancy buckskin vest embroidered with flowers and says it reminds him of Lakota beadwork.

"Whatever you wear, you got to be yourself, Martha Jane. Don't let anybody manhandle you," he advises.

It's like something a brother would say. Being with Teddy reminds her of how she felt as a girl, safe and yet looking forward to an adventure, on the trail coming west with Cilus.

They drink plenty, whatever's available, but not as much as Martha does when she's alone. The conversation's that good— and can that man tell a story—so she stays clearer to catch every word. His statements are like verses of song, and she keeps the word-rhythms in her head to practice later. Teddy's drawl is warm, musical Texas, like most cowboys', but there's a little purr of England breaking through, an exotic flavor from his British daddy.

Teddy has a simple knack for storytelling, relating pure facts as more exciting than any tall tale, and more believable, for being grounded in his sincerity. He always gets quiet when a story's coming. He tips his chair and tilts back his hat, tucks one thumb in his belt loop, and scratches his whiskers with the other hand. Acting like the idea just came to him, he mentions a three-legged dog or a peculiar thing that befell a buxom farmer's daughter. He may bring up a cavalryman lost in the Tetons, a fateful meeting of old lovers on a train, or a swooping blizzard that froze oblivious homesteaders in their fields. Listening to Teddy, Martha Jane can forget to let out her breath until the story's end. She swears she'll someday spin tales that well and leave her audiences awestruck.

She's sure of this: if she could choose to be any man, but couldn't be Wild Bill, she'd live, breathe, and talk as Teddy Blue Abbot.

Barring that, she'll strive to be his best friend.

Teddy and Martha Jane hunker in the damp, shrinking inside their lumpy coats on a loose-nailed, swaying bench outside the mercantile. In front of them, rain rushes off the roof in silver strings, while soaked, hungry-looking Indians slog through ankle-deep mud in the street.

Martha Jane holds up a hand, calls them names, and snickers.

Teddy side-eyes her and doesn't laugh but crosses his arms and squints. After shooting a stream of tobacco at a passing cat, he asks, "I ever tell y'all how I run off to be Pawnee?"

Martha Jane shakes her head, wondering why anybody'd want to be Indian. They look like the lowest of the low, as she sees them, even several social steps lower than the misbegotten Cannarys that kicked her into the world. Those stories she's heard about scalping and arrows and massacred homesteaders send shivers down her spine. She'll never forget, either, that smoldering wagon train discovered by the Newton-Jenney expedition with the slaughtered family and the turkey vultures.

Martha Jane crosses her arms and aims her chew at the same cat, now hunched in a different spot. "They're just killers, ain't they? Why'd you go with them?"

Teddy huffs. "Martha Jane, you don't know shit. The Pawnee were the finest people I knew."

"Well, excuse me," she says, miffed, widening her eyes and shifting in her seat.

Teddy doesn't excuse her but sets his jaw and leans forward to make his point. "I have Pawnee friends, dear girl. Down around the Loup and Republican Rivers in Nebraska when I was a tyke, they'd move back and forth for their buffalo hunts, or their summer and winter camps. They'd come by our place, and I'd play with the boys. Most spoke good English, and they taught me how to live off the land without plowing every last inch of it to dust. Those boys were damned good riders, too."

Out of respect for Teddy, Martha Jane shrugs off the insult to her intelligence. She'd like to tell him to go to hell, the way she does most fellows who cross her, but he's a good friend. Martha Jane pooches out her bottom lip and squeezes it between her thumb and finger, considering. Teddy's a good man, all right, and he knows more about the world than she does. Still, she's never heard anybody say one good word about Indians. Teddy saying one first makes a deep impression.

She glances over at him, wondering how angry she's made him. "So you run off with them?"

"Packed me a bedroll and shotgun and hightailed it after the hunting party. An elder made me go home, though. Said I'd make trouble for them, that my folks would accuse them of stealing me. He said white people believe Indians steal everything, even their white children, when every Pawnee knows white children are nearly impossible to raise up right." Teddy chuckles and scrapes his boot on the boardwalk. "That elder looked at me and tried not to smile when he said that."

"So he made a joke? I'll be." Martha *tsk*s and furrows her brow. Will wonders never cease. An Indian with a sense of humor.

"Besides, in plain fact it was white folks who stole everything from Indians. He didn't say that, but I knew it." Teddy finally looks over to see her reaction.

She nods, feels him looking, and pushes a greasy strand of hair up into her hat. "So did you get a lickin' when you got back?"

"Nah. My folks never noticed I was gone. But I set my broken heart on the next best thing to being Pawnee, being a cowboy. I'd never be a farmer, a nester like my father."

Martha Jane lets out a great sigh. "I never figured you for an Indian lover, Teddy."

"That supposed to be an insult? I respect any man or woman of good heart and honest disposition. 'Course, there are exceptions. Nesters, who cut up the range with bob wire, for one, can't be trusted."

"I'll make sure to remember."

"And don't tell false stories about Indians, neither, just to make yourself look good. That rubs me wrong as a new saddle. They got troubles enough."

Martha Jane's face reddens. So he was listening when she told that stretcher about Sioux trying to scalp her and how she shot down five of them, after. A pack of lies, of course, but she's grown attached to the tale. It almost feels true.

Shifting her chewing tobacco to the other cheek, Martha Jane spits again and ponders her scolding, muttering, "All right, then."

As if he hadn't said a cross word, Teddy hums, "Cotton Eyed Joe" and picks a splinter off their bench.

Grinning and still a little peeved, Martha shifts her heel in the soggy gravel to bump against his boot and says, "Teddy Blue Abbott, any other man correcting me that-a-way might get himself a black eye."

He chuckles, crosses his arms, and squints. "Any other man

mighta made the mistake of sitting on your left when he did so, but I studied on your right hook. I ain't stupid, Calam."

She promises herself that from then on, when Teddy's listening, she'll leave out the Indian battle dramas. It's a shame, though. Folks' eyes sure light up when she describes the tomahawks and glinting knives, and they crowd in close to see the little scar up by her hairline, the one she really got from falling down drunk and hitting her head on a barrel. But Teddy's too soft on Indians to see how little the truth means, sometimes, and can't understand the love and strength she feels in the telling, as if she touches those people who love her stories. Those stories ain't even about any real, particular Indians, to do them any harm.

After all, the truth's hardly ever the best part of any story. Ask any child. There's what happened, but then there's where you sprinkle embellishment, like a dash of salt in your beans; you can hardly swallow life without it.

Yet if Martha Jane learned anything from experience, it's how low-down she's felt when wrongly judged and despised. It gives her a pang to think she's done that to anybody, even a beat-down Indian she never met. With fresh sympathy, she eyes the ones huddled across the street.

Teddy snores beside her, having suddenly slumped against the mercantile wall, into a shallow nap. She lifts the bottle from his hand and takes a swallow, studying his face while he's unaware. He sure is tenderhearted, her Teddy, and she learns from him. He shows her things she never thought of and even makes her uncomfortable sometimes, the way he treats people like everybody's equal. Truth is, Martha Jane wouldn't want him any other way but kindhearted, especially when he's considering her.

CHAPTER TWENTY-THREE
SISTER JUDGE

1884

Lonesome and at loose ends, Martha Janes rides a bone-jarring stage to Lander, Wyoming, where Lena's settled with John Borner. Lena's eleven years married and four kids along. Martha Jane hopes Lige might be there, too. To see her brother and sister again would add some weight to her boots and connect her to this earth, which she feels she's been shaken loose of lately. Friends, drinking pals, even men in the night pass through and leave her behind like locomotives grinding through a city.

But family. They're the folks who got to take you in, no matter what, she tells herself with a grin. Even if they know how terrible rotten you are.

She wishes she could assemble herself for a better impression for the reunion. Her dresses are threadbare, she's missing a few teeth, and her face is pale. She'll have to ease up on the drinking at the Borner place, or at least keep her bottle tucked inside her buckskin vest. John Borner always held a low opinion of Martha Jane, and she can't imagine how she might improve it. She hopes to stay a week or two with the family and practices saying, "I find myself between situations presently and missed my dear ones. And look at these beautiful children." She reminds herself not to point out how they resemble lovely Lena, which surely they must, and not their homely father, which, please God, they must not. Martha Jane smiles, eager to meet those little ones. She'll teach them to juggle and conjure coins out of midair. Children are easy, always ready to laugh.

It's grown folks she has trouble with, and, as if to remind her of that, Lena meets her sister with a tight smile and a stiff hug. Lige is his same old self: loose-limbed and easy-slumped against any pole or wall. His sheepish grin says *don't you be looking at me,* but his eyes shine more love than he can put into words. His hair's cut short, almost bald, and bags under his eyes look like a hound's. *He looks half-dead,* Martha Jane thinks, and, when she hugs him, she feels ribs like sticks and muscles like leather straps.

Lena, Lige, and the children lead her past the laundry shack where Lena works, where the ground is dark with wash water and outdoor tables overflow with dirty laundry.

Inside the little farmhouse, Martha gives her sister a closer look and decides she's haggard, too. "He's working you like slaves," Martha comments, biting her lip. "Where's John? I'll talk to him."

Lena denies it, tells Martha Jane to simmer down, and insists she's happy with John, who's a better man than she expected to marry. "We ain't exactly fine folks, Martha Jane," she says, wiping sweat off her freckled forehead. "We've got to work hard, but John's a good Christian. He treats me and the kids fine."

A blond-haired, blue-eyed kid with Lena's hair and John's deep-set eyes sidles up to Martha Jane.

"I'm Tobe," he whispers.

"You say you're a toe?" Martha teases, chucking him under his chin.

He shakes his head, eyes wide. "No, I said . . ."

"I know you," she says, laughing. "Don't you know a joke?"

He shrugs and catches her big hand in his little one, clinging. Martha shivers, sensing the boy's afraid. Is this another sign of John's hard ways?

Lige murmurs, "He's the tenderhearted one."

Martha darts a questioning look at Lige and asks, "Who's poking around his heart to make it sore?"

Lige shrugs. "Borner swears he'll make a man of Tobe yet."

"He made one of you?" She glances up and down, looking for bruises but doesn't see any. Maybe she's wrong and John's not so bad.

"John works me hard, but, thanks to Lena, the victuals are good." Lige pats his little pot belly, which looks to Martha Jane to be more like starvation than plenty.

"You sure you're all right, sister?" Martha Jane can't let it go; something feels wrong, like one flat key on a piano.

"Don't look for trouble where there isn't any," Lena warns, "or you'll find it." She leads her older sister by the arm into the kitchen and says, "Settle here and I'll fetch you some soup. Then a bath. You smell like cigars and whiskey. John'll have a fit." She bites her lip, ducks her head, and leaves the room.

With a full stomach and after a long soak in a galvanized laundry tub, Martha Jane feels more like herself than she has for a while, meaning she's miserable. Sober as hell. Lena found her whiskey flask when she went through Martha Jane's clothing, and that little do-gooder absconded with it, scolding, "This is a Christian house."

"Damn. She spirited away my spirits," Martha Jane mumbles, leaning near Lige's ear. "I can't just cut it out, sudden-like."

Lige nods and says he'll fix it. When he steals back and returns her flask, Martha Jane's so relieved, she limits herself to a sip or swallow or gulp once every hour, as if she's taking doses of medicine.

John Borner, who has been away on an overnight trip, unloads his wagon and stables his horses just before sunset. Seeing him in the yard, Lena hurries to pick up newspapers, used dishes, and Martha Jane's cast-off clothing. "He likes things organized," she fusses, tucking Martha's rucksack behind the settee.

Lena acts afraid of her husband. Martha Jane knows, from having nursed Borner's broken leg and catered to him for weeks, he's not so holy or high and mighty as he may be pretending to his wife. Didn't Martha Jane hold a jar for him to piss into when he said it hurt too much to walk, and didn't he cuss and howl for more laudanum? She may remind him about pain and weakness if she finds he's roughing up Lena or the kids.

But when he comes in, John brushes a dry kiss on his wife's forehead, greets Lige with a joke, and seems glad to see Martha Jane. He smiles, pats her shoulder, and says, "My old nurse."

It knocks the fuss out of her to find John warm, just as she's ready to take him down a peg. It's downright disappointing. When Lena reminds her, she steps out to wash her hands before they sit down to supper. "What the hell," she mutters. "Already? I just had a bath." While she's at the washtub, though, she dumps some cold water over her head and smooths back her hair, to settle herself down. She must be polite to the old German. Damn.

Roast beef, steaming potatoes, carrots, and fluffy buttermilk biscuits—Lena's served the best meal Martha Jane's eaten in years. It's been so long since she's tried, Martha Jane's not sure she still knows her way around a kitchen, but she offers to cook breakfast the next morning.

Lena declines, but Martha Jane pushes her so hard she finally says, "All right, then. Have it your way."

"And you sleep in, come morning. You're looking puny," the older sister says, casting an accusing glance at Borner. With so little whiskey in her, she's nervous, itching for a fight.

"I never felt better," Lena insists, glancing nervously at John, whose squinted eyes smolder like coals. "John takes good care of me," she adds, patting his calloused hand. His leather fingers curl around hers, keeping.

"Well, while your big sister's here, she'll take care of you, too," Martha insists, eyeing John.

"I'll do something," Lige offers, heaping meat on his plate. "Just tell me what."

"Goodness," Lena whispers, squirming. "Just leave me be, all of you."

John clears his throat, glares at Martha Jane, and asks for the butter.

Martha grins and pats her breast pocket for a cigar, then remembers. Damn, double damn.

Lige chuckles, smashing potatoes with his fork and reaching for the gravy. "Good to have you here, Sis," he says. "I sure as hell have missed your sense of humor. Imagine. You, up early and cooking breakfast. That beats all." Glancing around the room, he adds, "Things were so . . . settled without you here."

John clears his throat at Lige's language, so the younger man ducks and mutters, "Sorry," not looking a bit that way to Martha Jane.

Martha Jane sleeps late after losing count of the extra nips from her flask the night before. She snored so loudly on her kitchen pallet, John Borner couldn't sleep and now grumbles through the house like a spring storm, demanding coffee and something, anything, by God, to eat now because he has work to do.

Lena steps over her sleeping sister, nudging her with a boot toe now and then, to no avail. The aromas of popping bacon and the coffee finally stir Martha Jane out of her half-drunken sleep.

"Gol darn it, Lena, I said I'd cook," she says, shaking her head, combing her fingers through her snarled hair, and pulling herself up to tower over her sister. Watching Lena scurry, Martha Jane pours herself some coffee and sips, to wash the nasty taste off her tongue. Must've been that gravy last night, with the peculiar spice Lena added.

"John's used to starting early," Lena sighs, kicking aside Martha's bedroll to reach and set the table.

Martha Jane scoops up her blankets and takes them into the other room, thinking some people are awfully grumpy in the mornings. She meant to help, but Lena didn't give her a chance.

Martha Jane sits on the porch and watches a sour-faced John Borner ride away on his roan. It pains her to think of her sister living with such a hard, bitter character, but while Martha Jane's here, she'll lighten Lena's load.

After splitting half a cord of firewood, Martha wanders into the laundry shed. Lena's small, standing not even up to Martha Jane's shoulder, but she lifts and scrubs and wrings so fast, Martha struggles at first to step in, and then to keep up.

"You know," she says, "with my help, you could take on more laundry. I could help pay for my keep that a-way."

Lena shrugs at her offer, but, when Martha repeats it to John at dinner, he encourages Lena to accept. "We could use the cash, with another mouth to feed," he mutters.

"See?" Martha Jane slaps the tabletop. "I told you it was a damned good idea."

Tobe's eyes widen and he giggles behind his fingers. John slaps the back of his head and the child's eyes fill with tears.

"Hey, now. I'm the one you ought to slap," Martha Jane retorts, looking John in the eye.

"Enough," John says. "Get more work as soon as you can."

Lena sighs and nods but slides a scowl at her sister.

"It'll be easy money," Martha says. "I sure as hell won't mooch off you good folks."

John blinks and scrapes back his chair from the table. Lena sighs. Martha Jane asks Lige to pass the potatoes, please.

Within a few hours, Lena fills her delivery cart with laundry from three more families. Seeing it stacked so high, Martha Jane's taken aback; it's more than she counted on, but she dives in and takes charge. Building hot fires, heating water, and dissolving soap flakes into tubs once the water's boiled, she waves Lena back from the hottest water. Martha Jane slops in and stirs the soiled linens and clothing with a long stick, then lifts the steaming wad into a rinse tub. With her big, hard hands she scrubs the clothes on a washboard, then wrings them through two clearer tubs of cooler water.

Martha Jane works hard. Her head pounds, her hands shake, and she's on edge. The flask is empty and John Borner keeps a dry house with nary a tonic, so there's nothing to borrow. Work's the only thing that keeps her in her skin—that and hoping to shine in Lena's eyes. She won't let her sister down or look like a fool in front of John Borner. Martha Jane can tell, when Borner looks at her, he expects her to fail. The man thinks his wife's sister is no-account, a bum come to his honest home looking for handouts. She'll show him.

In truth, Martha's always found comfort in work, despite her jovial aversion to it. When she has to, she can stoop and lift, chop and stack, so the laundry business isn't too much for her. She sees the toll it's taking on Lena, though. Maybe she should stay on a while to lighten her sister's load. She tells herself her sister needs her here, with all this work and four children, too. It's too much for one woman.

With each day that passes, Martha Jane increasingly resents both John Borner and the uneasy sobriety he demands. Still, she tells herself she belongs at Lena's side, easing her sister's load. After all, they're family.

After her third night of nausea, sweats, muscle spasms, trembling limbs, and nerves so on edge she can't sleep, Martha Jane sneaks out the creaking front door and off the Borner property. It's a sticky, hot night, and she follows a moonlit lumber road into Lander. On Main Street, she finds what she craves, the company of good time fellows and a ready flow of whiskey.

Short on cash, she finds a sympathetic new pal and promises to treat him when Lena pays her. For a split second it pricks at her conscience; she's not assured any pay, as she may be working only for room and board. The details of the deal she made are fuzzy in her memory, but having to lean on credit and feel beholden to strangers, even kindly ones, makes her resent Borner more. The old German's working two women to death now, she tells herself. She'll have to convince Lena she needs cash for clothing or shoes, or there's Lena's egg money in the tin on the top shelf, left of the salt cellar. Worse comes to worst, Martha Jane could dip into that to settle her growing debts. She'd soon pay it back, and Lena would never know.

After two weeks of night visits to the saloon, Martha Jane's credit dries up with her new friends. To regain goodwill, she does borrow from Lena's tin but doesn't give it enough thought to remember to pay it back.

Lena notices the shortfall when she stacks the quarters, nickels, and dimes to count them. Knowing the thief had to have been her sister, she fumes and fusses at Martha Jane about everything but the missing money.

"What's gotten into you?" Martha asks, after Lena scolds her for missing a grease stain on an apron.

"Now it may not come out, even if I re-boil it," Lena scolds. "You don't take things seriously, Martha Jane. You think life is one party after another. You always have."

Stung, Martha Jane squats quietly back on her boot heels, water dripping off her chapped hands back into the suds. She studies Lena's belly and wonders if that old German's got another baby in her. That'd make anybody cross. The borrowed money's passed from her mind, and she can't imagine what's riled her little sister, unless it's Borner.

"Did John do something to you?" she asks, standing and wiping her hands on her skirt. "Did he hurt you? I know him. He's got a nasty temperament and thinks he's better than everybody."

"John isn't my problem!" Lena cries, slapping the wet apron at Martha Jane. "It's you. Ever since you came, things are upset. You brought trouble into my house."

"That's a fine thing to say," Martha Jane sulks. "I'm pulling my weight here. And not so long ago, I pulled extra, for you and Lige."

"You did plenty, didn't you? You should be ashamed, and it's not on me!" Tears streak Lena's grimy face as she shoos Tobe out of the laundry shed.

"What I did," Martha Jane says, trying to keep her voice down, "was what I had to. And I ain't ashamed. I was just a kid, orphaned. Alone and trying to find my way."

"Oh, believe me, I know," Lena cries, wiping her eyes with her sleeve. "I heard it plenty of times, what all I owe my sister. But we had a ma and a pa. It wasn't all on you."

Martha leans against the wall, feeling gut-punched. She sees it for the first time. "You don't remember, do you?"

Lena says, sighing, "Enough to know decent folks don't behave that way. No matter how hungry they are."

Martha Jane draws in a ragged breath. "Then you don't remember it at all." She dries her leaking eyes and walks out of the laundry shack with Tobe in step beside her.

She wants to punch something but clenches one fist in the other. She wants a drink. She wants to disappear. Anything to stop this feeling.

"Aunt Martha Jane, can you show me again how to juggle?"

"Sorry, Tobe. I'm leaving. Your ma's got enough to handle here, without your old auntie making her tired and sad."

Tobe tugs at her hand, kisses it, and says, "She was tired and sad before you come."

Martha crouches down to hug the boy. She pictures her heart as a stone. "I'm real sorry to hear it, but there ain't nothing I can do for your ma."

In the house, Martha throws her few belongings into a gunny sack, while all four children, gaping like baby robins, watch her with Lena's blue eyes.

"You behave, or I'll come back and make you. Help your mama. Don't make her cry, never. Not the way I do," she adds, under her breath.

Giving each child a kiss on the forehead, Martha breathes in the sweet and sour scents of their hair, breath, skin, and sugar-sticky hands that pat her cheeks, painful pleasures. Saying goodbye, she longs again for a child of her own, then slams the door shut on that room full of risks and terrors. But if only her baby had lived, she might've made a home by now, a place where she'd belong and wouldn't be resented. A place where she'd be known and welcomed, anyway.

Brushing aside Tobe's long bangs, Martha feels a wet rip in her womb, like unseasoned firewood that won't split clean.

"Be good, kids," she chokes out, leaving before she distresses them with her tears.

She's gone a quarter mile down the lane when Lena calls after her, but Martha Jane walks faster instead of turning back. She won't fight with somebody she loves or defend herself with hurtful words. She won't apologize, either, for being who she is, or for any hard choice she had to make.

Martha Jane senses she'll never fit into anybody else's life. She won't even have a place in, and can't revise, her sister's memories. Each woman has to follow her own story where it leads her, and then she gets to decide if or how to retell it. In her own silence or her own words, to suit herself.

Martha Jane's on her own. She digs some tobacco out of her jacket pocket, tucks it beside her gum, and squints into the orange-and-yellow, sun-striped clouds. No siree. Nobody else gets to judge her. She'll decide which parts are told, and which are forgotten. It's her privilege to tie it all into a tale that makes sense to her. This, she senses, will be the hardest work of her life, because folks are so eager to decide her.

How will she tell herself? Some parts she'll pretend happened. Others are true and they'll stand. She sees now how she's already been whipping together the rest from imagination, to set things the way they should've been. As for her sins and faults, she'll settle them with her conscience, best she can.

It's the damnedest thing, and a terrible loneliness to bear. She's yet to meet, even among soiled doves or murdering soldiers or her kin who suffered with her, one person who understands Martha Jane Cannary's pain-shredded heart or her volcanic mind. In this human race there may be not one person with a lick of mercy, or one eye clear enough to see her for who she is.

So, she thinks, squaring her shoulders and spitting on the ground, *to hell with them all, in a handbasket.*

Martha shivers as the sun dips and drags down its colors, leaving her to drown in chilly blue evening. She's weak without her whiskey and imagines how cool a bottle will feel in her fingers. Tucking solitude around herself and taking longer strides, she plunges toward a new town, with a new saloon and kindly strangers with coins, folks who haven't yet heard her stories.

CHAPTER TWENTY-FOUR
CUTTING LOOSE

1884–1888

Cast off by her family, she drinks and fights it out, and any man or woman looking at her sideways is soon sorry. She might pull a gun but hardly ever shoots level to the ground, because a warning shot into the air clears a space around her and gets her a write-up in the papers. It can also land her in jail overnight in the more Christian towns, and sometimes she's satisfied with that. It's not bad having a place to sleep indoors, instead of on a stack of crates in an alley or huddled near a burning barrel of trash, with icy fingers tucked in her armpits. Most jails even serve breakfast.

Sometimes she'll start a fight over things nobody can hear or see: that knife-like stab in her womb, a little wrapped bundle in a nightmare, a baby not really dead, but buried anyway. Was she careless, too quick to give up on the little one? Terror breaks her into a cold sweat, so she gulps down some relief, picks a surly target, and comes out swinging.

In those long minutes before she falls asleep, she can't help thinking about what happened. Maybe she never should've left her husband, but how could she and Frank ever look each other in the eye without always seeing what lived and died between them?

Martha Jane tells herself she never loved Frank, anyway. Not him or Lena or Lige. Say those things often enough, and they almost feel true.

Leaning on street corner posts, chafing my butt sore on horseback, and perching high and looking down from borrowed wagon beds, I tell the Martha Jane out of me and the Calamity Jane in. Thinking I can get good folks with money to listen, I call adventures out to their feathered-and-ribboned hats as they bob past me, but those folks got me all summed up. For all their charity talk, they figure there ain't nothing deep or worth saving or feeding in this loud and sinful woman.

These rich churchgoing ones with gloves and pomade surely hear me shout because they glance over. Turning pink and too late pretending they didn't see me, they flinch and fasten their eyes on their pretty each-others and talk loud about God and the new things they'll get and pile and paint onto the fine things they already got.

When they look away so fast, I get a feeling they're scared. Maybe my eyes are a mirror and their ears are doors. If they see themselves in me and if they listen to my story and like it, they might like me and we might stand on the same level ground, and what then? Will they ask Calamity Jane over for dinner? It makes me laugh to think of my shitty boots on their rugs and my cigar smoke stinging their eyes. Not to mention how the ladies would faint when I'd cut loose.

So it's the folks with dirt under their fingernails and bear grease stinking in their hair who stop to listen. These ones, who ain't got a penny to spare, toss me a widow's mite out of their light pockets. Bless them, my brothers and sisters in sin and want and failure. Blessed are the poor—we will save our sorry, damned each-others.

A fellow in a houndstooth jacket and a yellow hat sidles up to me and asks for an interview. I talk to the newspaper men sometimes, to slip a few of my words into the lies they'll print anyway. I don't care for what they write about me, but as long as those lying sonsabitches don't pester me when I'm seriously drinking, I don't fuss. Their little scraps of newsprint add up to me being somebody strong, wild, free, and never ending, even if their Calamity bears not the least resemblance to me. A woman's got to be seen, don't she, to be remembered?

Words in the air and on paper keep me from disappearing, even if those words leave out the little girl lost. When I get sloshed, I almost tell the fellows with the pencils and notepads about little Martha Jane, thinking they'd care about that orphan girl and her troubles, how she got run under the shoes of better people, plumb forgotten, and left to starve. It sure would be good if somebody knew who I really am and who I was, but it sticks in my throat, thank goodness, because behind the story of that orphan is a bottomless hole. My old cold lonesome breathes stinking air from that pit and I could fall in where that little girl died but still walks around with her sad eyes rotting in her head. This would be a nightmare if I could sleep, but I am wide awake and she is always there.

So I make up better things to tell and hope that like Hickok, the buffalo, and the Indians, when I am dead I will hang in the wind and stick to people's boots, caught and kept forever in the dust and mud of the West. There surely ain't no place for me in a blue-sky, harps-and-wings heaven, but my ghost could hang lower to dance forever with the fiddles, pianos, and boots scuffing schottisches on hardwood floors. Because I come to believe this—remembering is a kind of forever.

I don't doubt the fellowship down here will be better; I can almost hear Hickok, the Utters, and my dear Teddy Blue laughing, cussing, and bluffing lousy hands so loud the good folks in paradise will think it's thundering below them.

Ranging from town to town on railroad cars, stagecoaches, or horseback, Martha Jane orates her version of the world. When it feels flimsy, she spices it with romance, naming Wild Bill as her true love. This romance never was, but now it is, simply because she says so, and the man's not here to holler any different. Wild Bill. Charlie Utter. Teddy Blue. Even Custer, or at least the United States Army. She names them all, the living and the dead, then weaves herself into their battles and sometimes, even into their beds. Martha Jane revels in the power of story. If people want to believe, she'll give them a creed. It's the same storytelling magic Buffalo Bill's conjuring with the show he put together last year in Omaha. His Wild West is pure theater, nothing but gun smoke and whoops in an arena, even though the hired Indians are real Sioux. And, back in '72, Hickok and the gang put together that buffalo hunting exhibition at Niagara Falls for the rich Eastern folks. Made some good money, too. So the West is becoming something new.

The same way an orphan gets taken in by a church lady to be bathed and dressed in nicer clothes—hell, the same way Martha Jane herself was—in that same way, rough stories of the West get adopted and dressed in costumes to make this country feel good about its progress. The wealthy folks, especially, want clean miners, sheriffs, Indians, and cowboys gussied up in satin instead of buckskin or linsey-woolsey, and those actors best be shining with gold and silver, not toting lead and tin. Americans crave gunshots and even a little murder, as long as it's the road agents or Indians who die, with red dye spilled for blood. Martha Jane sees a gussied-up nostalgia helps folks forget the true ugly parts, where good people and poor people died and still are dying. The pay's good, so she plays her part, but the dishonesty irks her into drunken brawls more days than not.

This chaps her, too: as the West gets civilized, young folks strut and pretend. They ride out on a train and talk about the hardscrabble, shoot-'em-up days as if they were here from the start and tamed what once was wild. It makes her blood boil. Martha Jane paid the price. She rode west with a wagon train, fought to survive in the mining camps, and has been on her own her entire life, right here in the West—her bragging rights cost her plenty. She may edit and embellish a little because it's her goddamned life and she'll tell it her way, but hell, didn't she play poker with Wild Bill? She'll fight anybody who says she didn't.

Keeping in mind the folks who do stop to listen, she memorizes and practices in private to craft a consummate performance. First, she lifts a hand and waves toward an imagined sunset. Then, touching the corner of her eye, she relates how she first knelt beside Wild Bill in a pool of his blood, only to run down his murderer with a machete and corner that coward for the sheriff. In another scene, she rests a hand on her six-shooter, ready to fire on a horde of invisible Indians.

If she could read and write, she might put the story down for print on paper, but she enjoys the way it lives and moves from her mouth, with nothing between her and her listeners. She holds the storytelling the way she savors a juicy steak or swishes whiskey before swallowing. She likes to play with the delivery, changing her speed or tone of voice, to draw in her listeners. It's a tonic to her to see the audience's expressions change, and how she moves them. She sometimes thinks she might be some kind of artist, inspired by something outside herself. Most of the time she's afraid of losing what she's made, so she repeats it like a rosary against forgetting when she's too drunk to organize her thoughts, which is nearly every day.

Whiskey may steal the story from her. It may also kill her. She almost hopes it will, and soon. Until that happens, she'll cover the cold lonesome pit with better lies to keep down its truth—the dead baby, cruel men, lost family, and things that might have been—with drinks and a grand performance.

The season blusters in hard and demands a change. Feeling the pinch of frostbite through her boots, Martha Jane rounds up eight dancers and sporting women in Livingston. They board a train, then switch to horseback. Riding through a storm with woolen hoods pulled down over their faces, they brave savage, snow-choked winds and perilous terrain. All-suffering, these women would bring succor to the desperate, gold-burdened Coeur d'Alene miners at Jackass Junction, the last stop on the wintry route to hell.

Calamity Jane and her girls unload their packhorses while men stare. Like magicians conjuring a dove from a scarf, they grab every scrap of bright cloth, interesting gee-gaw, or pretty thing they see. Their eager onlookers raise a tent and pound together a pine board stage, to be paid only with alluring smiles, fluttered fingers, and hints of more to come. The girls hang a red calico curtain on a rope to hide their secret doings and banish the curious men, who linger, smoke, pass bottles, and escalate each other's hopes. Whispering things they've already seen and hoping to see far more.

In only two days, the crew stitches, hoists, paints, and costumes their full-blown theater show. The prettiest girls those men had ever seen appear in lovely gowns somehow unrumpled, none the worse for wear for having been crammed in saddlebags, soaked by snow, and frozen. Footlight lanterns burn yellow in the tent, flushing skin and speeding up hearts, banishing what's real into cold shadows.

One girl plays the piano like it's a circus calliope, and she'd be a credit to her wealthy family back East, if only they knew where she was. Four of the girls draw all manner of human emotions from fiddles, while a third one warbles, like to break all hearts in her woeful soprano. The young ladies offer costumed vignettes, both sentimental and sorrowful; one from Greece features virginal statues draped with silk and boughs of satin flowers, their white-powdered, tender bosoms heaving. Another calicoed scene evokes home—mothers and sisters wring hands and wait for wartime news, pining for husbands, fathers, and sons in pretty poems, bringing homesick tears to hard-blinking eyes and grizzled cheeks. A third is a feverish, bedeviled fit of piano music, hitched and flounced skirts, and necklines dipping perilously low as the girls kick high and throw kisses at the crowd. Cigar smoke hangs thick, rendering every scene a vague and beloved memory. Homesick miners, railroad men, and vagabond husbands climb and fall from mountains of emotion, dissolving into impulsive fights, cheers, and grateful weeping before the gaslit beauty of it all.

Martha Jane lets the lovelier girls take the stage for an idyllic shepherdess scene, again featuring the heartbreaking soprano, while she steps to the back of the tent. There she draws the more unsettled men behind yet another curtain, to a makeshift barroom and rowdy roulette table. Later, when the saucy redhead finishes her burlesque dance onstage, the last act featuring the other girls, Martha hurries out the back for her act.

After she ties on a bandanna and settles her hat, she emerges from backstage into the footlights, standing tall. The men hoot and holler, begging for the redhead to come back and show a little more leg, or for this new one to drop her buckskins, so she draws a pistol to redirect them. One shot through the tent canvas ceiling, and they laugh, stomp, and applaud Calamity Jane.

Appraising the unshaven crowd, she tips back her hat, puts her hands on her hips, and waits for them to settle into what passes for quiet among men: dyspeptic belches, coughs, soft oaths, and boot soles scraping the plank floor. She feels their eyes on her, not with the same hot need they fired toward the other girls, but with mild interest and curiosity. They tip back their hats and tilt their heads, as if wondering what her true shape might be under the leather and wool. Maybe she reads in their eyes a little respect, uneasily given; it's what she's always hoped for, the rough camaraderie of men, a place at the bar she didn't buy with her body, and a seat at the poker table with no whispered innuendo.

She's patient, looking each man in the eye. Once she's captured them and feels their unsprung energy focused on her and gathering in her chest, she sings out her tale as if she's that lady Scheherazade, the clever gal who saved herself with stories.

She begins:

My maiden name was Martha Cannary; I was born in Princeton, Missouri, May 1, 1852.

Martha Jane falters and swallows. Well, there's the first stretcher, and it leaped off her lips like a grasshopper. She's made herself four years older than she'd memorized herself to be, but right away she sees why. These rowdy fellows need to see her in the West's childhood, riding with the army and fighting Indians as a woman grown. So she's said it and it's true, just like that. Who's to argue with her? Besides, she'll shoot any man who calls her a liar. She puffs out her chest, settles one hand on her gun, and glares at a pig-eyed fellow in the front row. He frowns, breaks eye contact, and looks down at her boots. *Yes,* she thinks, *just look away.* Clearing her throat, she continues:

My father and mother were natives of Ohio; I had two brothers and three sisters, I being the oldest of the children.

And the only one looking out for them, most days, cleaning up shit and piss, and begging for food, but who wants to hear about that?

As a child I was fond of adventure and outdoor exercise, and horses. I became an expert rider, being able to ride the most vicious and stubborn of horses.

In 1865 we migrated by overland route to Virginia City, Montana; took five months for this journey. While on the way, I was at all times along with the men when there was hunting, excitement, or adventure to be had.

By the time we reached Virginia City, I was considered a remarkably good shot and a fearless rider for a girl of my age. Many times in crossing the mountains, the trails were so bad that we had to lower wagons over the ledges by hand with ropes, for they were so rough and rugged that horses were no use.

We also had exciting times fording streams, for many of the streams on our way were noted for quicksands and boggy places where, unless we were careful, we would have lost horses and all. Then we had many dangers to encounter in the way of streams swelling on account of heavy rains. I on more than one occasion had mounted my pony and swam across the stream several times merely to amuse myself.

Her voice catches in her throat as Cilus's face rises up in mind. *Dear brother,* she thinks, *you were the best of us all.* Hot tears rise, but she blinks them back, swearing under her breath at her own tender heart and viciously resisting the real past. It's hard, but she forces more words.

I had many narrow escapes from both my pony and myself being washed to certain death, but as the pioneers had plenty of courage, we overcame all obstacles and reached Virginia City in safety. Mother died at Blackfoot, Montana, 1866, where we buried her.

Martha Jane pauses as if she can see Calamity Jane's voice floating on their murmurs and smoke. Charlotte's grimace revisits her, and Martha nearly forgets the rest of her speech. A pang twists her gut. Stalling, she hollers out over the crowd. "Goddamn it, I forgot my necessaries. Somebody fetch me a bottle of Thistle Dew, so I can forge ahead."

The men guffaw and pass up an uncorked bottle, which she holds up to the light before muttering, "Cheap sonsabitches. This ain't but half full," then gulps it down. Wiping her mouth on her buckskin sleeve, she lets out a formidable belch. "That's a far sight better," she quips, tossing the empty into the crowd, conking one dozing fellow on his bald pate. To their laughter, she adds, "If you want a story, you selfish sonsabitches better keep your eyes open and the whiskey coming."

They stomp and roar, loving it, loving her, and she tears into the next part, which feels liquid and easy now, flooding and drowning Charlotte's bitter, dying face. Calamity, undaunted, showers words over every acid memory that assails her.

Up to this time I had always worn the costume of my sex. When I joined Custer, I donned the uniform of a soldier. It was a bit awkward at first, but I soon got to be perfectly at home in men's clothes.

Then on about Arizona and scouting with the Indians. She doesn't think about the words now but instead finds herself caught up in how the men below the gaslights look up at her. There's power in the way she's intruding on their imaginations, and the cold lonesome recedes as the cowboys and miners lean in to join her adventures.

When she finishes, the crowd erupts in cheers. She sees it; every last sorry sonofabitch believes in Calamity Jane. She steps behind the calico curtain and listens to them stomp and chant her name, and she feels she could live forever like this. She doesn't move until three of the pretty girls push past her, adjusting their flounces and parting the thin curtain for their encore.

Back behind the bar, she pours whiskey for fifteen cents a shot to men who've been gambling, the restless rabble-rousers who didn't gather around the stage to hear her story. She's ordinary, or merely peculiar, to this bunch. As she relaxes, she releases the electric charge she felt, up front. Clinking together dirty glasses, tossing old bottles into a crate, and bantering across the bar, she settles back into being Martha Jane. From a bottle under the plank bar, she keeps herself lubricated, too.

She may be drunk as a skunk, but Martha Jane can still tell when a sharp fellow tries to slip her a slug instead of a nickel, and she's still right enough to wrestle troublemakers out to the street, especially those rascals who try to cut ahead in line to claim a girl for the after-show dance. Martha Jane's eight satin-gowned gals waltz, polka, and reel until their feet nearly bleed from being stomped on by staggering men. The party spins until dawn with enough fights, and even a couple of surly gunshots, erupting in jealousy over slathered feminine graces, that in the morning the snowbanks are splattered red. More than one man loses a toe to frostbite that night, after getting too hot with whiskey to feel the weather and falling asleep in a drift, and then finding his pockets empty to boot. But still, the general sense of the town was a good time had, and couldn't those sweethearts dance?

Martha Jane counts the money and divides it among the girls, who of course keep whatever else they earned, off their feet and in their makeshift cribs. She'd do better as a madam, Martha Jane sees, and thinks maybe she'll save her money to open a house in Billings or Butte. She's not a foolish girl any more to play sex games, and not since the baby, anyway, does she have the heart to be that close to anyone.

She'd rather manage the girls, so they travel as a group for a few months, taking all the coin, gold nuggets, and dust they can finagle from ready miners. Martha organizes the acts, settles tiffs, wrestles out disorderly customers, tells her stories, minds the bar, and keeps the purse. It seems a good arrangement until the usual arguments and jealousies erupt over percentages, stolen petticoats, or slick-haired, handsome customers with bags of gold dust. Jealousies and gossip, the usual things that divide self-proclaimed sisters, suddenly burned too hot for Martha Jane to manage and melted down the merry company. Sitting up all night with raging, aggrieved parties, she thinks, *God save me from the sharp tongues, tender hearts, and copious tears of womenfolk.* When one sworn lifelong best friend scratches another's face, and the traveling bordello divides into two screaming camps, Martha Jane's glad she's not limited to the feline companionship of women.

After the eight divide up the horses and goods and straggle out—one penitent to her Methodist mother and the others to bordellos in Denver and Cheyenne—Martha Jane bucks the hip-deep snowfall, coaxing her exhausted horse south and east. Picking up her rounds through familiar saloons, she settles her nerves alongside men's deeper laughter, flirting, and joking. Together, she and they nurse their more restrained, liquor-soaked griefs and grudges with faro, poker, and the odd fist-fight. When she runs out of money, she decides these saloon fellows aren't her answer, so, at least for a while, she resolves to leave them behind.

She's sworn off love, more or less, and keeps that vow for a while, riding into Wisconsin with the "Great Rocky Mountain Show." As Calamity Jane she hones her speech until it sounds like music and rolls out as easily as whiskey flows in. She doesn't mind the parades, riding with the Indians, or playacting the stagecoach attacks. Sometimes the staged shows seem almost real, and she can see past the cheap costumes and paint into something that really happened; her heart pounds in terror at the whoops and screams, the tomahawks and arrows falling around her. She makes a few drinking friends in the troupe, but before she feels at home there, Hardwich's show goes bust, and she's on a train headed west to Montana.

She's not looking for anything or anybody, just earning however she can, preferably on her feet. Scrubbing laundry, tending bar, dealing faro for drinks and maybe a plate of food. But most of her nourishment is Old Kentucky snake bite prevention, so she figures any rattler that bites her will surely die of inebriation.

A hunger hardly ever wakes in her that whiskey can't satisfy. She forgets to eat for days at a time, and soon her dresses hang loose, with her breasts drooping flat behind the calico and satin. When she puts on her man's outfit against the cold, the buckskins nearly stand up around her, stiff with grease and too large for her shrunken frame.

She likes how light she feels inside the leather, though, as if she could step off the earth and leave it behind. When the whiskey shots burn a straight line from her lips, around her heart, and into her anxious gut, she finds a loose, hot happiness in being alive. The drink unties her from her body and lifts her spirit into a sense of angelic being. Meanwhile, she empties curses and punches into any sucker who crosses her path. Dizzy, staggering, and swinging, in whiskey's blur she sometimes wonders, how can it be that she rises, feeling divine, only to fall without fail, sore and filthy, into the gutter?

This is no ordinary salvation, no church religion: Martha Jane has abandoned these, which first abandoned her. Her only hope is to burn out her thirst and her flesh, and, in the end, to die. In the meantime, she cherishes her secret part that sings, cries, and begs to God when she's plastered; this fragment of her eternal soul is what may still weigh on God's mercy, beyond the veil. This is Martha Jane's hard spiritual journey, her slow act of dying. When she awakens with a throbbing head and pissed trousers, she curses the life that chains her down and the sickness that drives her.

William Steers rolls like a spring squall across the high plains. He's a scrap of man with hard shoulders, come from Honey Creek, Iowa. He whispers in her ear, swears his gray eyes are a perfect match for hers, and insists he's meant to have her. A brakeman, he has steady work with the railroad, so he courts her with drinks, jokes, and rolls of ten-dollar bills.

After the first drink he buys her, she walks away, trying not to favor his wit with her laughter. When he follows her out to the street, she tells him he's nothing but trouble, all the while shivering inside her trousers, because trouble's the very thing that draws her.

When he gets mad that she ignores him, and then picks a fight with a bigger fellow to blow off steam, she looks back. She would've thrown a punch, too, reacting to that same frustration. Here's a man ready to fight for what he wants; she's the thing he wants, and maybe he's what she needs. Could be she's been mistaken in the past, looking for too good a man. Just as her mother was too wicked and too strong for Martha Jane's father, maybe Martha Jane needs a firm lead. Maybe this one, with his quick hot temper, is her match, the lid for her own crooked pot.

She's bone-deep tired of fighting, proving she's the strongest person in any room. Martha Jane's weary of her latest occupation, warring with her own, so-called gentler sex in brawling, knock-down wrestling matches, taking on women as big as she is, and some even bigger. The fistic arena seemed like an easy place to make some money off bets, and she knocked Blanche Danville to the grass in one punch. Not so the policeman who arrested her, after, and locked her up, costing her in fines the nearly twenty dollars she'd made. Martha Jane, billed for that Rawlins fight as Mattie King, has more moxie than muscle, and now, at thirty-four, she already feels too old to fight or poke for a living but may still be young enough to settle in as a wife.

Bill Steers sets her to thinking. There are advantages for the fairer sex, Martha Jane knows, as long as a girl behaves, so maybe she should try being cared for, for a while. Her oversized clothes are so rank she's even noticed them, and she hankers for a clean dress and some new, soft stockings—maybe even kid leather boots as fine as those that boy stole for her years ago. And how about a ring for her finger and a comb to hold up her hair? She could slow things down, drink a little less, and maybe settle with somebody, but most men are too weak to stand up to or beside her. Her average saloon Joe can't even look Calamity Jane in the eye, let alone stand toe-to-toe with her in love's match.

She figures it's been her own fault, playing rough and stretching stories about herself the way she does. She's made herself bigger, louder, and fouler than life, all calluses and shaggy edges. Dripping snuff from the corners of her mouth, she's barely even a woman, and no man's idea of a dream. She may have plenty of friends in the lower saloons, but no lover.

Bill Steers may be worth cleaning up for. Damned persistent, he keeps playfully nudging her elbow at the bar, and he knows enough to keep her drinks coming, even when she shoves him off and tells him to piss at the moon. When he twists one arm behind her back and kisses her, pressing her hard against the saloon wall, she feels overpowered and overcharged, lightning-struck. In his grip, the black part of her that went cold dead after Little Calamity flares and throbs to life like a banked and blown-on woodstove coal. She teases him back so he'll wrestle her harder. When he pins her by her wrists against the wall and kisses her breasts, his growl vibrates through that hard bone that covers her heart. Feeling her soften, he nuzzles, bites, and then lets her go, leaving her hungry for the rest.

Martha Jane tells him maybe she will. Encouraged, Bill Steers sets her in a wagon, then winds her through the mountains on trains to take her to Cheyenne. He buys her new shoes, petticoats, and dresses, and when she's all decked out, he tells her she's a handsome gal. This claim builds up his character in her eyes; if Steers had claimed she was pretty, she'd have called him a liar and punched him, but handsome, that she can find in the full-length mirror and believe. She looks at his reflection, too, and thinks that, even considering the fine clothes, her strong, set jaw and tired, gray eyes appear to please him to an unreasonable degree. *Maybe*, she thinks, *love has warped his reason.*

They've been in Cheyenne for about a week when Steers

seats her at a linen-draped hotel table for a steak and potato dinner, promising strawberry shortcake for dessert. He watches her eat, then orders her a second helping. They drink a little, just for fun, and he teases her about all the different Calamities he's read about in dime novels.

"So you solved crimes and chased ghosts with that Deadwood Dick?"

Her full belly relaxes her into truth. "I did not."

"But what about rescuing that little gal from a runaway team of horses?"

She shrugs and chuckles, "Well, I never" and gnaws a bloody hunk of steak, wishing she hadn't lost those teeth. The beef juices trickle over her chin, so she dabs herself with the napkin from her lap, ladylike. For Bill, she'll act the part.

He raises a ruby glass and eyes her tenderly until she squirms. He asks, "So dear, who the hell are you?"

She crosses her knife and fork over her plate the way she's seen ladies do and wonders, what's the right answer? Does he want Calamity Jane? She ponders, swallows, and dabs her lips again. Her mouth is dry, so she sips her wine.

"Martha Jane Cannary," she finally whispers, and tears come into her eyes for no reason she can call to mind. "Just a girl."

He pushes back his chair, comes to fetch her from hers, and walks her upstairs. She tingles where his hand presses the small of her back, guiding her the way wind pushes a ship. As he unlocks the room with its skeleton key, she glances down the hall, embarrassed and scared. Maybe she should run before he sees what's real about her, under the fine clothing.

The room shines in silks, oiled wood, and beveled glass and smells like oranges. Martha Jane feels finer just standing in it, yet small and frightened, too. As he unbuttons the back of the scarlet gown he bought her, she shivers. She's too old to feel this childlike and innocent, as if she's never done this before.

He undresses her, kissing each part he uncovers, even her rough fingertips after he pulls off her kid gloves. She wishes she'd kept herself softer, if only for him. She prays to God, if he's listening, to keep Bill from seeing her scars and sags, and to prevent her from blowing this good thing to hell. She feels close to a canyon edge, wanting this man and this love, so much.

He eases her, and, looking into his eyes, she considers her cards. Letting him press her onto a rented goose down bed's brocade coverlet, Martha Jane decides to bet it all, and Bill Steers makes her as happy as a bride.

She marries him in her heart. To conform to her new man, she calls herself Martha Steers, Mattie Steers, Jean Steers, or whatever name he prefers on any given day. He's younger than she is, but firm of hand. He leads her horse, drives her wagon, and directs her mind. She becomes changeable, rising to his desires. She fears and respects him as she has no other man and interprets this terrible passion to be the love she's needed but never known. Trembling, she seeks his favor. When he smiles, she imagines herself safe from his talons, close under his wing.

He quits his job at the railway to spend more time with her. She's not sure how they'll live, but Steers says he has money in the bank, so they travel town to town, drinking. Staying in hotels, she watches him write in the registers *Mr. and Mrs. William Steers*. It warms her, to see him claiming what she believes.

In Meeker, Colorado, Martha thanks a bartender for her drink, and Bill flares up, jealous. Swiping his shot glass off the table to shatter against the wall, he calls her a whore. It's the first time he confirms her fear of his rage, and, as she struggles out of her chair, she trips on her skirt hem and staggers back, whispering, "Dear, it's nothing." With her soft hand on his arm and a tender word she tries to settle him back into being good, gentle Bill.

The curl she loves still droops over his forehead, but his eyes are bloodshot and mean. Martha can't understand where her husband has gone or why this man is here. Twisting her arm again, but this time with no playful kiss, he pulls a knife and presses it to her bodice.

A bystander shouts and grabs Bill from behind, getting knocked down and kicked for his trouble, but the heroic interruption gives Martha Jane a chance. She ducks into the alley, swearing at herself for having traded her gun belt for a corset. Imagining Bill in pursuit, she hikes up her skirt and petticoats, to run faster. Fine kid shoes splash behind a line of horses, through manure and puddles of piss. She hears him; Bill's boots pound and breaths rasp behind her, so as he yanks her arm, she bends and grabs a cold chunk of granite. He spins her around and punches her, busting open her lip.

Martha staggers, telling herself that didn't just happen. She can't see straight but widens her eyes to stay clear, to watch his bleary eyes. Pressing her free hand to her swelling lip, she tells herself he's had one too many. He only means to protect her from strangers, and maybe she did flirt too much. She cries out, "Bill, it's me, your Martha. Your Jean." He pries the rock from her fingers and strikes her on the head with it, his lip curling as she falls to the ground.

As he walks away, he drops the chunk of granite but keeps the knife in his left hand, and she feels a strange gratitude. It could have been worse, she tells herself as she tastes her own blood. Tomorrow's newspapers could've read, "Calamity Jane Dead in an Alley, Stuck Like a Pig." She almost laughs, then cries.

The saloon customer who took on Bill rounds the alley corner and finds her there. He tells her Bill Steers deserves to hang for beating a lady. She's not certain she agrees, but Martha Jane wobbles to the sheriff to swear out a warrant against her man or, at least against her fear of him. In court she swears he was no true husband to her, so her beloved leaps over a table to attack her. Two men standing by restrain the accused as the angry judge pronounces William Steers guilty, then to be jailed.

With Bill locked up, Martha drinks first to his imprisonment and then to her own foolish sorrow. Missing him, cursing him, wondering what she did wrong, to make him turn on her. She sits with sympathetic men who tell her, drink after drink, Calamity Jane deserves better. And why, they ask, didn't she just whoop his ass?

Bolstered by her new friends and tired from a dreadful hangover, Martha Jane bars the door when Bill comes to her hotel room the next day, released on a fine and his own good word. Soulful and repentant, he begs, but she refuses him, even as she rests her fingers on the doorknob.

He begs and cries, scratching his nails on the outside of her door. He seems to her most pitiful, a repentant, broken man, and she, he claims, is the one who broke him. Sorrowful for her power over him and heavy with love and guilt, she opens the door to his sloppy remorse and affection. After they make love, she packs a bag to travel alongside him to Rawlins. Nobody else has ever begged for Martha Jane, or sinned, or nearly died for love of her as Bill claims he might. Nobody's ever tried to kill her for love, either; this passion awes and terrifies her, but surely this is real. For a man to be so ready to fight for her, or to strike her down to keep her only for himself, this must be the rarest of love, true and eternal.

On the trail he leans from his horse to hers, thoughtlessly kissing her hard on the swollen, red wound he opened on her lip. She winces but doesn't complain. In Rawlins he's gentle, though, even courteous in helping her down from her horse. At the hotel, he opens doors for her and carries her satchel. She tells herself he'll do better, and he is, after all, only a man.

She cares for him tenderly and edges around his temper, easing him with sex and gazes.

Six weeks later, after a quarrel over a not-hot-enough dinner, he cracks her skull with a monkey wrench. She escapes through a window, wraps a handkerchief around her bloody head, and complains to the sheriff. Despite the pain Bill's caused her, Martha Jane stumbles to the saloon, weeping, wailing for her man. Three whiskeys into her fog, the officer comes for Martha Jane because they can't find Bill, but he'll take in Mrs. Steers for her own protection. Afraid to go back home, she spends that night in jail.

Bill Steers, after riding hard and long to Colorado, is captured a week later. The court gives him thirty days, and Martha Jane leaves him behind and tours saloons in Rawlins, Douglas, and Carbon. Taking her whiskey neat with chasers of more whiskey, she drowns that passion for Bill with her greater love for the spinning, the heat, and the forgetfulness; amber shot glasses sing like angels before her.

She travels by stage through rain and heat, from town to town, so drunk that, when the stage stops, she needs a guide to the first saloon and, later, into its nearest alley to pass out. Covered with flies, snoring, she slurs curses at boys who nudge her with hard-toed boots. Only in the hard light of morning does she call out to some grubby sweeper or trash collector, maybe even the same child who tormented her the previous night, "What town am I waking in, Skeeter?"

The answer changes, but the boys and the towns look the same.

She doesn't know how he could have found her, unless by the newspaper stories that track her escapades. Later she will blame the journalists, those lying sacks of shit, for giving her away, but for now Bill Steers brings whiskey and promises enough to draw her in.

Together they board an upholstered train car for a trip to visit his family in Wisconsin. It's strange country, wooded and as alien as the moon. Martha Jane's restless between the hills and fearful of what's coming, certain the state's dense trees shelter disaster. Hell, she can't even see the weather coming.

Bill's family receives her quietly. Sensing they may disapprove, she sets out to win them over with her cleaner stories and help in the kitchen. Bill doesn't drink around his brothers or his ma and pa, so in his sober gentleness, the couple get along like newlyweds again, rumpling the covers and stifling laughter in bed.

After three months, they board a westbound train for home. Martha Jane's sorry to go. She's enjoyed the close comfort of Bill's family, who seemed to warm to her. As the train rattles and jars her, she thinks, *it's strange how a place can shift people into better versions of themselves.* She and Bill didn't fight in Wisconsin, and her thirst wasn't as bad without a saloon nearby. Maybe it was the security of family that eased her. She glances at Bill dozing beside her and wonders if they can stay calm and happy back home.

Halfway to Cheyenne, she feels dizzy and faint and loses her breakfast off the back of the train car. Dear Lord, is she pregnant again? The prospect terrifies her. What if this one dies, too? She won't survive another little grave. Maybe she'll lose it early. That would be easier than getting attached, and for now, she won't tell Bill.

In Wyoming, her so-called husband doesn't adjust well to the absence of his loving, teetotaling family. He drifts into saloons and drinks, so she drinks, too, and their fights resume. Soon Martha Jane must wear swooping, wide-brimmed hats to keep her calamitous, bruised face hidden from the press. He reminds her in hard and sudden ways; Bill doesn't like Martha Jane drawing attention to herself, and he believes rumors about her and other men, no matter how absurd. He wants wild Calamity Jane in bed but insists on docile Martha or Mary or Jean on his arm—Bill picks and changes her names to suit his temper. When she must call herself something, she settles on Mary Jane Steers, expressed only in whispers so he can't overhear and take issue with her choice. Leaning into her angry husband and struggling to anticipate his needs, Martha Jane steels herself for a terrifyingly quiet life in Cheyenne as a wife and, maybe soon, as a mother.

Whiskey calls Martha Jane by many old names—Martha Jane Cannary, Calam, Maggie Cosgrove, Mattie King, Calamity Jane—in a voice too loud to ignore. Most frightening of all is the idea of being called "mother," so she won't accept the pregnancy is real. Another child to fail or lose will only prove Martha Jane to be as bad a mother as Charlotte was. After the first few weeks, the nausea settles down, so she tells herself it's not happening. Besides, isn't she too old? Maybe age is making her monthlies irregular, as women say it will.

Soon Martha Jane struggles to squeeze the truth down under her corset, but if she tells Bill, this child will give him more power than he's already staked to claim over her. Watching his eyes and his moods, she wonders if he'll be happy to be a father. Maybe her condition will make him feel more like a man. He loves to show her off in the saloons, claiming he's tamed Calamity Jane, even as he stink-eyes other men, especially reporters, daring them to come near her. Always itching for a fight. But if she gives him a son, Bill might be proud to publish that; every man wants a boy. Martha Jane ponders how to frame the announcement, how not to rub him the wrong way.

Stuck in the saloon corner beside him every night, she's lonely as an angel in hell. Bruises and twisted joints throb and burn. Since that punch in the alley, her jaw still clicks when she chews. She knows she should leave him, but with this baby coming, she can't be choosy. *If this one lives,* she tells herself, *I'll do better. Surely, I will.* She tries not to wonder whether she or the baby can survive Bill's rage.

As her man simmers beside her, Martha Jane throws back another burning shot to quell her imagination and steady her trembling hands.

Things fall apart. She can't remember the details of that night, but she has a vague sense Bill set her up with too much drink, then tore up the saloon when she flirted. After the bartender kicked them out, Bill bloodied an unsuspecting cowboy, or so Martha Jane's been told. With his fists in the privacy of their little house, Bill's kept it up for three nights, now, punishing her for losing control of herself and getting him into trouble. Weary and sore, she admits he's a mean sonofabitch, but then she swerves off the truth and blames herself for provoking him.

She wakes with vomit on her bodice, recalling she sweet-talked her man into making up after their fight, but then Bill raged at her, stormed out, and left her alone at that Eddy Street saloon. Out of her mind, according to the long-suffering sheriff, she busted up chairs and left the lawman no choice but to arrest her. Benefiting from a tenderhearted judge, who heeds her whispered confession and a doctor's testimony about her delicate condition, Martha Jane goes free after suffering his temperance lecture.

On her way home, she's terrified of finding Bill there, so she stops to buy a bottle to keep down the shakes. Using Bill's credit at the grocer, she buys victuals to cook for him, offering a savory peace any man would appreciate. God only knows what waits for her in their little house, so she swigs off the bottle and sends up a desperate prayer, in case He's listening.

Bill welcomes her home in bad humor and with the blank

memory of an infant asks where the hell she's been. She shrugs and smiles, then fries up potatoes and side pork, his favorites. The meal satisfies him. After he dozes off, Martha Jane drinks down the raw edges of her nerves, so she can sleep, too.

Martha Jane fidgets and ferments for months until finally Jessie Elizabeth is born in October, 1887, full sized and chubby cheeked. The baby girl has a voice like a bawling calf. After counting fingers and toes, Martha Jane's relieved she hasn't weakened or harmed the baby with her drinking. Hand to God, she resolves to do better.

Bill doesn't take to the newborn, and Martha Jane hears him mutter, "It should've been a boy." At night, as he sits drinking at their table, he eyes the baby with suspicion, so Martha Jane leaves Jessie Elizabeth with neighbors while he's there. When she and Bill are alone, he treats Martha Jane better, singing to her, holding her in his arms, and swearing to always love her. It's better, she tells herself, to be alone with him, to keep her and the baby safe.

One night after they make love, Martha Jane stands at her window, looking past her neighbor's parlor drapes and watching another woman rock Jessie to sleep. Bill's snores rip like a sawmill behind her, and she sighs, remembering how she used to juggle on the street, keeping walnuts, stones, pocket watches, and trinkets suspended in the air, desperate to keep them from thudding in the dirt. She did it to survive then, and it's the same now—juggling food, sex, jokes, and fake smiles, she's keeping Bill happy so she and Jessie don't fall and get hurt.

Bill goes away for a week, bullshitting her with an excuse about finding work. She suspects he has a woman in another town, but Martha Jane's relieved when the door slams behind him. Because she needs to believe it, she tells herself she still loves him enough. He's Jessie's father, after all. But then she pictures some shadowy fate befalling him, some tragedy great enough to prevent his return. Or maybe just that suspected other woman winning, giving him another lip to bust or arm to break. Another fool falling for Bill Steers could be the answer.

The neighbor tells her that Jessie's sick with a fever and should stay where she is, to rest and recover. Terrified of her sick child, Martha Jane agrees. Restless though, with too much time on her hands, she cuts loose while Bill's out of town and gets arrested again. The officer's a kind man, but she sees Bill's anger when she looks in his eyes, so she strikes him and scratches his face. Struggling to hold her, the lawman accidentally rips her dress at the shoulder, and she cries at the top of her lungs to the saloon clientele that he's dishonored her.

The next morning, the bandaged officer explains his belief that she has a sort of sickness, and the only cure is for her to stop drinking altogether. "It don't agree with some people, you know," he says, murmuring to her from a safe distance, opposite the iron bars.

Martha Jane softens a little at his voice and mutters an apology for wounding him. He talks gently to her, as if she's a child who needs consolation, but she's lolling, dizzy, and sick with need for another drink. She begs him for hair of the dog. When he refuses, she asks him to go away, so he does. *Lord save me from do-gooders,* she thinks, pressing her hand to her pounding forehead. Still, she wonders. Wouldn't it be something, if she's not bad, but only sick?

The next day, once Martha Jane's wide-eyed and steady on her feet, the officer gives her a plate of steak and eggs his wife cooked—medium rare and sunny side up—to the prisoner's preference. Humbled, Martha Jane devours the meal and offers thanks. When the officer reminds her to stay off the snakebite medicine, she ducks her head and shrugs, saying she'll try. Then, feeling the best she has in a long time, she tracks down her baby girl, who's recovered and having a lovely stay at the preacher's house. *If all it took to get well were a reason,* she thinks, *a perfect child like Jessie Elizabeth should be enough to inspire her.*

When Bill returns, Martha Jane covertly sniffs him for another woman's perfume but detects no scent of betrayal. He's cleaned up and looks better than she remembered, so she welcomes him back. After a roll on their old feather bed and mutual apologies for what went wrong that they can't quite remember, they decide to pick up baby Jessie from the preacher's wife. Restless and meaning well, they travel to Pocatello, figuring the best way to settle each other down is to make their union legal. Get married as an actual fact. In a big Victorian house they find a justice of the peace, a Mr. Fisher, who hitches them on May 30, 1888. It feels like a good thing, a new beginning. They'll have to get it right now, for Jessie's sake, Bill explains. Martha Jane can't be running around now that she's his.

As they ride away from the justice's house, Martha Jane holds Bill's arm and wishes she could steady her feelings. Bright and airy with excitement, she's certain she's made a terrible mistake but scolds herself for only remembering to shut the barn door after the horse got out. God help her, she's the one locked in now.

With all the force and false cheer of sober good intentions, Bill and Martha Jane settle back in at home with their baby. For a week or so, it's like playing house. Bill's sweet, the baby sleeps at night, and the cooking's hot and tasty. Domestic bliss rules the days, and Bill's lovemaking is tender at night. Martha opens to him, feels herself both loved and loving.

But missing the whiskey sets Martha on edge, so she's churlish and pesters Bill about hiring back on with the railroad. She warns him to pay off their account at the grocer, or they'll starve; in truth, she simply wants him out of the house. Nervous under his watchful eye and exhausted from his demands, she can't maintain much longer without a drink. Her hands shake unless she grips one inside the other, and she feels her emotional seams are splitting like an outgrown dress. When she breaks out in a cold sweat, she knows the sickness is close, so she sets her mind to slip out. First, she has to get Bill out of the house.

Martha Jane hears her voice get too loud for the little house, warning him—unless he wants her in the cribs, he'd best support her and his child. Blowing up at her angry husband and needling his sore spot about her vivid past, she cringes as the words pass her lips.

Bill shouts back at her, asks what kind of wife would turn so easily to whoring, and says if she didn't drink so much, there'd be food a-plenty in the cupboard.

It rankles Martha Jane. She hasn't had a drink in nearly a week, but she knows she did drink up a lot of his pay before Jessie was born and fears her husband is right.

Her hands are damp and slippery, and she's clumsy with the shakes as she prepares their meal. When she drops and shatters one of their only two china plates, Bill jumps up to shout at her and rolls the baby off the settee, where she's been sleeping beside him.

Stumbling over to scoop her screaming Jessie off the floor, Martha Jane scolds him. "You clumsy oaf, you'll kill her."

Bill erupts. "I can't take another minute of you nagging me." He slaps at Martha Jane but grazes the baby, bringing up a lump and red mark on her head.

The baby gasps, shudders, and screams. Martha Jane breaks down and shouts, "You son of a bitch!" It was one thing when he hit her, because she surely had it coming. *But now, the baby,* she thinks. Trembling and blaming herself, she rages even louder.

Bill follows her room to room, yelling his defense. Says he

never meant to, and what kind of animal does she think he is, to hit a baby? When she won't stand still to listen, he grabs her arm.

Martha hesitates at something she sees in his eyes. Maybe it's fear or regret, but she's been too angry, for too long, to believe him now. Shoving him off, she locks herself and the baby in the bedroom, while he beats on the loosely hinged door. The louder he yells, the more she fears he'll break through, so she rummages through the valise under the bed for her guns. She hasn't worn them for so long, she's forgotten where she put them, if she brought them to this house at all. Maybe she sold them for ready cash, to drink away. She can't recall. Damn.

Bill hammers until the door cracks, yelling, "Mary Jane Steers, you come out!"

"You break through that door, I'll shoot you dead." Empty-handed, all she can do is bluff.

She finds one of her six-shooters wrapped in an old satin nightgown in a bottom drawer, unloaded. As Bill throws himself against the door, Martha Jane dumps out the drawer, shuffling through her unmentionables for bullets, but finds none. She shakes and cries, her nerves torn ragged from Jessie screaming on the bed. Crouched on the floor, Martha Jane chokes out sobs, ashamed she let any man hurt her child; even bitter, drunk Charlotte protected her own better than that.

"I ain't her," she yells, meaning Charlotte or Mary Jane or whatever the hell Bill Steers would call her. "I am Calamity Jane and by God, I will lay you in your grave!"

She scoots over and leans back against the bed, making her stand between the baby and the door with the cold pistol in her sweaty hands; empty, the Colt might slow Bill down, should he break through and find it aimed between his eyes. Hearing him swear, then weep and beg as he slides down the door, Martha

Jane keeps the pistol pointed where she figures his head would be.

The door creaks as he rests his weight against it. After snuffling and muttering self-pity for half an hour or so, he quiets. The room where Martha Jane's huddled goes dark with the sunset, and only a little lamplight seeps in under the door, on either side of Bill's shadow. She thinks maybe he's fallen asleep, but he works himself up again, finds his second wind, and swears with renewed gusto.

She's weakening, hugging herself with one arm while propping the pistol on her knee with her right hand. She looks down at the ring on her left finger, the one Bill slid on with a vow. She'd tug it off to throw it at the door, but her knuckle's too swollen. It means nothing on her finger, and it'd mean less thrown away. When the baby sobs, then hiccups herself to sleep behind her, all Martha Jane can do is murmur "Shhhh, shhhh" and start to sing in a whisper "Bye, Baby Bunting." But at that first line about "daddy's gone a-hunting," Martha Jane swears to her Jessie that if Daddy comes hunting through this particular door, she'll bash his head with the pistol grip before he harms baby bunting again.

But thanks to the God who hardly ever hears her prayers, Bill gives up. Scraping his boots across the floor, he slams the front door.

Martha Jane counts to ten. Afraid of a trick, she creaks open the bedroom door with a shoulder and a boot wedged against it, ready to slam. Once she's certain Bill's truly gone, she jams a chair back against the front door knob to keep him out.

Packing a carpet bag with what she'll need for the baby, she also wraps a loaf of bread in a rag and stuffs it in next to a nearly empty whiskey bottle. There's not enough whiskey left to do any harm, she tells herself, and not enough to make the future clear, but maybe a swallow or two, for courage.

She won't know if Bill returns, because by sunrise she's traveling, her baby rocked to sleep in the rhythmic racket coming from below a railroad car.

Martha Jane rubs her tight neck and tries to relax on the hard seat, telling herself if she's good and keeps her head down, Bill won't so easily find her again. She knows she'll be looking over her shoulder for some time, though, and wishes she had family to hide behind. Recent rumor holds that Lena's dead from a farm accident, and it brings tears to Martha Jane's eyes to think of her baby sister in her grave. Not to mention, those children are left motherless; sweet little Tobe and the others are left with only that sonofabitch John to raise them. Martha Jane longs to visit, but she won't face Borner's scowl and judgment over a runaway wife. Such is the way of the world, with not enough mothers to go around, and those that survive ain't worth much, herself included. Martha Jane leans her forehead on the vibrating window glass and vows to do better, to be more like Lena. Sweeter, more patient, and sober. Or maybe, if she tries hard, she'll make two out of those three.

Martha Jane thinks how pretty Lena was, taking after Charlotte with her delicate chin and turned-up nose. Martha Jane searches for traces of that inherited beauty in her baby girl and finds in the sleeping face a memory, a surprising resemblance in the tulip curve of the baby's upper lip. *That's Ma and Lena, there. Little Calamity had the same,* she thinks, but then pushes that thought away.

Martha Jane closes her eyes and strains to picture her brothers and sisters, those helpless babies in her charge so long ago. Their faces waver behind Martha Jane's tears as if they are underwater, drowning, and she still can't save them. Shivering, she tucks the blanket around Jessie against the window's chill. Thinking how tattered, hungry, and sad they all were, Martha hugs her baby tighter to her chest.

God help me, she thinks, biting her lip and fighting down the urge to drain the bottle in her bag. Hoping some chance or divine generosity will offer strength to start over, to leave behind another mistake, Martha hums to her baby girl as the hills outside her rattling window flatten into plains.

★ ★ ★ ★ ★

PART FOUR
HER STORY

★ ★ ★ ★ ★

CHAPTER TWENTY-FIVE
DEADWOOD AGAIN

1895

After sixteen years without Calamity Jane, Deadwood's a sight for Martha Jane's sore eyes, yet unmistakably changed; its rough edges are sanded down and varnished and the people, far better dressed. Martha Jane rides in on the stage with Jessie, who's grown into a wiry eight year old with gold curls trailing down her back. Her daughter's begged to attend school, so Martha Jane's vowed to settle in her good old town, hoping she and her child might find a welcome, some sentimental donations, and cheap, warm shelter against the winter winds.

"People here know who I am," she tells the girl.

Jessie eyes her too wisely and quips back, "Everybody gets to know you pretty fast anywhere, Ma. You do raise a ruckus."

Martha Jane sees the girl's eyes twinkle and answers her teasing. "I do make friends easily. It may be my finest quality."

Jessie steps down off the stage after her and grips Martha Jane's callused hand. She blinks against the dust, rubs her eye, and leans on her mother.

Her nervous child's weight against her calms the woman, who's not as confident as she's putting on. She whooped up a lot of hell in this town, most of which she can't remember. The newspapers and gossip talked her up plenty, even putting it in print, back then. Will they remember the good she did and be glad to have her back?

Martha points up to the hill where Wild Bill is buried.

"There's my friend, Bill, the fellow I told you about. My dog, Henry, is buried there beside him."

"We should get a dog," Jessie says, looking thoughtful.

"We should," Martha Jane agrees, taking their valise from the stage driver and handing him a coin. Maybe for her generosity, he'll spread kind words about her.

After a few easy nights in the hotel with running water and a soft bed, Martha Jane recounts her coins and rents a rickety little house. *It's not bad,* she thinks. It has a plank floor and a kitchen cabinet to hold a basin. There's a black stove with no apparent cracks and no rats Martha Jane can smell.

"Sorry for this," she apologizes. Jessie seems cut out of fine cloth, and Martha Jane wishes she could provide a better home for her. She hopes to raise her daughter's sights by giving the girl a chance to learn manners and reading. With education, Jessie might find a place in better society. For the time being, Martha Jane's slim funds are better spent on new dresses and shoes for the girl, so the other kids don't make fun of Jessie. A nicer house can wait.

After shopping, they return to the little shed with its gapped planks. Seeing the girl shiver in the cold winds that wail through, Martha Jane says she'll stop those holes tomorrow, with rags and mud.

Jessie nods and lies down in the gunnysack-padded bed Martha hammered together from crates. Martha Jane sits beside her, feels her for a fever, and asks, "You ain't getting sick, now, are you?"

Jessie shakes her head, but Martha Jane can't move away. She stays beside the girl, stroking her hair and making sure she's asleep.

This time she has to pay attention for the little signs of disaster.

There's only the one bed and no chairs, so Martha Jane settles on the splintered front stoop. She's torn with nostalgia, watching the sun sink behind the pine-whiskered Black Hills. As it falls into shadows, the town's quieter than she remembers, and the people who pass look near as swanky and healthy as city folk. You notice when they smile, they have more teeth, too. Martha Jane's heard there's a sort of hospital in town now, an improvement from the days when she nursed miners during the smallpox. There are gaslights now, flickering like rows of fireflies along some of the main streets below Martha's shack. As purple-water dusk fills in Deadwood's gulch, Martha thinks back, and then ahead.

Her West is getting civilized, and it troubles her. How will she fit in? Change is the strongest opponent she wrestles, and it generally pins her.

"I am what I am," she whispers, poking the air with her cigar, for emphasis, then taking a puff. "But I can do better." It's already October, so Jessie will be late starting school at the convent, but the girl will be fine. For her daughter's benefit, Martha Jane's determined to reconcile with Deadwood, her oldest lover.

Blowing smoke rings, Martha Jane feels a tug from the music that drifts up from the saloons below. Her heart beats faster, but she tells herself to keep her head down. "Drink in private here at home," she mutters to herself, "but don't be cutting didoes with the boys." No matter that folks would expect no less of Calamity Jane. "This ain't about me now." Putting Jessie Elizabeth first, Martha Jane won't make herself a laughingstock or a byword. The old days are gone, and Deadwood could be Jessie's town now.

A few balding old-timers gather around her in the sheriff's office, to welcome Calamity Jane and chew over the old days.

"Didn't figure I'd be back here at the jail so all-fired soon," she joshes, leaning over for a fellow to light her cigar. She draws, puffs, and creaks back in her chair, watching the blue smoke curl up. "You there, Whitey. You done got old, when here I am yet, young as springtime," she quips, as the man in question cups his ear to hear her, bobs his head, and grins back yellow teeth.

She explains to the eager circle how her husband, the man who is Jessie's father, may soon follow his beloved gals to Deadwood, and they all will settle here. "Clinton Burke and me, we had us a ranch," she adds, "but it wasn't my kind of life."

The old-timers chew and nod as if they believe her, and Martha Jane sighs. *Sure, Clinton ain't truly Jessie's father,* she thinks, *but he's a sweet enough fellow. The girl will be better off saying it's him.* Since Clinton first told Martha Jane he liked her johnny-cake at that Montana logging camp, he's stuck tight. Clinton's the sort you might marry if you weren't already hitched, so Martha Jane can't figure why she fled him for Deadwood. Maybe she's testing the clean-cut, hardworking man, to see if he'll look for her. Maybe she wearied of his little calf-eyes mooning, brimming with love—Clinton's constant attentions can tug like a bridle. Or maybe she got thirsty, and that preacher's son scowls a thundercloud whenever she calls for a fourth whiskey shot.

Martha Jane pulls herself back to her audience. She holds court, delighting in their tilted heads and skeptical eyes. The first time they call her "Calamity," she corrects them, but then that old name falls down over her like a favorite shirt. *It's all right if they call her that,* she thinks. In time, they'll see she's still that fun old gal, but better behaved when it matters. Forgetting the new impression she's hoped to make, she tells her well-rehearsed story with all of its rowdy adventures. She jumps up out of her chair to wave and stomp through the exciting parts as a reporter from the *Black Hills Daily Times* jots in a little book, licking his pencil and scrawling too slowly to keep up with her tale.

With sweat beading on her forehead, she settles back into her chair at story's end. "But them was the old times. What I desire most of all," she says, "is a good education for my daughter, so she won't need to rely on any man to survive." Martha Jane's smile slackens as she remembers the men who've failed her, and she glares at the glowing tip of her cigar and mutters, "That's the most important thing." She confesses she's in demand for Wild West shows and exhibitions across the country, hell, even in Europe, but the traveling life ain't right for her little girl.

The men question the story she just finished, and she embellishes to hear them mutter, "My land," and, "That does beat all." With a sidelong glance at the scrawling reporter, she pointedly suggests that somebody, maybe a faster writer, could take down that whole story she just told and print it for posterity.

Not her true life of course, but the version she's been working on for years. She wonders if she could sell her tale on paper. The newspapers sure do. A gal could go hoarse telling and retelling her life the way Martha Jane does, up to a dozen times a day. And then, after all is said and done, some cheap bastards don't even give up a coin for her trouble. For a little book, Martha Jane could set down the perils and pride of Calamity Jane word for word and sell it, getting her money up front. That's just good business. Martha Jane smiles, squints, and flicks her glowing stub of cigar at the reporter's boot, making him jump. Yessir, it's a damned good idea.

Rewarding their own Calamity Jane for her newfound maturity and moderation, the up-and-coming city of Deadwood opens its arms to her. It's a comfort to Martha Jane, to be in a familiar place, but it itches at her, too, to pick up where she left off her old, hard-partying ways. She paces and talks to herself, insisting this restraint is only temporary. She'll spend these nights here on the hill, guarding the shack door as her girl sleeps, protecting her until it's time to place Jessie with the nuns at the convent school.

After dropping off her daughter at the boarding school, Martha Jane celebrates the end of her virtue. In the midst of saloon laughter and music, she falls back into friendships, whiskey, pranks, dances, and gambling in hazy back rooms.

Blessing Calamity Jane's good intentions, Deadwood's Green Front saloon patrons pass a hat for contributions and promise a percentage of one night's take, for little Jessie Elizabeth to stay in school. After all, isn't the child's mother a local legend? And didn't she nurse those sick miners, back in '78? Deadwood owes Calamity Jane a debt of gratitude. Besides, it's just damned good to have her back, with her lively memories of things they'd almost forgotten.

Overcome with gratitude, Martha Jane tearfully accepts the money and endearments. She stands two rounds of shots for the donors before they can curb her generosity and remind her the night's donations are for the girl. As she falls into a stupor, one kind soul relieves her of the purse so all won't be lost by morning.

As Martha Jane sees it, the churches in Deadwood have taken their toll on history; Calamity Jane's old-style hell-raising isn't as welcome now as it was with Wild Bill at her side. Since his death, and in Martha Jane's absence, her rowdy Deadwood has veered into the unthinkable, cherishing civilized oddities like steeples and hymns, and law and order. The returned heroine awakens frequently in custody behind bars, usually without any cash to post bail. Deadwood doesn't seem as glad to see her now, and she wonders if this old lover, too, has betrayed her.

When Martha Jane visits Jessie on weekends at the convent, the girl glares at her mother or weeps because the other children, informed by their parents, tease her about her drunken mother. And each time Martha Jane leaves the angry girl behind, guilt spins the mother back to the saloon, where she drinks her failures and hard feelings down. Bored with her stories and looking for new entertainment, the other patrons wind her up, place bets on how long she'll last, and then stand her shot after shot. When she finally hits the floor and snores under a table, the bartender checks his pocket watch. Cheers and groans erupt, coins and bills change hands, and Martha Jane floats in oblivion.

When Clinton catches up to the woman and child a few weeks later, he finds Martha Jane's already outstayed her Deadwood welcome. The papers publish her as a no-account, a joke, and a blight on their cleaned-up town.

As Clinton tries to dry out the woman he loves and looks for work, Martha Jane sneaks out of their shed. As she walks the streets, she clutches her whiskey bottle to her heart. *How soon they've forgotten,* she thinks. This can't be the same town Wild Bill knew and loved. Raising her fist, she belts out the most elegant curses and filthiest ditties she knows at passersby, then spits on the jailhouse's front door.

"The hell if I'll stay where I'm not wanted," Martha Jane cries. When she trips on a step she'd swear never used to be there, Clinton fails to catch her, and she bruises her head on a building's brick corner. Bricks. Another dangerous, new development. "Town's gone to the dogs. It ain't even safe to fall down here," she mutters in her lover's ear as he leads her uphill, toward home.

Martha Jane's invested their little nest egg in pacifying the judge with fines and bail, so Clinton suggests they leave Jessie in school until summer. There's no work for him here, and they'd best move on, he argues, to somewhere Martha Jane's not so well remembered.

"You're easy pickin's for that sheriff," he says, shaking his head. "With what you paid, they oughta name a street after you. What they write up in the paper only makes it worse."

"But that, Clinton dear, is my bread and butter. That they know me."

Finally she admits he's right, and she also counts the thing he doesn't know—that Calamity Jane's reputation is ruining Jessie's life. Seems Deadwood isn't her town, after all.

Martha Jane shares with Clinton her plan to find a writer and printer for her stories. He agrees they might make a Wild West show of their very own. Soon Calamity Jane will be even more famous, telling her story everywhere but Deadwood. The little gulch town may be full of itself, so high and mighty now, but when folks see her fame, they'll wish they had appreciated her. It'll be too late, though. They've taken to calling her a no-account and a drunk, and it makes her smile to think how they'll eat their words.

Maybe Montana will be a friendlier Wild West stage for Calamity Jane's one-woman show.

CHAPTER TWENTY-SIX
GO-DEVIL

1896, Montana

Bill Hickok was a hell of a man, and she adds it to her story that Calamity Jane and Wild Bill were in love. Clinton doesn't mind. It's playacting, like most everything she recounts. Besides, who wouldn't want to be with, and then brag about, a man like that—quick with a gun and good-looking as the devil himself? On a good day, he'd put up with Martha Jane, wouldn't say she smelled bad, or might even let her sit in on a hand of poker. He was more than glad to take her money, anyway.

Martha Jane chuckles, remembering, and thinks, *if that ain't love, it's near it.*

Of all the men she's known, Wild Bill made the deepest impression, not only with how love could be unrequited, sharp as a blade in your gut, but even more with how he proved the goingness of things. The way you can never hold on to anybody, because of a gunshot in the back or some other fate you never saw, and never will see, coming; this dark knowledge sets Martha Jane on edge and keeps her from holding Clinton Burke nearer to her heart. What if she were to truly love him, and he were to die or leave like all the others? Martha Jane knows there is no "if." A woman seasoned and grown, she knows the sudden inevitability of tragic endings. Hard and fast they come, like a swung sledgehammer, and always from behind. Martha Jane expects an expression of surprise on every face in heaven, and a knowing smirk on every one in hell.

So Martha Jane can't help wondering how her death will be, and what story people will weave around it. Will she become a legend for the manner of her passing? She considers the story value of a stab in the back, a rifle shot, or a heroic self-sacrifice. Living, Martha Jane has learned, is the dreadful aspect of being, given its private burdens of shame and bitter memories. So, were she to write her own ending, she'd compose a death that's both elevating and memorable. Done well, her death might leave bystanders breathless, sorrowful, and even envious. But most days, it seems boredom or guilt will catch her in their crossfire, glory be damned, and only drinking eases her despair, that down-sucking sense of drowning in all her wrong choices.

Martha Jane wonders, though, how much choice is there when your blood is bad, when you're damned from your whiskey-soaked cradle? God knows, crazy is a squirrel that runs every branch of the Cannary family tree, and not one Cannary child truly survived Robert or Charlotte. Some just rotted younger. Even sweet Lige with his heart of gold fell into crime; he's locked in a Wyoming prison for some cockeyed scheme of driving horses onto a railroad track to get them killed by an oncoming train, so as to collect damages from the railroad. *That boy ain't right*, Martha Jane tells herself. *Not one of them is, including myself.*

And now Martha Jane's failing as a mother, too. The rip in her heart is as fresh as if it happened yesterday, so, whenever the whiskey fog lifts, she racks her brain to figure what she did wrong, to let Little Calamity die. She can't divine it, unless it was a punishment for her sins. She was even sober in those days and still failed the test. And, while Jessie Elizabeth at first seemed to be a second chance, now the girl's a second torment to Martha Jane, a smoldering disaster like a coal seam fire underground that lacks only oxygen for ignition. The anxious mother keeps her distance, as if her absence will prevent the explosion, but her certainty and terror keep Martha Jane sleep-less and rarely sober.

Martha Jane wishes that, instead of Bill Steers, Clinton Burke were Jessie Elizabeth's father, so she fashions the story that way. Even though Jessie met Clinton less than a year ago, the girl is glad to call him Papa and play along. She's too young to remember those violent days with Bill, and Martha Jane would rather not enshrine them; if only there were no marriage license recorded back in Pocatello, Martha Jane's fiction would stand clean. She trusts nobody will care enough to check that register. Here in the West the law is like a net full of holes, easy to slip through. It also seems true that most plains and mountain people consider it rude to ask personal questions, so the truth easily bends with telling.

Besides, her girl should have this good sort of father, so Martha Jane insists on this story version, for Jessie's sake. Clinton Burke doesn't drink much, usually tells the truth, and never gambles. He and Martha Jane don't fight, and the restaurant they run together would make money, if only Martha Jane stuck to dealing faro and didn't drink up their profits. But what's the point of owning a bar, she figures, if you can't drink for free?

Martha Jane watches the father and daughter, glad for how close they are, but almost feels shut out. It's a sadness and a relief to watch them as she drinks. Still, she can't find fault with him, and maybe he'll save Jessie from Martha Jane, in the end. He has a genuine way with the child. Clinton tickles Jessie's cheek with his beard but pulls away at the right time. He holds her, gentle and chaste, away from himself, lifting her with both hands up into her saddle. He takes his time, shortens the straps, and presses her feet into the stirrups to make sure her little boots won't flop free. He never looks that girl up and down any way he shouldn't, the way some men can't help doing. Clinton fries her bacon crisp the way she likes it, not half-raw or burned, the way Martha Jane does because she's either too hungover to pay attention, or in a rush. He gives Jessie nickels for hair ribbons and ice cream and holds her back from running in front of wagons in the street, if she gets overexcited and forgets to look.

Martha Jane likes Clinton, maybe even loves him. After so many, she's not sure how to tell what is love, and what isn't. He's a fine-looking man, with flecks of Colorado in his blue eyes. He has a sterling character and is married to the truth, for better or for worse. Always patient with her, he muscles his thick shoulder under her arm to ferry her home when she's drunk, then peels off her dress or her buckskins to tuck her, reeling and pitching, into their feather bed. He doesn't even take advantage of her then, she can tell, because she's never sore down there in the mornings after he brings her home. He's a rare man, all right, to pass up a free poke after all his trouble.

When she's sober, they often make love with a tenderness that brings tears to their eyes, or sometimes, with an abandon that leaves them breathless. Their bed business is so fine, and he makes her feel so clear and light that while he's inside her, Martha Jane imagines she'll never need to drink again. That Clinton will be her new whiskey and her everlasting peace.

Yet she fears he's too good to be real, with some invisible crack ready to split wide. He doesn't drink too much or beat her like the other men did. His virtue almost blanches and steadies her heart, but then in the next second, it makes her a nervous wreck. Sometimes she wants to egg him on, so he'll hurt her as much as she hurts herself. If she could make it an even game all around and prove he's no better than the others, then she could refuse him and retreat into her bottle, where it's safe.

He wants to marry, and she refuses. When he insists, Martha Jane negotiates a compromise; instead of making it legal, she tells their union into story by calling herself "Martha Burke."

She eases into him, but Clinton's goodness is a caution, like a needle pressing her skin. She looks warily at him as she does at all good people now. Since she met him in Boulder and he sized her up with a lopsided smile, every time since that he's cast his eyes upon her, she trembles with love and with fear. Will this be the time he judges her unworthy? How long will he hold on, before she drives him away?

Martha Jane hates how, time and again, she places her soul like a fledgling into a stranger's calloused hands. She's not even certain she picks them, but these men seem to find her. They appear suddenly—on horseback, behind store counters, at faro tables, or busting through the doors of roadhouses—her sudden lovers, her appointed judges. Weakened by her cold, lonesome need, all she can do is cast herself on their mysterious wisdom and their tender mercies, hoping one might find her worthy of love and keeping.

Clinton Burke now holds her fate, or at least he holds Jessie's, and it's the same because Martha Jane feels the strands between mother and child unraveling. Jessie Elizabeth is separating from her mother again as surely, if not as cleanly, as when Martha Jane sliced the umbilical cord. This separation requires no knife; Martha Jane's long, drunken binges and sleeps abandon Jessie to Clinton's steady care.

Watching her child and her story-husband from a whiskey distance, Martha feels herself melting like ice. She considers another beneficial but painful cut she could make, if only she could love her child enough to let her go.

After three nights of blackouts, Martha Jane wakes to find Clinton frying up breakfast for Jessie. She stumbles outside, her head throbbing and eyes barely slits. The mother's stain of shame won't rinse off in the stock tank, but she scrubs her skin raw as a sort of penance, slips a clean dress over her damp back and shoulders, and sits to table. Leaning back in her chair, she presses a hand to her mouth and tries to avoid smelling the plate of food Clinton sets in front of her.

Jessie twirls a curl around her finger and chatters about a plover nest she found in the creekside grass. Martha Jane stretches a smile and nods, feeling her failures and the tension strapped across Clinton's shoulders as he stoops over the stove. Martha Jane would like to say something bright and loving to her daughter, but she might undo what's left of her motherhood with one wrong word. And Clinton is listening, thinking, waiting for something. Dear God. The thirst is already drying her mouth and picking at her mind like a scab. Martha Jane presses a hand on her neck against the agony and tries not to weep.

Clinton keeps his back to both of them, but his whole body opens the way dry ground holds its breath for rain. Even that dark curl behind his ear seems tuned to her, expecting a confession, a sign, or a change of heart. The poor fellow still believes, but Martha Jane knows the cavity inside her heart; she holds nothing but disappointment for this man and this child.

Martha Jane sighs. She should never have taken up with a minister's son.

The coffee steaming in Martha Jane's cup is as strong and black as the story she's brewed for Jessie, her confabulated gift to her beloved girl that might still help her forget. Martha Jane can't stop drinking or change people's low opinion of her, but she may still prevent her daughter's shame. Better yet, she can prevent Jessie's inevitable fear of becoming like her drunken sot of a mother. Martha Jane knows that fear and suspects it holds a curious inevitability—didn't she herself become a spitting image of Charlotte, the mother she despised?

Taking a deep breath, Martha Jane leans in to clear up the misunderstanding with the lines she's rehearsed. Jessie argues at first, saying it doesn't make sense, then tilts her head to consider. She nods, glances sidelong at Martha Jane and asks, "Is this the truth? Are you sure?"

Martha Jane glances up at Clinton, who's turned to face them both. With the cast-iron skillet in one hand and a spatula in the other, he peers at Martha Jane and gives her a barely perceptible nod. She sees it now. This is the very thing he'd hoped for; Martha Jane's heart sinks, then strengthens, under his low opinion. She's rising to do the best thing for her child, but she sees she's already lost her lover, too. There is no faith on earth, and she doubts she can stand alone.

Martha Jane ignores her own wanting. "Yes, dear. I'm sure." Like a rock careening down a mountain, Martha Jane can't back up or even slow down. Pushing words past the knot in her throat, she explains she kept this special secret until the girl was old enough to hear of her true mother. Belle, Martha Jane's sister, was a good but frail widow who died in childbirth. "You are the very image of her, beautiful in body and soul," Martha Jane explains, picturing Lena, stroking Jessie's hair, and blinking back tears. She tells herself that like every other one of her false stories, this one will get easier with retelling.

"So," the girl asks, tracing a letter "B" with her finger on her greasy plate, "who does that make you to me?"

"Your . . . aunt. Or better, let's say your granny. From now on, you cherish the memory of your mama and call me 'Grandma Calamity' instead of 'Ma.' "

Jessie purses her lips and nods again, so readily. "All right. That'll be fine."

The child sits up straighter and pushes fallen hair out of her eyes, then sighs, seeming relieved. In that instant Martha Jane realizes she'd been hoping for resistance, a cry of "please, no, you are my only ma." As a great space opens up around Martha Jane, she draws a painful breath, pats the girl's hand, and lets go. "All right, then."

Sighing, Clinton sets the pan back on the stove, then scrapes and wipes it clean with a rag. When he turns back to squeeze Martha Jane's shoulder in approval of her sacrifice, she runs ice cold with rage and shrugs off the hand she had loved only moments before. How could he let her cut out her own heart, and then approve? A true husband would have taken her side and found a way for Martha Jane to keep her child, to be better. Feeling how he despises her, how he agrees to this abandonment, Martha Jane feels sick. She finally admits his condescension was always there, masked by his forbearance and steady good deeds: the oh-so-patient sighs, the mild-mannered corrections, the unspoken "how could yous?" in his eyes. How had she borne holy Clinton Burke this long?

Loathing is a coarse shirt; you can abide it if you sew it yourself, Martha Jane realizes, but if somebody tailors it for you, the garment stings like nettles and scrapes you raw.

"Your mother was a beautiful woman," Clinton mutters to Jessie, who smiles up at her gentle, beloved father. "I knew her, too."

Jessie doesn't even ask Clinton if he ever was, or still is, her pa. Of course he is. Fathers are above question.

Martha Jane feels like her brain is bleeding as it screams for whiskey. *Soon*, she thinks, *soon she will drown herself beyond feeling any pain or loss or hate*. But now she studies the knife Clinton left on the table after slicing the bacon. She imagines how hard she'd have to push to drive it into his sacred heart.

After enforcing Martha Jane's lie with his own, Clinton shuffles over to kiss Martha Jane's cheek. *Judas*, she thinks. *Go hang yourself, and damn you to hell*. Pretending she doesn't notice his hand on her arm or his leaning in, she stands to take Jessie's empty plate to the basin. Even as his eyes follow her like ravens claiming something dead, Martha Jane ignores him until he leaves her house.

Taking Jessie out to ride, Grandma Calamity Jane shows the girl how to shoot from the saddle.

"Squeeze a little with your legs to hold yourself on. Blueberry's a good horse, and she'll stand still enough, until the gunshot. Then if she sidesteps or rears, you reach down with one hand and grab the reins you wrapped around the pommel."

The shotgun's not as big as the old Henry, but it's still heavy for the child, so Martha Jane leans closer, to support the barrel with her gloved hand. "That's it," she coaxes as Jessie squints one eye and sights. "You're another Annie Oakley, I'll wager," she says, feeling proud but wishing she had more to teach this girl, who's smart as a whip. Jessie ought to be back in private school, not passing through one-room schoolhouses wherever Martha Jane's signed on for a dime show. But those kids back at the Deadwood convent wouldn't believe the story about Jessie's real mother but would singsong "Calamity Jane, Calamity Jane" until the girl refused to go back. She needs a new school where nobody knows the old story, but Martha Jane hasn't found the right one for Jessie yet.

The gun barrel scorches Martha Jane's supporting fingers through her glove. Jessie winces at the sharp report, then slides a smile. "Is that right, Ma . . . uh, Grandma?"

"Grandma's real proud, and so is your ma, who's looking down from that cloud." The lie is getting easier, but her old motherly heart still clutches in her chest when the girl slips. Martha Jane blinks her stinging eyes and points at a stacked cloud fat as a cherub's belly. "From heaven."

Jessie studies the woman's face. She says, "What . . ." then changes her mind and hands over the shotgun as blue smoke still twists up out of the barrel. "That's enough. I'm tired."

"But you had fun?"

"Sure," Jessie says, gathering the reins and clicking to the horse as she heels it with her rawhide boots, the ones Clinton bought her. "I'm just tired."

Martha Jane's horse falls in beside Jessie's. "I love you, girl," Martha Jane mutters.

"I love you, too," Jessie agrees, drawing her thin brows together in thought. "Can I ask you something?"

"Sure."

"How did you say my real mama died?"

Martha Jane sighs at the question that's finally come. "I feared you'd ask something hard, like arithmetic. Like I told you, she fell off a horse and broke her neck."

Jessie shakes her head. "You said she died when I was born."

"Are you testing me?" Martha Jane snaps, then forces a laugh and a congenial tone. "You're a pistol, ain't you? No, I never said that. You were three months old when that mare threw your mother." Martha Jane tries to sound certain, but cold sweat chills her neck. She doesn't dare look the girl in the eye. Maybe Martha Jane did tell that other story; her memory has holes in it like cheese, and she can't keep a story straight. The drink befuddles her mind, she knows, so she tells herself she'd best cut back by half, for Jessie's sake.

Jessie's sudden fever rages. She sweats through her blankets, sees spiders on her skin, and screams for her pa, Clinton.

Martha's lied for weeks that Clinton is traveling to buy liquor for the new restaurant they plan to open. But the man's long gone, except for his salty, honeyed sweat, the sharp, grassy liniment he rubbed on his knee, and the clove oil he dripped on his toothache—these hover over Martha Jane's bed and dreams like spirits in a graveyard.

Jessie cries in delirium for him to come, and Martha wishes

252

he would hear and answer. She's tried two kinds of tonic, and the girl's only gotten worse. Clinton's the smart one. He'd know what to do.

On her fourth day of fever, Jessie's eyes are sunken like gray holes in snow. Dragged by sickness beyond her usual good humor, she accuses Martha Jane of lying.

Martha Jane covers her face with her hands. "I'm sorry, girl."

"Was I bad?"

"There's no bad in you. Men get over me easy."

"I love Papa."

"He loves you yet. He only couldn't abide me another day." Martha Jane's voice cracks. "Your ma . . . your grandma is a sure-fire cure for love."

Jessie gazes at her with wide, blue eyes, so illogically shaped and colored like Clinton's instead of Bill's. Can a child come to resemble the father she was promised, the one she craves, instead of the one who sired her, even with no blood inheritance? Is love for a father, or for any man, so powerful it can change not only the soul, but also the body? It's not only the girl's eyes that echo Clinton Burke; her voice rises and falls in his very rhythms, and even the soft hairs at the nape of Jessie Elizabeth's neck curl the same as Clinton's. Thanks to Martha Jane's complicated storytelling, Jessie's not only no longer Martha Jane's child, but now she mirrors her false father. Martha Jane's lies return now with a backlash of justice and retribution.

Jessie closes her eyes, coughs a deep, hard rattle, and turns away from Martha Jane. As the child's eyes close, Martha Jane prays silently, *Please God, only to sleep and not to die.*

She stumbles outside, cussing Clinton for breaking the child's heart into illness, and disassembles the woodpile, tossing logs aside in search of that half-full bottle she stashed for emergencies.

The child can't be blamed for her misplaced devotion to

Burke, led on as she was by her mother, but Martha Jane cusses herself; she ought to have known better. Again she let love slam her like a go-devil, a maul splitting her soul into halves, while she told herself in desperate abandon, "Ah, it's divided I'm meant to be, with my body and heart exposed to the sun and air. And these inner rings, signs of all I've suffered and become, were formed only to fall into broken curves." So again she'd allowed it, all the while glad and raw in love with her insides outside, split and revealed. She forgot the truth again; the go-devil splits and tears you only to burn you down to ash.

Martha Jane longs for her wise rings, protective bark, and secret self to be restored.

She swigs from the cold bottle she found and wipes her mouth. From where she sits on the chopping block, Martha Jane cringes at Jessie's cough hacking through the shed wall behind her.

Her nerves settle. Before she's too drunk to decide anything, Martha Jane admits she's no good for the girl now. She decides to wrap Jessie in a blanket, set her in front of her on a horse, and deliver her to Mr. and Mrs. Ash, those good folks who gave Martha Jane a few dollars for food last week. They're proper parents with healthy, living children. They'll know how to nurse a sick child.

Jessie's illness terrifies Martha Jane, and the best mothering she can offer now is to hand over Jessie, to give her a chance. Any confidence she'd gained from nursing those sick miners in Deadwood abandoned her at Little Calamity's graveside. Besides, whenever one of those men died, she'd been able to console herself by saying, "He lived a life." But a sick child is terrible with potential, yet as fragile as dandelion fluff stuck in mud. Like a seed, a child is meant to live, and if she doesn't, a small world ends.

Before this fever Jessie never had more than sniffles. What if this is pox or typhoid? Martha Jane's nursing knowhow is as thin and useless as a quilt full of holes.

Before leaving her girl with these near-strangers, Martha Jane declares in front of the couple, "Your grandma is too old to nurse you right," fearing the suffering girl will fall back into needing and calling her "mother." But Martha Jane's good girl closes her eyes and nods, agreeing to their lie, or maybe by now believing it, about who Martha is. Or maybe, Martha Jane fears, she's dying and beyond such cares.

The parents glance at one another, surprised and then relieved. The mother chuckles and says, "So that's it. We couldn't quite believe it before that you're her mother. You don't seem . . . a domestic sort of woman."

The words hit Martha Jane like a punch in the stomach, but since she asked for them, she laughs, too, and thanks them for taking in her grandchild. She adds, "I'm surely a hell-raising mess, not to be trusted with a child." And isn't it true? A good mother would've noticed something so wrong it could carry off a two-week-old infant in his sleep. Even sober, Martha knows she's no fit mother, and lately, sober is an impossible way to stay.

Mrs. Ash clutches an embroidered handkerchief, folds her hands over her starched apron, and nods. Her nose wrinkles, and Martha suffers it as a righteous judgment against her own body odor; it has been some time since her last ablution, too long ago to remember. Or maybe the woman's upset that Martha Jane in her stumbling has overturned their good sitting room chair. Martha Jane widens her stance and resets the chair before the hearth.

"Yes," Martha Jane mumbles to herself, "I'm a little lubricated today." All the better. It proves she's doing the right thing, leaving that precious girl to steadier hands and clearer minds.

Martha Jane balances on a spindly parlor settee while Mrs.

Ash settles Jessie in a clean bed. As they walk upstairs for the grandmother's goodbye, Martha Jane asks the woman to register Jessie for school, once she's strong enough. Mrs. Ash sighs but agrees.

Martha Jane crosses the long, wavery distance across a red rug to the girl's bed and manages not to stumble once before leaning over. "You mind these good people and get well," she whispers to Jessie. She lifts the girl's braid and kisses it before letting it fall back on the clean pillowcase. "Grandma will come back for you, and we'll have more high times when you get strong."

On horseback half a mile down the road, Martha Jane feels watery, giddy, empty, and free of the burden she's laid down. All the same, it hurts to leave behind her child. Love, that go-devil, hacks her open again. But she's done right to give up the child, to save her from Martha Jane's inevitable failure, hasn't she? She tries to feel proud of herself for her sacrifice, but a voice like Charlotte's tells her she's selfish, dirty, and cold under all her good intentions. Martha Jane tells that voice to go to hell but breaks down into weeping.

Mixed-up and thirsty, Martha Jane goads Jessie's Blueberry to the nearest establishment. Her pockets are empty and her prospects dim. Still, while she may not be as storied or loved or hated here as she is in Deadwood, nearly anywhere she appears, somebody will stand Calamity Jane a drink.

Although she's convinced herself it's the best thing for Jessie Elizabeth, Martha Jane can't leave the girl behind. Her new idea is to edit her story, to change herself from the failed mother into somebody Jessie can remember and feel proud of, while keeping occasional contact. Kohl & Middleton provide a job, a stage at their dime museum where Calamity Jane can shine.

When she hears in May that Jessie's sick again, Martha Jane

takes a leave from the show to visit. Afraid the girl could die while thinking her Grandma Calamity doesn't care, Martha Jane sits soberly beside her bed with the wary Ashes looking on. Relieved again to leave Jessie in their care, and certain the girl feels loved and will recover, Martha Jane boards a train the next morning to return to the dime show and her new friends.

The next summer, when the child is well and stronger, Martha Jane takes her on a whirlwind tour to see more of the country, riding trains. They deboard to enjoy the sights and events, taking in towns and cities from Minneapolis to the East Coast. It's a fast circuit of ice cream, circuses, and sideshows— any public place Martha Jane can strut in her buckskins as Calamity Jane, while bystanders and audiences smile and clap. Martha Jane imagines Jessie Elizabeth watching the shows and recognizing how her grandmother's legend spans the United States, printed in newspapers Jessie can read for herself.

On the day Martha Jane finally tells Calamity Jane's life story to a biographer who writes it down to print on pamphlets to sell, Jessie's a witness in the room. While the ink is still fresh enough to sting her eyes, Jessie reads the copy back to Martha Jane. The child learned a lot in that convent school, enough to make her grandmother proud, but she may be a little too quick. Because the story mentions a baby girl, Jessie stops reading and asks, "Am I that girl?"

Martha Jane pats Jessie's cheek and dances around the girl's question. "This is show business, darlin', and people like to think Calamity had a child. You were Belle's daughter, but you are mine in my heart."

"You lie every day." Jessie nods at the paper and studies Martha Jane's face. "Who's to say you're not lying now?"

"Well, nobody. But ain't you learned yet, little girl, the truth turns in the telling?" Martha Jane winks and tickles her chin, but the girl only sighs and studies the little pamphlet.

"And no matter what you say, this isn't how I remember things."

Martha Jane figures she's looking at the dates and trying to do the math. It won't add up, because Martha Jane fudged those, too. How do you tell such a smart little girl that life isn't in the numbers and never adds up?

Jesse glances sideways up at her. "You swear I'm your grand-daughter? That I was Belle's?"

The child is as sharp and disconcerting as a rifle shot. Martha Jane resists her last opportunity to stitch the girl back under her motherhood. It's all lies upon lies now, from what she told that biography fellow to print down to what she says in this moment. Martha Jane hesitates. What was it Wild Bill liked to say? Sometimes when you look at your rotten cards, you got to bluff. Go all in and the chips may fall your way.

Martha Jane shoots tobacco juice into the biographer's brass spittoon. "Sure, Jessie darlin'. My dear grandchild ever and always, but you remind me more of your sweet angel mama every day." She tips her head forward then, so the biographer can't see, and winks.

Jessie puffs out a sigh of disgust and rolls her eyes. "Do you even know the truth anymore? I think it's been a long time since you two had a conversation."

Martha Jane shrugs, grins, and thanks the biographer. "Come on, sweetheart. Let's have a treat to celebrate all these papers we got to sell." At the drug store, she pulls coins from her leather purse, money she'd planned to use for whiskey. Feeling guilty and eager to play the hero, she buys Jessie two scoops of ice cream and then, at the ladies' shop, a new gingham dress.

Martha poses and performs on boardwalks and in parks. She calls out her stories and sells those new pamphlets, along with cabinet photographs of herself in buckskins, while Jessie rests under trees and reads. Sometimes the child looks up, shading her eyes with one hand, and when she catches the famous woman's eye, the girl smiles and waves. It fills Martha Jane with bubbles of joy to have her girl near.

Each evening, Jessie retells the stories she's read. Together they act out scenes from *Tom Sawyer* and from Twain's newer book, *Huckleberry Finn*, with their best accents and gestures, then fall laughing on the different towns' hotel mattresses, exhausted by the long days. While Jessie sleeps, Martha Jane fights the urge to leave her, to go drinking. Instead, she studies the girl's face, to memorize it against their time apart. She tells herself, soon enough the girl will be back at school, and Martha Jane will be alone again. With the girl beside her, she doesn't feel so cold or lonesome, and she dreads the coming autumn of their separation.

That summer, Jessie tries twice to teach Martha Jane to read, but the letters jumble together. "I don't see what you're seeing," the woman complains, then tousles Jessie's hair. "You're so good at it, you just go on reading to me." She feels the same shame she first felt as a child, at not being able to learn, but acts like it doesn't matter.

Standing in the sun, bragging and storytelling for money to support her child (and those coins for the secret bottles she sneaks from in the most desperate hours of night, after Jessie's asleep), Martha Jane hopes the girl's proud of her grandmother, the legend Calamity Jane. She hopes Jessie will treasure this summer together and tell her children about their shared golden days. Maybe the bad times, when Martha Jane was or wasn't Mama, when she got sloppy drunk and let things slide, will fade from Jessie's mind. Maybe the girl will forgive her for driving her Papa away. It could happen, if only the girl is better at forgetting childhood than Martha Jane has been.

As summer winds down, so do their good times. Martha

Jane's drinking more in secret and finds herself tested by the girl's endless questions and sass. Jessie notices a drug store calendar marking "August" and asks to go home to start school by September. On the train back to Sturgis, Martha stays sober so she won't miss a minute with her girl, but the shakes grab her hard, and her head pounds, needing whiskey.

Jessie notices her illness, squeezes Martha Jane's hand, and whispers for her to take her medicine before it gets worse.

Martha Jane blinks back tears and thanks the girl for her kindness. "Darlin' girl, your grandma is sick to the bone and sorry for it, but what can I do? I got this way when I was no bigger than you. I can't remember a time when I wasn't drinking. Promise your grandma you'll stay away from the whiskey."

As Martha Jane tips up the bottle for a swig, Jessie nods and looks out at the passing hills, never letting go of the woman's hand.

It's a hot day when they arrive in Sturgis. Dust coats their sweat-sticky dresses, so Martha Jane parts with some precious coins at a bathhouse, spiffing them both up with long soaks and clean clothes. She rents a rig in town to drive the girl to the Ash homestead in style. No longer a pauper, and now a proud grandmother, Martha Jane would have them greet a successful woman bringing their daughter home.

Jumping down from the rig, Jessie hurries to the Ashes on their shady porch, greeting them with hugs and calling them Ma and Pa. She thanks Martha Jane for the dresses and fun, blows her a kiss, and approaches that white Victorian house like she owns the place. With that other woman's motherly arm cradling her shoulder, Jessie slips behind a doorway shadow Martha Jane can't see through and leaves her past standing alone.

Climbing back in the rig, Martha Jane straightens her hat, flicks the horses, and beelines back to the livery. The pain in her chest testifies to her good deed, she knows, because doing what's right always hurts. From how deep this one stabs, Martha figures this is surely her finest hour. Bone-deep sorrow grips her for again deceiving and leaving her girl, but she promises herself not to bother the child again. Martha Jane knows she'll never be better for the girl than she's been this summer, and she wouldn't want the girl remembering worse.

May Jessie remember this one shining summer on rails, when the lies became a legend. Better for Jessie never to be ashamed of a drunken mother. Better that she might brag to her own children about that great woman, their great-grandma, Calamity Jane.

Martha Jane crisscrosses the West and plains with stories. She calls out to strangers on the street, holds out the paper she can't read, and stomps after them in muddy boots as she teases them to buy. Some pay to get rid of her. Others spit on the ground and shrug her away.

In a few passersby Martha Jane senses something different. It may at first be only curiosity or pity for her plight, but then some folks receive her with a need that matches her own. When she looks into their mirrors and they look back into hers, their mutual recognition opens both teller and listener to something new. Martha Jane leans in, and there, in the suspension of judgment, in the willingness to cross boundaries, the storyteller comes to life as Calamity Jane. The listener is transported. The West rises up out of the dust and lives.

Those glorious moments are usually days or weeks apart. Most mornings, she's shaky with nausea and squinting to block the hardboiled-egg sun that makes her head throb. She's sober before noon, so her voice is steady and strong, and she sells more pamphlets and pictures then. After midday, when she starts to sip from her flask and slur, more people ignore her catcalls and shove her away until she thinks, *to hell with them all,* and enters the soft, half-dark comfort of the nearest saloon. Friends and drinking strangers hail her and offer her a bottle or shot. It's a homecoming, the next best thing to family, here where a weakness for drink isn't considered a sin.

Without Jessie beside Martha Jane to retell the book-locked stories, Martha Jane has only her new, printed story to speak. That memory usually buys her first drink. Whiskey mumbles over the older tales, the memories she can't even admit to herself now: Charlotte whoring and Robert gambling, dead brothers, sold sisters, and her own baby eternally newborn and dead in the ground.

Excruciating and elusive as they can be, stories enliven and drive Martha Jane. They draw people to her and keep them at a distance. In her heart Martha Jane knows her secret stories will kill her someday; too many fault lines of sorrow crack her granite mind, and too much sorrow chokes her heart. Too many lies tangle her reason, and the only things she dares believe about herself are the lies she's memorized. With the whiskey, she finds a terrible relief from the truest things, but when she's drunk, she suffers a fast-fading certainty of what or who was ever real. The drink roars, rocks, and then abandons her, the way an oncoming train speeds up your heart, then rattles bone and steals breath, only to thunder into nothing beyond a *V* of shining track.

But Martha Jane only knows story, so when she's too weary to carry her own words, she lets the whiskey tell her. Whiskey alone can burn out the cold lonesome, so the colder Martha Jane feels, the louder the whiskey shouts and the harder it swings, no matter who tells whiskey to shut the hell up. The whiskey is strong. It is love. It is god. It is rest and strength and black forgetting. That place beyond story, beyond truth and lies, that silence of whiskey is the only relief Martha Jane can trust.

Its blind ease binds and breaks her, keeps her restless, and brings with every sunrise the enchanting birdsong wish to die.

CHAPTER TWENTY-SEVEN
THE NAME OF A RIVER

1898

Despite her best intentions, Martha Jane can't leave the child be, even when the girl is sullen and reluctant to receive the strange old woman who claims to be some family relation. Martha Jane sees Jessie's slipping away from her, so she works to tease her out of it. She buys the girl gee-gaws at the mercantile or takes her out to shoot at tin cans or birds. If she happens to make Jessie laugh with a bawdy joke, Martha Jane feels she's won a prize. After that first laugh, the so-called grandmother offers something bigger, a trip or a shopping excursion. For some reason, maybe curiosity or avarice, the girl usually says "yes."

Jessie Elizabeth looks more like Lena every year, but unlike her unknown aunt, has grown tall as a pasture weed. She's smart and funny and like Lena bites her tongue while failing to hide her judgment of Martha Jane. At times she appears to enjoy their little train rides between mining towns, especially when they dine in hotels, but the girl gets homesick after only a few days. Trying to get by on less whiskey, Martha Jane grows irritable, calls Jessie ungrateful, and nags the girl about picking her nails and twirling her hair until Jessie breaks down and cries. In the end, Martha Jane always apologizes, buys another gift she can't afford, and escorts the exhausted girl home. It still catches like a stitch in Martha Jane's side when Jessie hugs that other woman as if she's her real mother.

It's not always easy to act as grateful as she should be for the Ashes.

Robert Dorsett is a sweet talker with gentle hands. He's good for a nice poke now and then, and he's never mean. The more he drinks, the quieter he gets, a fine quality in a man. Martha doesn't find in herself the same hot-blooded gumption about him that she felt for Clinton. She feels nothing close to that over-the-moon thing people sing about and call love, but Robert, whom she calls Robert Dear, is a hard worker and shares every damned dollar he has with Martha Jane. He has an honest enough face and aims to make her happy, so she doesn't sense betrayal coming. She never suspects such a giving man would someday steal the thing she loves most.

She seems to recall they had a wedding, but she'd run out of whiskey that day and finished off several cans of suds too, so the memory is fuzzy. Was there a preacher? Robert Dear's memory is clearer than hers, and he insists a judge said some lawful words. She doesn't worry much over it, as she's probably still married to somebody else, Steers or maybe Burke, depending on which state law applies. Marrying Robert Dear was a lark, and that judge may well have been only an actor from that theater farce they went to see, the one about people getting married.

But married to her or not, Robert Dear's a good fellow, and she likes being with him. He laughs at her stunts. His favorite is when she walks up to folks, asks to see their purses or wallets, then takes out a few bills and thanks them for their charity. He loves it when she borrows and rides a horse into a saloon, then calls for an auction, driving up however many free drinks Calamity Jane needs to ride that beast the hell outside, preferably before it plops stinky apples on the floor. Robert Dorsett, also known as Bob, enjoys all her pranks.

Martha Jane loves the way his mustached lip pulls up like a bow and how his eyes crinkle when he doubles over, laughing. She can't let him in, though, the way she did Clinton. A woman's only got one or two great trusts inside her, waiting like seed underground. Still, to comfort the high-toned, church-going people of Utica, Montana, she calls herself Mrs. Dorsett while she lives with him. Taking Robert Dear at his word, Martha Jane adds his account of their marriage to her ongoing story.

Calamity Jane in love is good for business; folks always feel better about a woman if she's some sort of missus, and Martha Jane sells more pamphlets if Calamity Jane has a lawful fellow, sometimes even a little child, in her wake. Because times are changing, it improves everyone's sense of humor about Calamity Jane to see she's settled an inch or two inside the law.

Still, sometimes when she tries to act like a lady and stay out of trouble, folks miss her wild side. Baiting her with cigars and drinks, they wind her up in hopes she'll bust up the joint, and then they call in the law. It's as if landing her in jail overnight is part of the Wild West show they gladly pay to see.

Bob's a pretty good sidekick. Understanding whiskey's like medicine for her, he sees she gets her drinks when nobody else is buying, or when she runs through her washerwoman dimes too fast. When she spins too high, he talks her down, and when she falls too low, he hides her guns. Last time she started a fight, he stepped in and took a cowboy's fist to his own jaw. He gets her home safe.

But he can get Martha's goat, too. He takes offense when she goes on a toot while Jessie's visiting, even though she always tucks the child in at a good-enough hotel with a new book to read. He tells Martha she's no proper mother for swearing in front of the child, when not one of those words is new to Jessie after several summers of expanding her vocabulary at Martha Jane's side. He couldn't know this because he's new to the family and doesn't know the girl the way her own mother does. Still, he preaches. Meanwhile, Bob decorates his own orations with those very same damned words, only behind Jessie's back.

So it makes Martha Jane sore when Robert Dear acts high and mighty. About once a week he gets saved and figures everybody else should dry out, too. He even goes to church, knee-jerking back off his own sins and dragging Jessie into his pious playacting.

It gives Martha Jane no small satisfaction, then, when he's weekly fallen-down drunk by Friday evening—all his Sunday through Thursday hymn-singing be damned—and it's Martha Jane who fetches Jessie's supper of cold beans and bread. Martha Jane rubs his nose in it on Saturday mornings, how his holiness liquefied so fast. She reminds him not to be thinking he's somebody.

Martha Jane admits she's not perfect, but she's no hypocrite.

But then Robert Dorsett breaks Martha Jane's heart. Pulling the wool over her eyes by saying he's going to visit his mother in Livingston, instead her rapscallion Robert Dear rides away with Jessie in tow. When she sobers up, Martha Jane's not sure how many days he's been gone, so she asks around the hotels and bars to find Robert Dorsett left no word with any of their drinking friends about if or when he plans to return. Martha Jane quickly assumes the worst, because it's what she believes she deserves. He's gone and left Martha Jane, same as Clinton Burke did, but the goddamned hypocrite has added kidnapping to abandonment.

Martha Jane mourns her girl hard from inside a whiskey glass. She tells everyone she's going to look for the child, swears she can't let her go, and then fires up a three-day fuddle. She leaves the booming laundry-for-hire, her most recent livelihood, to pile up in a stink by her washtub. When her drinking money runs out, she lures some coughing, out-of-work working girls to boil, scrub, hang on lines, and iron the mountain of cloth, to be disappointed in the end with a dollar they'll split three ways.

Damn that man. It was one thing for Martha Jane to leave the girl to be raised by another family, a mother's prerogative, but quite another to have the child snatched. Suddenly gone, Jessie's alone with a man Martha Jane realizes to be little more than a stranger. As if Martha Jane hadn't already felt guilty enough, now she sinks deeper.

Her drinking coins run out. She asks around to take in more laundry, even knowing she'll have to wash it herself but can't gather much; the soiled doves got wise and started their own business. Too broke to print more pamphlets, Martha Jane spills her whole story on the street for a penny. She tells it rote with the same words every time, but memory fails more often than not. At the slightest distraction she loses her place and has to restart from the beginning. "My maiden name was Martha Cannary . . ." If nobody interrupts her, it follows like a river rushing snowmelt down a canyon.

She still raises hell like nobody's business, but causing a ruckus, even shooting up the street, doesn't deliver the thrill it once did. Angry as hell most of the time, she's itching for a fight, ready to throw down a bad poker hand and bust a chair over a cowboy's head, but her heart's not in it. Afterwards, she feels sorry. She gives the bartender a quarter for the chair, mumbles apologies, and buys the cowboy a drink. Then they both ruin it by apologizing back to her, instead of fetching the sheriff.

There's no fun to be had in Utica.

After three weeks Robert Dorsett, no longer considered Dear, still hasn't returned, so Martha Jane pronounces herself abandoned by another husband. The newspaper picks up the story, or so she's told, painting her as the heartbroken mother.

She told them "grandmother," but they printed it wrong.

Brokenhearted, Martha Jane lets folks toast her and pat her on the back. She puts on her best dress and thanks them, in two or three towns over the course of several nights, by tossing back the free drinks they offer. Sometimes she feels close to washing out the feelings, but she fears for and misses Jessie. What will she tell the Ashes?

Teddy Blue shows up, puts on her feathered hat, cavorts in the street to cheer her up, and, when he runs out of cash, he swears he'll pay back the money he owes her. She says, "Hell, no" and buys him three more drinks, to stay in somebody's good graces.

In Gilt Edge she sobers up, despite her best efforts. With her senses cleared, a particularly brilliant orange sunset catches her eye. It speaks to her of a wider, more beautiful world, so she quits Judith Basin altogether, this time on a borrowed horse. Having heard Robert Dorsett's mother lives there, Martha Jane sets out for Livingston to look for her girl.

The high peaks of Yellowstone light up with stripes and patches of aspen gold, while early October snows sugar the peaks. The cold, clear air snaps her out of her dismal funk. Her spirits rise with altitude as her horse ambles higher. The Yellowstone River is a circuitous guide, and she elbows back within sight of where she came from, time and again. Martha Jane sips from her flask, trusting the water to provide direction.

Rising higher, she pronounces to her horse that all the evils of the world can be attributed to people crammed too close together in dirty little gulch towns, dark mines, or sprawling cities. She urges the horse, whom she nicknames Henry for a beloved old friend, ever higher along the narrowing canyons.

In Livingston, no one will admit to knowing Robert. There's no sign of her girl, and, as she tours the saloons, Martha Jane senses the town is keeping that secret from her. Sorrowful and yet feeling guilty relief, she restocks her liquor. After spitting on the street and loudly cursing the stonewalling citizens, she takes her leave. Henry carries her higher into the mountains, blowing white clouds of steam from his nostrils and rocking her in the saddle as if in a cradle. As the temperature drops, Martha Jane pulls tighter the moth-eaten beaver coat she just won in a poker hand, while full whiskey bottles clink together in her saddlebags.

Against the quiet she sings a bawdy chorus about a gal with yellow bloomers and chuckles as the frosty stones ring back her staggering chorus. She shivers, though, as mountain chickadees chide her and the wind's susurration erases her echoed songs. An enfolding force quells her bellowing, and she shivers under its firm hand, while aspen leaves flutter and purr like yellow cats twisting through the pines. Falling below Martha Jane, the Yellowstone River waters flash bits of sunlight through the trees, piercing her eyes. The water that was her companion and comfort no longer leads her but now follows, lazing golden green in shallows and leaping foamy white over tumbles of granite. Teasing, abandoning her, and Martha Jane's heart chills with loneliness. Everything goes.

After countless dead-end trails and a full afternoon scrambling over rock, her horse finally puffs and blows its way to a summit. Dizzy and bleary-eyed, Martha Jane approaches the canyon overlook above Yellowstone Falls to look down. Thanks to the whiskey, she's near oblivion, but the rumble sobers her a little, pitching her first into awe, then into despair. She wants to run from the noise and power but urges her weary horse forward.

Her new Henry balks and refuses, tossing his head back and forth. Martha Jane has to settle for a safe distance from which to wonder, how might it feel to fall or jump into that immensity? She's nearly numb but probes her soul for fear, and, once stirred, that terror curls her inward; she ponders what a small thing it would be to die. Nobody would miss her, she tells herself, and she flinches as a needle of self-pity pierces her soul with something like satisfaction.

Martha Jane's heart beats faster. She tips up her light bottle to catch its last drops but is again disappointed by emptiness and shatters the glass against a bouldered wall. She shushes and pats her startled horse, comforts him with his new name, and reins him back to the rocky trail where they both might feel safer, if not well. The air is thin, and the horse walks with his head down. Martha Jane has to expand her chest until it hurts, to get enough air at this altitude. She feels poorly, like a twig snapped underfoot by somebody stomping over. Yet, tracking along the canyon edge, she senses a part of herself that is immortal. A terrifying, enduring part of herself that won't let her go. Martha Jane swallows hard, draws a hard breath of cold air, and squeezes the pommel. Glancing around, she's just sober enough to appreciate the prettiest country God ever made, but she struggles to feel she belongs or should stay; this seems the kind of place a person would only come to, to die.

Through an opening in the trees, she again tries to rein her horse near the top of the falls, where he stumbles. He's winded and spreads his legs wide to bear his load, while resisting the edge. *Smart horse*, Martha Jane thinks. He's afraid, as she should be. As if thinking of someone else, she wonders why she isn't. Because it doesn't matter. Since the worst things, she has no fear of what else might happen.

Loose rock slides and shining stretches of weather-smoothed stone create a barrier, a barren no-man's-land. Beyond it, tons of catapulting water funnel into a narrow waist, then break free to fall, foam, and roar. But where? The chaos is a kind of magnet, and Martha Jane's pulled like iron. From horseback, she leans and peers over but can't see the bottom. Henry, whinnying and nervous, feels her movement and tries to turn back.

Martha Jane pats him, mutters, "Good Henry," and dismounts, wrapping the reins around the pommel to secure him before she leaves common sense behind. It flits through her mind, *he can find his way down alone.*

This close, the sound is overwhelming; she can't look up at what she most wants to see but watches her loose, flap-soled boots scrape left-right, left-right over sparkling bits of stone. Time and pounding water seem to have fractured the mountain's skull into chunks, crystals, and powder. Or was the mountain, like Martha Jane, born broken? Yellow-and-black shattered pieces of something that once flowed cut through her exposed socks like knives. She staggers and falls. Noticing a crescent slice beside her thumb, she raises the wound to her tongue, licks, and tastes her own blood. *Iron,* she thinks as she stands, *I am iron.*

She scuffs, inhales, raises her eyes, and bends forward. The water spins, dizzies, and draws her in like a sweet-talking man. If only she could overcome her body's recoil and force herself over, she'd never be thirsty again. She'd finally escape the emptiness, the cold lonesome she's running from. The water thunders its reasons, and she listens, edging closer.

She wants to die, she tells herself, but then feels a whisper of distinction—she simply doesn't want to live or feel. She's run herself ragged to numb the tender parts left raw, red, and swollen with unstaunched blood and unsuckled milk after Little Calamity. She tried to bury those parts of herself with him, and it seemed to work; she didn't flinch at the terrible open wound of motherhood when Jessie Elizabeth was born. But, by protecting herself, she failed the girl.

Martha sobs and scuffs another step, feeling mist settle on her face. She closes her eyes. Don't look. Just topple over and the guilt will die. The legend will live on, and people will believe the better story, the one about a woman dressed like a man, a mule-skinner, an Indian fighter, a cavalry soldier, and Hickok's one true love.

As she hesitates, the whiskey thins, separates, and scuds off her mind like high, icy clouds. Snatches of her senses return in bodily jabs and throbs. Her feet stick to her socks, blood-saturated rags stiffening in the cold where those lava stones sliced through. Tears freeze and crackle like old face paint as she grimaces in pain. Her nose runs. What's that pain? She rolls and rubs her shoulder. It feels torn loose in the socket, probably from trying to catch herself when she fell on the rocks. That cut on her hand is swelling and won't clot, so she wraps a hanky around it, tying a knot with her teeth. The spreading blood on the rag gives her a strange satisfaction, a tickle of life. Her stomach growls and spurts a nasty reflux of whiskey up her gullet. Martha Jane sighs, reluctantly taking up her body again.

Glancing over the canyon edge, she sees past the crashing falls to the boulders that would pummel and shatter her bones. Would she feel the impact? She broke her arm once, and it hurt something awful. Still does when a storm's coming. Would she drown right away or get sucked under? Her lungs ache already, determined to pull life from this thin atmosphere. It's hard enough to drink herself out of this world; God only knows what a beating her hard body would suffer before losing consciousness. Martha Jane might be ready to knuckle under, but Calamity Jane wouldn't go down without a fight, or she'd have already drunk herself to death.

Martha Jane's heart races and blood rushes in her ears. Panic clutches her gut. "Damn it all," she mutters, clutching her dirty skirt and taking a step back. Passing the edge might end the pain, but it would hurt like hell first. Truth is, those thundering falls she now feels vibrating up through her worn boot soles terrify her worse than the idea of living. *Damned coward.* Calamity Jane, who claims to fear no white man or Indian, is knock-kneed and too scared to jump, to let go, to fall into oblivion.

Death may not be so bad, but dying looks dreadful from this height.

Reasoning above her desperation, she gulps and considers, what if God is, as they've always claimed, a man? What if He won't give her credit for nursing men with the pox, saving run-over dogs from the street, or giving coins to orphans? What if He hates the liar, the painted cat, the gambler, and the drunk—every dark woman who occupies her soul. If what preachers say is true, there'll be no mercy to catch her, only a fiery basket in the suicide's hell.

Stepping back, she leans against a boulder to steady herself. Hell might not be fire at all, but suffocating torrents of ice water. Whiskey's a warmer way to die. And maybe the god she senses under the drink is woman enough to look for the good in Martha Jane, the sort to give a gal another chance.

Martha Jane scrapes the ice-mask of tears off her face with her furry sleeve, gathers up her skirts, and scrambles over the glassy stones. Henry lifts his head and nickers, so she pats his nose and offers him a handful of oats from her saddlebag. There's a bottle she'd forgotten there, to settle her shudders and warm her heart. Encouraged, she mounts, levels her hat, and points Henry's nose downhill and south, toward the next river town.

Martha Jane takes sick in Helena and, penniless, lands in a poorhouse to recover. A country doctor tells her she'd better give up the drink, that her liver's enlarged. If she keeps it up, she won't see the new century.

"Hell, doc, I'm just getting fat," she jokes, waving him away from the clean bed the county's providing. "I'll get cherk if I get some sleep."

Once back on her feet, she sells more pamphlets, then drinks down whatever the loose change can buy. Folks seem to crave the Wild West in a new way, as if it's a precious, bygone thing. Calamity Jane is part of the drama lost. After their surge of nostalgia, some of her customers eye her with pity, while others leer in disgust. Most, in the manner of young things, feel indifference and would forget her, if not for her tintype card artifacts displayed in their china cabinets.

She creaks her joints into a comfortable seat at Billy Jump's Pisor saloon, where she likes to sit with the owner and chew the rag. Her memories are softening around the edges, almost as if they happened to somebody else, so she likes to listen to other people talk about her. The fight's gone out of her since she looked down the throat of Yellowstone Falls, where she decided not to die but couldn't quite decide to live. She feels she's been on a long walk but senses a gentle ending not far down the road. If she's careful it won't come in a fight or shootout, not in any blaze of glory—no jealous wife will have cause to take her on. Broken-down, abandoned, and losing her teeth, Martha Jane figures she's too ugly to be wanted, so she pretends she doesn't want a man.

She'll pass out sleeping in a bed, if she's lucky, not facedown, drowning in an alley puddle. Maybe the spot won't matter; she figures she'll be too blasted on whiskey to know. As for what comes after, she doesn't give a shit anymore. God can do with her as He likes. Heaven or hell, it's all the same to her. Which begs the question, for judgment, which name would Saint Peter read out? Martha Jane Cannary, Martha Burke, Jean Burke, Mattie King, Jean King, or Mattie Dorsett? She's called herself all of these. Even the saintliest saint would throw up his hands after sorting through so many documents, so maybe Peter will hand her up the chain of command to God Himself. Maybe He'll be the one to find her on the scroll and holler out the right moniker, "Calamity Jane!"

She and God might differ on many things, but they'd agree she's had more names than a river in Indian country. Martha Jane pulls her bleary thoughts together and explains to Billy Jump, she's like that Yellowstone River, the one that scared her off jumping to her death, forever setting her course on a slower demise.

Billy squints and draws his eyebrows together like caterpillars meeting. "You sayin' you almost killed yourself, Calam?"

"Maybe I did or didn't almost, but I didn't for sure." She waves a hand to clear the air for her own words. "But I was saying. That particular river, the Indians called *Mi tse a-da-zi,* or Yellow Rock River. French trappers came along and called it Roche Jaune, or Pierre Jaune. Yellow rocks in every language, whole mountains of them." She unlaces her boot, pulls off her stiff sock, and props her foot on the bar. "They're sharp little sonsabitches, too. See these scars?"

Billy blinks and gently nudges her bare foot off his bar but holds his smile. She's good for business, sure, but there's something likeable about the old girl. He likes having her around.

Martha Jane wonders if she should trot out a new name, just to keep things interesting and maybe to get herself written up in the papers again. "How about Whiskey Jean?" she mutters as she tries to replace her twisted sock and fails. She drops the holey thing on the fallen boot and turns back to her host. The room spins. She grips the bar.

Billy says, "The name of a river depends on who's drinking from it, I suppose. But it's always the same river."

This is profound, so Martha Jane nods, considering the name, the same, and who's drinking? Whiskey Jean or Calamity Jane? Belching, she gives Billy a gap-toothed smile and asks, would he be so kind as to stand her another round? Whiskey Jean will pay him tomorrow.

Shaking his head and tipping the bottle, he smiles. Sentimental and generous, he pours two fingers for the old gal he's always known as "Calamity Jane."

★ ★ ★ ★ ★

PART FIVE
IN A WHITE DRESS,
LIKE A BRIDE

★ ★ ★ ★ ★

CHAPTER TWENTY-EIGHT
MADONNAS &
MOUNTAIN HOWITZER

1901

It troubles her mightily. She'd always thought of it as a good deed, but had giving up Jessie been just another sin? No, she argues against herself. It was as hard and as ugly as cutting off her own thumb, and it still throbs, but it wasn't selfishness that drove her to it. But was it the thirst?

If only whiskey were God, or God, whiskey, to ease her into whatever's coming, even death. Maybe when she's dead the thirst and the gnawing cold lonesome will ease.

The thirst, the thirst.

Looking out her train car window, Martha Jane's forgotten where she's headed, and she can't find her ticket to see what's stamped on it. It doesn't matter. Her flask is warm in her hand. She sips and thinks about how hard she's tried to do right, how she's put down the bottle only one time less than she's taken it up. Was her first drink with Cilus, or before? Her thirst for whiskey's all wrapped up with first memories, maybe with her mother's milk. With the milk, to keep the babies quiet. Yes, whiskey is like mother's love, that easy, warm, and natural. But if being a mother is natural, why couldn't she do it better?

Martha Jane takes a long pull off her flask. The lady two seats over side-eyes her and fumbles her rosary beads, talking to another Mother, Jesus's own. Martha Jane's uneasy with that Madonna too. So pure, she was a perfect mother, and even those consarned Mormons who tried to adopt Martha Jane insisted that Mary stayed a virgin always. How that worked, Martha can't imagine. But Martha Jane can believe this—that Virgin never offered her Son a rubber-nippled bottle of mountain howitzer to hush him. Only a devil would. *Or maybe,* Martha Jane thinks, feeling a little guilty, *a devil's broken daughter.*

Two rows down, the woman with the beads mutters, "Pray for us sinners."

The thirst, the thirst made me selfish, made me give my child away. Holy Mary, will you cast merciful eyes on poor, besotted Martha Jane?

It shames Martha Jane to think it. That Madonna, unlike herself, kept her baby to raise. She kept that boy alive too, until he was grown and they crucified him. Poor mother. How she must have cried under the cross. Did she watch while they buried her beautiful boy, or did she have to ride away and let his Father do it?

Martha Jane closes her tearful eyes, drifting through motherhood's journey, through fitful dreams. From childbed to cradle to crucifix to grave, Martha Jane twitches and moans. When she cries out, "No!" the woman with the rosary stiffens in her seat and mutters back, "Mother of God."

Reformers get ahold of Martha Jane again. Goddamn.

That fast-talking lady journalist Josephine Brake is a handsome woman, but she is the devil in disguise. She said she'd look into the pension Martha Jane is due from her service in the U.S. Army. After promising Martha Jane the lap of luxury and a comfortable retirement, she tricked her into an interview with her cousin, who works for one of those yellow rags in St. Paul.

Only a few weeks into their association, Martha Jane sorrowed and raged to learn Miss Brake's true intentions. Calamity Jane was not to retire but had been procured for a sordid destiny, for exhibition purposes and that novelist's financial gain. Claiming it was for Martha Jane's own good, Miss Brake pressured her into that New York Pan Am Exposition with Cummins's Indian Congress, where Calamity Jane appeared for long hours in parades, staged shoot-em-ups, and horseback demonstrations.

Worse, Miss Brake took the lion's share of every dollar Martha Jane earned, leaving the star of the show a mere thirty cents, plus meals, for a whole week's work. Then that New York hellcat had the gall to frown upon a little good-natured drinking, even as she got rich off Calamity's rowdy reputation. Oh, the hypocrisy of Christian folks, and how they prowl the earth, hungry for sinners to redeem.

So Martha Jane's good old friend Buffalo Bill, the great showman himself, wired her gold coins sufficient to escape Brake and her designs, but not enough to get her very far west. So on this September afternoon Martha Jane's stranded in Chicago, drowning her considerable sorrows. She overheard two salesmen discussing how some anarchist sonofabitch shot President McKinley in the Temple of Music, there at the Exposition after Calamity Jane left Buffalo. She wonders as she gazes into the amber of a whiskey bottle as if it's a crystal ball: could she, Calamity, have saved the president? She can still draw fast enough. Folks could have seen Calamity Jane in all her legendary glory, a true heroine of the West.

She'd never have had to pay for another drink, for the rest of her life.

Just think of it. She drowses, resting her head on her arms. *I'd be celebrated as a heroine, but here I am alone and broke and less than a finger left in this whiskey bottle. And not a friend in sight.*

Propping her head on her fist, she admits she's usually been better off on her own. But these last few weeks she's been feeling poorly. Some smart-alecky fellow, an acquaintance who knew her back in Montana, passed through the museum in Buffalo and had the gall to tell her she's looking peakeder. Hearing that, she felt even worse. News rags have been saying she's on her way out, but she'll thrash any woman or man who tells such a lie in her hearing. She could have just saved the president, after all. It ain't her fault she left a day too soon.

Has it been a week, or two weeks, since she broke from that cold-hearted woman journalist? She was a liar and a cheat, but Martha Jane did get a few paychecks out of the deal. And, oh my, did she have herself a high time. Even got arrested, but the New York judge had a soft heart and suspended her sentence for her god-knows-how-many-really, so-called "first time" behind bars. Clearly, he never read the South Dakota or Wyoming papers, or he'd have known better.

Lord save all happy drunks from those who mean well, and may the devil take their charitable, profitable plots to save our souls. Because, as Martha Jane has learned from the likes of Josephine Brake, the road to heaven is paved with stuffed purses and not near enough whiskey bottles.

After being so badly used and cheated, Martha Jane spends nine months in a string of South Dakota towns, absorbing public appreciation: selling picture postcards of herself, occasionally buying rounds of drinks, or frequently letting generous admirers buy. It's a hard winter in Huron and Aberdeen, and the only way to keep warm is to drink and smoke cigars while hunkering down in saloons. Fights get her blood moving, too. She suffers a bad turn in Oakes, North Dakota, though, where on the way to Jamestown, she gives a fine, spontaneous shooting exhibition and makes those insolent cowboys dance. She gets no jail time, but the judge runs her out of town.

Alas, there is no rest for the wicked and no home, neither.

Not even in Jamestown, Livingston, Lewistown, or Red Lodge where she's made the rounds and worn out her welcomes. She's feeling sicker every day. She doesn't let on or complain but keeps peddling her life story for whatever she can get. She'd like to stay in one town to rest, but it's not to be; word's out that she's hell on wheels. She's the same old gal she ever was, and how is it her fault, she wonders, that times have changed? It's the West that ain't true anymore, and she says so at the top of her voice in every saloon she visits. She lives in the old days, still.

Now and again, she hears people snicker as she passes. Bone-sick and weary, Martha Jane hasn't the heart or ginger to fight them. Even Calamity Jane's too beat down to tell them to go to hell.

CHAPTER TWENTY-NINE
HOUSE OF JOY

1903, South Dakota

The spidery cracks in the lath-and-plaster walls don't trouble Martha Jane. The room's solid enough to keep out winter's wind, even if the corners are gray with dust, and it's finer than most places she's slept. She doesn't mind the slapdash rose-trellis wallpaper patterns that mismatch at the corners, the dust-clotted, silk lampshade fringe, or the thin-tracked Persian rugs, unmentionably stained. It's a cathouse, after all. Nothing goes on here that can disturb Martha Jane's peace. It's what's beyond Diddlin' Dora's red front door that makes her nervous. Outside is where Martha Jane's worst temptations lie.

The lye soap and hot water make her thumbs crack deep at the nail corners and bleed, tingeing the sheets, unmentionables, suds, and water pink. Martha Jane blinks at the steaming fumes that rise from the tub, dampening her cheeks and burning her eyes, but she's grateful. Dirty laundry, stained with other people's sweat, dirty feet, piss, and lust—these have kept her from starving more times than she can remember.

Once she gets the stinking cloths in the hot water, it's not such unpleasant work, even if it makes her shoulders ache. The heat from the tub holds off the January drafts. She likes the silence of the laundry room broken by the slap of wet cloth against the washboard, the rhythm of dip, press, scrub, rinse, and wring. The work gives her time to consider better days as her hands, like machines, scrub, plunge, twist, and flatten the cloth.

Without the drink, she's edgy, better left alone. Tingles like ants crawl up and down her arms, and her hands tremble.

She cooks for Dora and the girls, but Martha Jane can't taste anything but salt and pepper, so she seasons their food heavily. The girls gobble down her cornbread, dried-fruit pies, and elk stew anyway, glad for anything homecooked. Dora's a kind-hearted madam, only slapping the girls if they truly rile up at her or if they scratch each other, marking up the merchandise. She can't fry an egg or boil water, though, and the chef who cooks for the hotel guests is some skinny fellow with a handlebar mustache and a fake French accent; he'd sooner let the working girls starve than lower himself to fill their bellies. As if some people ain't people, and food ain't only food. It's all right for Martha Jane, though. They need her and that feels good.

She scorched last night's cornbread in its skillet, though, a first, so maybe she's losing her touch in the kitchen. She's been sober for two weeks, the shakes and nausea are settling down, and she's promised Dora she'll stay dry, because a drunk in the parlor is bad for trade. It's hard to fight the thirst, though. Stretching, arching with her hands pressed low in her back, Martha Jane also wonders whether liquor might have been the missing ingredient behind last night's cornbread disaster.

Belle Fourche is a lively town. When Martha Jane stretches out in bed at night, the muffled riot of the boys thumping against the cathouse walls conjures up old times, but it's not how it was. Belle Fourche has grown civilized in this new, twentieth century. Even Dora's place has a new outlook and a new sign out front—"Dining, Drinking and Dancing, a Place You Can Bring Your Mother." *Just keep her at the foot of the stairs*, Martha Jane thinks, chuckling. Upstairs is, well, still upstairs, where the sheets get extra dirty.

Dora's a good egg, a true friend, even if she insists on trying to save Martha Jane from herself, meaning, from the drink. Not out of piety, mind you, but thinking she can hold on to her friend a little longer. So if Martha Jane were to cut loose and raise some hell, which she tells herself she absolutely cannot do, she wouldn't do it at Dora's. She'd likely get a bottle at one of those places down the street, out of respect for what Dora's offered: a dry, soft place to sleep, clean sheets, a job, and three square meals a day, even if Martha Jane can't keep the victuals down.

No, she won't run after a bottle tonight, she tells herself, tossing on the sagging mattress. Two weeks is a good run, and her word to a friend has to mean something.

Her head's clear, and thoughts line up like bottles on a saloon shelf. That's neither all good, nor all bad, but tonight the cold, dark lonesome presses in hard enough to knock them down. To distract herself, Martha studies the gold-twinkling ferns of frost on the gaslit windowpane. Winter spills off the glass like a waterfall and chills her iron-frame bed, saturating her with memories of the dead. Her mother. Her father. Cilus and the babies. She shivers and pulls the quilts to her chin, pointing her mind to Teddy Blue and Charlie Utter and Wild Bill, high times and better days in Deadwood. *Maybe,* she thinks, *they'll share better days in a bawdy-house Paradise to come.*

The bed wires squeak beneath her. Her hip aches from that time she got thrown off the wagon. She smiles, remembering those damned oxen and their hard, broad heads where she'd scratch them and the tender spots on their flanks where she'd flick them with the whip. How they'd startle and beller, but then they'd lean away from her cussing, into the yoke. Leather would creak and wheels would turn because she drove them.

Her left bottom molar throbs, dragging her back from memory and denying her sleep, but she won't go to a dentist again. That Dr. Frackelton was kind and did a fair job, but even those teeth he filled have fallen out now. The rotten few she has left, she needs. To gnaw a steak is one of life's few remaining pleasures, with those red juices running out of the meat, salty, rich and raw trickling down her throat. Only she's not ever hungry and it hurts too much to chew. Still, no dentist with his pliers. There's no point.

Damn her thirst. Sometimes she thinks she'll go mad with the itch, the nag, and the sorrow unleashed. She doesn't like who she is without the whiskey—snappish, cold, and angry all the time. Slamming pots on the cast-iron stove, sloshing water over the rim of the pan, cussing under her breath at the curious, hungry girls. She misses Calamity Jane, the gal with her easy laugh, her clomping, dancing shoes, and her jokes. That Calamity slammed into the saloons with a "Hello, darlin'." She'd always forgive and forget. She'd run into hell or fire to save the other fellow, with no thought for herself. But that girl's gone.

Without a drink, Martha Jane can't even sing or pray. Christians don't know the truth—God's easier to talk with through a bottleneck.

Tonight she burns the roast and the potatoes. What good is she to Dora if she can't even cook? Martha Jane hasn't another night's worth of good intentions left. Not even for love of Dora can she lock herself in.

After the downstairs clock chimes two, she gets up, slides into her brown dress, and struggles with the buttonhook to fasten her boots. Her hands shake worse at night, so she leaves the top buttons undone and the leather flapping. She wraps on the heavy coat Dora gave her. It's too big around because she has no bosoms left, and it's too short because it was one of Dora's, but its thick beaver lining keeps the chill from biting through her bones.

She tells herself she won't drink, but she'll walk it off. She tracks wide around the establishments, leaving the snow-filled gulch and its saloons behind in favor of the stinking cattle yard by the railroad line. The manure and ammonia steam, sending up vapors to clear her head. The hard iron of the rail beneath her boots grounds her, while the wind slaps and chaps her cheeks the way it did when she was a girl. If she squints, she can see dozens of stars, not clearly, but fuzzy and white, like frost.

She imagines catching a train tomorrow before full light, while the sunrise is as thin as pink silk panties flung over the eastern hills. It's always better to be heading somewhere, than to be standing still. God, how she loves being on a train with the track rumbling and the car swaying and the steam flowing like Chantilly lace outside her window and the mountains ripping past like yesterday's mistakes, and she's putting it all behind her. In motion, everything never happened, or it still can.

On a train, she's not old but new, and none of her mistakes touch her when she's leaving. She can pretend she's still a girl first running away, still a legend waiting to happen. She can chat up strangers, introduce herself as Calamity Jane, sneak nips from the bottle in her carpetbag, and feel fine. Catching nickels in her gloved palm, she can hand over cabinet cards and pamphlets. She won't get falling-down drunk but just ride the wind, keeping her hands steady and her nerves down. She'll remember her smile, be ready with a joke, and make friends with all the fine people headed in her same direction.

On a train, the ground slips away and you can picture the old West coming at you with the tracks. When you're screeching into a station, somebody might be waiting for you there. Somebody who knows you and remembers better days.

Dora loves Calamity Jane more than anybody else does; she

says so every day. Dora may be sorry to find that bed empty, but she'll understand, even if Martha doesn't say goodbye or explain why she's gone to Calamity again.

CHAPTER THIRTY
HULLABALOO

1903

The ore train to Terry is a rough ride over small-gauge track, but at least Martha Jane didn't miss it. Looking out at July's scorched ground, Martha Jane sees the hills and scraps of plain as they once were, as they should've stayed. This place was better before the abandoned shanties and gouged, failed mines marked by piles of slag pocked the ground. She could almost weep over the hard-raped, abandoned earth.

Black-and-white-collared antelope run like snow-melt streams, surging up and down the gold-green foothills, over saltbush, cinquefoil, and yarrow, but Martha Jane can only glimpse their shadows if she doesn't look straight at them. Buffalo haunt the corners of her sight, too, faint as ghosts with remembered steam rising from their nostrils. The switchgrass, bluestem, and grama grass shush and bow as the bison graze and thunder.

Attracted to the shadow past, Martha Jane works hard not to see the hardscrabble homesteads with fences where cattle bunch in mudded bobwire-and-split-post corners. Trampled, cracked ground won't let grass grow. And all those crops in rows. Is that wheat? Alfalfa? What the hell?

She snorts and wipes drool from her chin, then rubs her neck, stiff from sleeping. Her mouth is dry and tastes foul. She needs a rinse of whiskey and a dab of clove oil for that rotted tooth.

She digs in her rucksack, not finding a bottle, but deals through the deck of photos and brochures. She still can't read the brochure but doesn't need to; it runs in her head and she reads it from there. Feeling as if somebody's watching and means her harm, she glances around for pickpockets or unsupervised children. That man's asleep, and that woman's playing cat's cradle with her girl. Nobody's looking, but feeling threatened nonetheless, Martha Jane hides those papers, her only livelihood, in the bottom of her bag. Leaning her head against the vibrating glass, she closes her eyes. Remembering. Wishing. Dreaming the legend into life. There was that party with Teddy Blue, and that dinner with Buffalo Bill. Then that other Bill, and Clinton.

The baby falls from her arms, startling her awake, but she can't shake the blame. The cold, blue face is her fault again. She blinks and presses her eyes with her fingers, but Martha Jane can't erase the nightmare from her throbbing, red eyelids. The small wrapped bundle, the black dirt, and the white snow spiked with frozen grass.

Desperate, she digs in her bag again, this time finding the cool, curved glass. The Burlington car rattles her, stabbing her right side and gnawing at her aching joints. She closes her eyes, uncorks the bottle, lifts it, and sips. Wiping her mouth, she coughs down the swallow.

Only bad mothers let their babies die.

She forces her mind off the grave, to the hurdy-gurdy house in Livingston. There she'd danced with so many fellows she lost the fat that baby put on her. She was glad when her breasts collapsed and lost their milk-memory, their accusations against her. Back then, the whiskey was enough to numb the tingle of Little Calamity's lips and his sweet tugging on her nipples. The rush and the warm drops of milk.

Martha Jane's milk never came in for Jessie, as if her body

293

blocked the chance and wouldn't risk another betrayal. She had to milk goats to feed that baby girl and feed her with a rubber teat on a washed-out whiskey bottle. Jessie took to that goat's milk as if she'd rather not bother with Martha Jane. At least there wasn't whiskey in the bottle, Martha tells herself. *I did better than that.*

But Jessie Elizabeth's all right, better off having been nursed by goats and growing up with that family where Robert left her. Not the Ashes, who fell on hard times and gave her up, but some other good Christian folks whose name Martha Jane heard but can't recall. She tells herself Jessie surely has a hard-working father and real mother, one who holds her and puts mercurochrome on her scraped knees, as bright orange as the center of a blanket flower. That mother doesn't get drunk, yell at her, and make her cry, and Jessie would never tell that woman to go away and never come back. But isn't Jessie grown now? No, that can't be right. She can't be more than ten years old, still. Martha Jane dozes, smelling hard candy and holding her girl's soft hand.

The pain in her side startles her awake, sharp as a knife under her right-side ribs. Even after Martha Jane rubs the sleep crusts from her eyes, the land outside the window is a blur. The buffalo and antelope wisp away, and she squints, bracing herself against a sudden wave of dizziness. Is the train going faster, or is she slowing down? Could it be this is how a life ends, like a train chugging into a station, knocking you off balance and blinding you with smoke and steam?

Martha Jane feels it—she's dying, hard and slow. She won't see Jessie again, but then, they won't argue again, neither, and won't throw more cross words that are hard to forget. Maybe someday Jessie will look back on the legends and forgive. Maybe she'll treasure their traveling days.

Martha Jane sighs in relief. Good. This ain't death, not yet, just her train braking, easing into Terry.

At the station she's too dizzy and whiskey-fuddled to deboard alone. She waves her hand in the air and calls out, "Help, please!" until the man with the funny hat comes. Martha Jane laughs at the hat, tears leaking from the corners of her eyes. When he frowns, she demands to see Hilton, the engineer. The conductor bites his lip, wrinkles his nose at the stink, and takes her by the arm. "The gentleman is busy," he says. "I'll assist you."

"I'm Calamity Jane," she tells him, wincing. "And don't pull me so hard. What's the matter, you got a train to catch?" He doesn't laugh, but she does, even harder, and has to sit down on another seat to catch her breath. Drawing a dirty handkerchief from her bodice, she dabs her brow.

"Ma'am, I know who you are." He glances down at his pocket watch, then pulls her to her feet.

When she stumbles down the steps onto the platform, he stays above her. Already putting the old woman behind him, he puffs out his cheeks in a sigh of duty. "Are you all right, then?"

"Fine and dandy," she says to his back as he re-enters the car.

Terry is still a good old stacked-up gulch town, with its own named peak hump-shouldering over it, to the west. Today the town simmers hot as an armpit. Like so many places Martha Jane's lived, Terry suggests a glitter of gold dust, slogs in ankle-deep mud, and clings to hillsides for dear life. There's a mine and more rock, but fewer trees than you'd expect, with most of the native pines cut down for firewood or rough cut into planks, for ramshackle cabins. Stumps stubble up like a miner's whiskers, tripping anybody who dares to look up while walking. Scrub brush survives out of spite and because it's too smoky to burn. There's a sad little cemetery with few markers, and Martha Jane shivers as she stumbles past it. Will they plant her here?

Her swollen liver fires another warning shot, nearly dropping her to her knees, so she asks a passing stranger to guide her, please, to Mr. Schaeffer's Calloway Hotel. That stranger discreetly raises a perfumed handkerchief to his nose but obliges the gray-haired woman with a stop at the saloon. She calls for a package of whiskey, her medicine, she explains, to ease her rheumatism. Seeing his gold watch and hearing coins clink in his pocket, she asks, "Tell me, sonny, did your folks ever tell you tales of Calamity Jane?"

Hearing that his elderly guest's breathing is labored, and that she rarely leaves her bed, Mr. Schaeffer invites Dr. Richards to attend her. She refuses care, saying she's inclined to follow her friends who've already passed over. When the dubious doctor asks to verify her name, Martha Jane chuckles and mutters, "Saint Peter will call it, heaven or hell." When he insists on examining her, she gathers enough strength to shout, "By God, you ain't paid for that privilege" and slaps his hand away.

While Martha Jane slumbers, a thirteen-year-old Irish maid enters her room, peeks into her bag, and finds the pamphlets and cabinet cards. A bright girl, she puts two and two together and later, while kissing the night desk clerk, divulges their guest's secret identity. Seeking favor and a raise in pay, he directly informs the proprietor.

The news blazes, spreading like a lightning-struck forest fire. Calamity's friends come on horseback and on the ore train, bearing gifts of whiskey and rye. She drinks with them, and, when they've ambled to the saloons so she can sleep, she drinks what they've left behind. With her friends filling the room—the ones she can see and the ones she can only remember—pain eases its grip. Her mind addles, but her hallucinations are kind;

beyond her fears and offenses, Martha Jane snores loudly in a fog that's almost rest.

Days later, the curious Irish maid brings linens again, only to find Martha Jane stiff in her bed. To be sure, she pokes the old woman through her sheet and feels her hard and cold, so with a shiver and without a word to the desk clerk who betrayed her confidence, she tearfully breaks in on the proprietor, who embraces her. Under his tender hands the girl from Ballyragget is not only consoled, but also pleasured and encouraged; in her employer's arms she imagines love, prosperity, and even marriage to the successful man, all thanks to Calamity Jane.

The rumpled, blushing maid straightens her skirt, lowers her eyes, and folds her hands as they carry the body out, shedding a tear for a woman she'd only just heard of one week ago. A good Catholic most of the time, the girl anticipates sainthood for Martha Jane, so she kneels and prays a quick rosary for the old woman's soul. After all, didn't she answer the little maid's prayers? It's surely the old lady's first miracle, *begorra*.

Beyond the hotel, news and heartbreak lumber less piously east with an old friend on a mule, but then the word speeds ahead to arrive in Deadwood on the Burlington with the ore.

At a saloon where Calamity Jane's old bullets still lodge in the ceiling, liquor sharpens Deadwood's memory and lubricates sentiment. Funeral plans are made and paid for. Terry's humble cemetery won't do for Deadwood's great lady.

Maybe she asked to be buried beside Wild Bill. Why, of course she did; at least four of Deadwood's finest gentlemen recall her saying so. Others consider it a fine joke to settle those two side by side for eternity, when all they did above ground was argue and cheat each other at poker.

The heartfelt pioneers of Deadwood tearfully, if not quite

soberly, demand that Calamity Jane be rescued from that muddy gulch, Terry.

When Calamity Jane, what's left of her, is carried off the ore train in Deadwood, the citizens dress her in white like a bride, weave false lupine and Indian basketflowers into her hair, and sneakily snip ragged, gray locks for keepsakes. They repeat the stories she published, then embellish these with personal accounts. They sing about her romance with Wild Bill, an ill-fated, eternal love that never happened. They remember and broaden how she whipped bulls, saved lives, doctored miners, and gave her last coins to the poor. They reprint her pamphlets and jack up the price. They write poems, preach sermons, sing hymns, and publicly bawl. Despite what would have been her certain protestation, they even drag her body into church.

A guard stands by her casket as thousands doff their hats to mourn. Prostitutes wail and righteous men dab their eyes, for it strikes them like a sledge on a railroad spike: the West has died. Calamity Jane gave them the West as they believe in it now, the West they couldn't exchange fast enough for theater seats, dry sidewalks, and trellises of roses. They sing of things they hardly remember—the gold dust, the mud, and the woman they bury here.

Two hired men, one Negro and one Chinaman, shovel a hole in Mt. Moriah beside Wild Bill. Fighting back tears, they let the ropes slide across their hard palms, to lower her body in. What's left of her is light, too light to hold who she was, the woman they remember. The gravediggers, her friends, will suffer but won't talk about this hard thing later, over the drinks her funeral buys. But they will clink their shot glasses together and mumble her name as if it's a prayer.

The hodgepodge of mourners, with the rich standing in front and poor in the back, is half-sober and serious now. Sensing what's passed with this woman, beyond them and their tintype memories, the gathered ones clear their throats and deny how they resisted and despised her. Stopped-up with grief, they gape at how deep her flowered casket lies and how the ground crumbles down every side of her grave. They file past her body for an hour, dropping clods and flowers to cover their own shame.

When the minister wraps up his folderol, everyone hesitates. The finality ripples and fades. Maybe it's one of her pranks. They half expect her to saunter up from the town, raise a bottle, and cuss their tomfoolery. Sure of what she'll still do, no rich man, working man, prostitute, or orphan dares to break the anticipation. With eyes on her grave, her people finally listen for her voice, itching for one last twist to her story.

There comes no interruption. Calamity Jane's last and lasting words drift as dust over her box, forever pitched beyond their hearing.

Beyond this hullabaloo.

Another here spills in behind her eyes. Dry, rocky hills wear old green coats of grass, not bright and leafy, but dusty, dry, and wide, dotted with blue and red and yellow flowers. Purple, rumpled-blanket mountains shrug up behind the hills, wearing sharp white hats. Their rocky chins are rough with evergreen whiskers. Blue sky bubbles high and clear as water to quench a body's thirst, and this forever opens so far, she can see what's coming. To run if she needs to, or to stay if she likes.

That horizon she walks to is teasing, wandering away. It knows her name. It's soft, too forgiving to cuss or beat or tie her down with a rule. More than a place, it's an invitation. A story somebody wrote for her.

West. A new land to cross and follow, like a dream.

ABOUT THE AUTHOR

Inspired by a lifetime in the West and study of its history, **K. Lyn (Kelly) Wurth** has published three other novels: *The Darkwater Liar's Account; Seven Kinds of Rain: River Saga Book One;* and *Remember How It Rained: River Saga Book Two.* Literary and online journals have featured her award-winning short fiction over the last thirty years.

Supported by her educational background and life experiences of Great Plains and Western literature and medicine, she researches and reimagines the complex history and characters of the American West.

A supporting member of Women Writing the West, K. Lyn Wurth now leans westward from rural northwest Iowa, where she lives with her husband, David.

The employees of Five Star Publishing hope you have enjoyed this book.

Our Five Star novels explore little-known chapters from America's history, stories told from unique perspectives that will entertain a broad range of readers.

Other Five Star books are available at your local library, bookstore, all major book distributors, and directly from Five Star/Gale.

Connect with Five Star Publishing

Visit us on Facebook:
    https://www.facebook.com/FiveStarCengage

Email:
    FiveStar@cengage.com

For information about titles and placing orders:
    (800) 223-1244
    gale.orders@cengage.com

To share your comments, write to us:
    Five Star Publishing
    Attn: Publisher
    10 Water St., Suite 310
    Waterville, ME 04901